Networks

First published in 2022 by the University of Sydney.

Funded by the University of Sydney Faculty of Arts and Social Sciences School of Literature, Art and Media.

Sydney University Press
Fisher Library F03
University of Sydney
NSW 2006 AUSTRALIA

Email: sup.info@sydney.edu.au

sydneyuniversitypress.com.au

 A catalogue record for this book is available from the National Library of Australia   A catalogue record for this book is available from the National Library of Australia

ISBN: 978-1-74210-510-9 (paperback)
ISBN: 978-1-74210-511-6 (epub)
ISBN: 978-1-74210-512-3 (PDF)

Design and text layout: Melissa Snook and Sophie Amos

Contents

Contents

Acknowledgements

The year 2021 saw a continuation of the unprecedented challenges we all faced in 2020; amid such a tumultuous and unpredictable year, having the opportunity to work on the *Networks* anthology has been a deeply rewarding experience for the entire team. As with any collaborative project, there are many people who share credit in bringing this collection to life, so we want to take a moment to thank them directly.

We would like to extend our thanks first and foremost to Dr Agata Mrva-Montoya. Despite another year of online communication and Zoom calls, you have brought the team together and empowered us to adapt and learn from every challenge that arose. Thank you for contributing so much of your time and experience to helping this project reach its fruition, we greatly appreciate your belief in our abilities.

We extend our deep appreciation to Distinguished Professor Larissa Behrendt, for generously contributing the foreword to *Networks*. We are so thankful to you for taking the time to read these pieces and craft such an impactful introduction to a collection of truly resonant works. It has been an absolute privilege for us to have you on board.

This anthology would not be possible without the fantastic contributions of the students, staff and alumni of the University of Sydney. With every contribution, you have all presented nuanced and creative perspectives on the role of networks at a time that arguably challenged our relationship to the concept more than ever. Thank you for trusting us to share your work with the world.

Without the encouragement and support of the Department of Media and Communications, we would not be able to bring this anthology to life and we value your support of this incredible learning opportunity.

We would like to extend a special thanks to Eloise Fetterplace from Sydney Environment Institute. Thank you to the wider University of Sydney Marketing and Communication team, academic liaison librarians, department staff, and representatives from various clubs and societies for helping to advertise our call for submissions. Your continued promotional and marketing assistance through remote working has been invaluable.

This publication would not have been possible without the following assistance: Marc Fernando from the Digital Media Unit, Katie Leach and Phil Jones from the University of Sydney Library and the entire team at Sydney University Press.

Lastly, thank you to the anthology team. The diversity of skills and experience that you all brought to this project have made for a truly rewarding collaboration. I'm so proud of what we have achieved together and I couldn't have asked for a better group of people to work with. Thank you for contributing your commitment, adaptability and passion for publishing to this 2021 anthology.

Foreword

Larissa Behrendt

Through the unprecedented modern crisis of the COVID-19 pandemic, we have all been forced to live differently and therefore to learn something about ourselves. As we had to lock ourselves away and borders closed, the concept of NETWORKS became more profound, more real. We utilised modern technology to reach out to each other across new geographical and physical limits. It forced us to connect increasingly in ways that had been already creeping into our lives – a social NETWORK through Facebook, Instagram, and Twitter with like-minded communities. We have created bubbles where we can feel culturally safe but have also, in other incarnations, created places that generate hate and division.

Technology has always been a blessing and a curse. It allows us greater freedoms and more ways to express ourselves; it creates vehicles for oppression and damaging, sometimes lethal, misinformation. It can save lives and cost them.

During the last couple of challenging years, I have begun to reflect more deeply on our NETWORK of interconnectedness. It is a central concept in Indigenous cultures. Through our totemic systems we are born with a matrix of relationships that carry responsibility, and through that system we know our place in the world.

In my own nation, the totemic system has three facets. We have a personal totem that connects us to our creation ancestor (mine is emu). We have a clan totem that connects us to other people (mine is the long-necked turtle) and a spiritual totem that links us to the spirit world (mine is the lyre bird). It is through these systems that I can find my responsibilities and connections to the people I meet and the world around me. It is why, when First Nations people meet each other, their first question is often 'where are you from?' We try and understand who we are in relation to each other. The mathematical explanations of kinship systems by First Nations scholars like Lynette Riley and Chris Matthews shows the deep complexities within a system that every First Nations child learns.

Understanding this interconnectedness, this NETWORK, is not just about knowing who we are, it is also about our relationship to country. Those totems and relationships give rise to obligations. Lying beneath that interconnectedness, was a system that understood that the relationship to the ecosystems around us was something we are a part of. It is not there for us to own or exploit ruthlessly. If we don't live in a way that keeps the ecosystem vibrant, then as it dies, we die.

I have to confess that when I was younger I found some of the appropriation of the concepts by the New Age cringeworthy. The idea that 'the earth is dying and the Aboriginal people are dying with it' was a view strongly expressed in that context and my instinct was to bristle at the idea that my people are seen as some kind of Noble Savage. To me, it is as dangerous as painting us as savages. I should just add, for context, that my father had a pretty ugly mid-life crisis as he sought to reconnect with his own First Nations heritage. Brought up in an orphanage, the son of a member of the Stolen Generations, he had known he was Aboriginal but didn't find his connection back to our family until he was in his early forties. He knew he was missing something and looked for it in may places. When he did find it – through tracing archival documents from the Aborigines Protection Board – he could place himself – and me and my brother – into that NETWORK that still survived even after such aggressive colonisation. I noticed a profound transformation in him as he found his place back within his family, community and culture. It is his most precious legacy to me that he has passed that down.

As I have matured into my cultural understandings – and come to appreciate that real wisdom comes from listening not speaking – I have come to understand the deeper importance of the First Nations worldviews inherent in my culture. We celebrate being the world's oldest living culture. One of the key reflections of that is how was that achieved? It was in no small part due to the fact that we knew how to live with and adapt to our environment. We didn't exploit it mercilessly for greed or gain.

But you don't become the world's oldest living culture by just living well with the environment. It is living with each other that is just as important. Since Australia was claimed by the British under the Doctrine of Discovery and the legal fiction of *terra nullius* used to sustain that colonisation, it was inevitable that the colonial narrative would be one that painted First Nations cultures as without any system of governance. The intricate NETWORK with country and people was wilfully ignored. Not having a stratified hierarchy like the feudal monarchies of the Europeans and having distinct but equal gendered roles seems to have been a benefit in ensuring people lived together in a cohesive way. And if you can't find a way to live together in a mostly hunter-gatherer society, you don't live. Everyone needs to pull together or you don't survive. First Nations cultures are framed collectively and communally, not individually and rigidly hierarchical.

It seems that, if we look at three of the great crises we are facing today, First Nations understanding of interconnectedness have some insights.

In relation to the climate crisis, First Nations knowledge systems remind us of the need for sustainability and for positioning ourselves within – not above – the ecologies around us. As we look at increasing social and political divisions within society around the world, First Nations cultures remind us of the importance of remembering we are connected to each other and if we don't work together, we can't survive. And in relation to the increasing sense of personal isolation and the associated mental strain and illness that is progressively endemic, connection to both country and people is a critical strategy in addressing that isolation.

For all these seemingly intractable, First Nations ways of being and seeing provides important insights into how to tackle them differently. And interconnection, NETWORKS, connection, is at the heart of it.

It is no surprise that meditation on the concept of NETWORKS at this moment in time inspires a diversity of reflection and personal insight. Thematics that weave through this anthology remind us of important life lessons. Displacement forces us to reconnect, to find a way to place ourselves within a new community. Disorientation does the same thing. Every time we lose our footing as an individual, we steady ourselves by finding out more about who we are. Who we are is not just defined by ourselves but by our relationships with others.

It is striking that one of the strongest recurring motifs throughout this collection of eclectic, inspiring, prophetic writings is that of trees. It's a simple metaphor of thinking of ourselves as part of a system – family trees, our roots. But there is something more profound underlying this seemingly simple metaphor. Trees are a quintessential example of good citizens. They live symbiotically with the ecology around them. Iron bark trees collect the lightning rods from storms, protecting the other trees around them. Eucalyptus trees share their properties with the plants around them, ensuring that they survive. Westerners often classify the natural world as a competitive hierarchy – a 'dog eat dog' world, a food chain, 'survival of the fittest' but there are other ways of looking at the relationships, even between predator and prey, that are far more respectful and symbiotic when not defined purely through an Anthropocene gaze.

Connection to Country is unique in First Nations cultures. In Australia, those connections can be traced back over 65,000 years – so many generations we think of it as 'deep time'. Throughout this anthology, it is clear that whatever our background or where we are from, place has a defining role to play. Lineal time is a very Western concept. I remember my father explaining to me that time in our culture exists in a loop. It was hard to get my head around but it perhaps felt most real to me when he took me to the spot out on our traditional land in north-west New South Wales where my grandmother had been taken from when she was removed by the Aborigines Protection Board. My being there for the first time, my return to that country, was a moment that existed side by side. We were connected through the land, not separated by years. It is, for me, of a reminder, of the many ways we are part of a NETWORK that we don't see and have yet to discover.

*

Distinguished Professor Larissa Behrendt is a Eualeyai/Gamillaroi woman. She is a legal scholar, lawyer, writer and filmmaker based at the Jumbunna Institute at the University of Technology Sydney.

Networks

Being a Part and Apart

Ana Mashi

(Literal: I am walking; figurative: I am leaving)

Diana Chamma

Moss squirmed under our feet at thirty-three kilometres into the walk. Somewhere in Balgowlah Heights my curls started to frizz as our bodies got warmer and the bush got denser. It was particularly stuffy when Abhi told me his older brother DJ killed himself. A few months after his twenty-four-hour, one-hundred-kilometre walk, his wife found him hanging in his bedroom on 4 January. Months of rehab before his walk created a healthy-looking DJ, one who seemed willing to live. The shock of his death still lingered, five years later, and haunted Abhi's twitching eye. Silly Walk Sydney, which Abhi founded in 2019, became the commemoration, his fixation, raising money for charity. He broke the walk into categories, from 'Very Serious' one-kilometre walks to the 'Very Silly' one hundred kilometres. People joined the walk at different intervals from several locations, depending on the kilometres they preferred to do. Four men and I chose to be very silly together.

'A kid now,' Abhi blurted.

My pinched eyebrows and the question, 'What kid?', prompted him to spell out e-c-h-i-d-n-a, pointing at the hedgehog. I stared at the Australian hedgehog with a strange name and thought about the lack of animals we see in Dubai. Abhi's pin-prick eyes, peeking through thick black lashes and onto his phone, confirmed that we were at a good pace to reach the beaches on time.

'But no von asked,' the twenty-three-year-old's voice rang in my ear with a nasal shrill. I moved closer to Abhi while phrasing a question in my head about DJ leaving a note. Holding back, I remembered how Colin Tatz explains that 'there are many evidentiary signs of suicide apart from a note.' What's evident to me is that four days into 2016, *kill self* was at least one of his New Year's resolutions. He must

1

have viewed notes as 'an exaggerated facet of suicide, deriving from nineteenth-century fiction and twentieth-century films'.

When I moved to Sussex for my first master's degree, I was tempted to fill my pockets and walk into River Ouse. Woolf's depression spiralled after losing her home in London to the Blitz – she had good reason to drown; I thought I didn't. Her note had no impact on me – she says it herself, 'You see I can't even write this properly'. However, the one note that really kills me is in the excerpt from Tumarkin's *Axiomatic* that asks its readers to 'Please do not assume you know why … it is simply the best thing to do. The mechanism telling me not to kill myself is broken'.[1] It could be that most suicides are preceded by a broken mechanism; I'm not completely sure.

The muffins at the Corso lured me in like expensive prostitutes I couldn't afford. We walked into a shoal of Greek gods and goddesses – a parallel universe where paunches and muffin tops did not exist. I felt like a seal and wished to be eaten by a polar bear. As we walked into residential areas, I peeked into the houses reminiscient of Dubai. Males in polo shirts and thongs roared in their prides, gulping Carlton Draughts – how Manly! The vastness of architecture remained unimpressive despite my current living space, which is *ad koss el-'a'rabeh* – Arabic for 'the size of a scorpion's vagina'. In that room in Surry Hills, I dragged a desk into the Victorian terrace to sit with a eucalyptus tree. I exchanged morning greetings with rainbow lorikeets, magpies, and cockatoos. When a galah rocked up one morning, tears burst onto my face and I fell head over heels for Sydney. Being stranded in awe by a bird, let alone anything pink, felt like a homecoming. It was on that day that I decided to stay, rather than go back to the UAE. First and foremost, because there's about two trees in Dubai … and not one galah.

Time: ten hours, forty-four minutes, thirty-one seconds. Distance: fifty kilometres. The robot woman on the Nike app declared all this through Abhi's phone. He twisted his legs like Shah Rukh Khan and pulled an arm out for high fives. Jesus slapped his large palm into Abhi's while the rest of us crumbled on the building entrance in St Leonards. We waited for Abhi to make a phone call about codes and keys and

---

1   Tumarkin 2018, 31.

I watched him transform from a white Aussie accent to an Indian from Mumbai. Another walker ripped his shoes off with a groan and wrapped blisters with used bandages. *Blister Guy needs a foot fairy for the remaining fifty kilometres*, I thought. But given the complex logistics of fairy visits, it might be better for him to be home attending to those wrinkly, peeling chunks of foot. The door opened and five of us wedged into a one-bedroom, one-bathroom. My wet bun perched atop my head as I ate through a Woolies whole roast chicken. Abhi warned against sleeping to avoid cramping up, while Blister Guy's head wobbled in agreement. Jesus, Twenty-Three and I sardined onto a queen. My eyes fell shut as nausea travelled through me – three quarters of a chicken might have been a large feed for a vegan stomach, but Twenty-Three also breathed like an aircon from the nineties. At three in the morning our feet lined up for another mission. 'To repeat something is to make it possible anew'[2] – Anwen Crawford's phrase hummed in my chest and inoculated my mechanism of not wanting to kill myself. Blister Guy smelled like ginger chutney.

Ethnic Aussies put up with being too brown, too curly and not Vegemite enough. When their migrant parents packed *naan* and *dhal* in their lunchboxes, their Australian-born children were ashamed of their exotic (now expensive Newtown) food. As they grew into different Aussie Shapes, they became coconuts – a derogatory term for a brown man who behaves like a white person. In Arabic, describing someone as *albo abyad*, white on the inside, refers to being good hearted. When I called my Indian friend a coconut, he got insulted and ruined my favourite snack. My mind started to play games: honeydew melon for white-washed Asians, sushi for Africans, lychee for …! This is what Tatz means when he says that the 'devaluation of their culture and self-identity' together with a 'sense of anomie, hopelessness, despair and depression' creates a common resort to suicide.

The tedious journey from St Leonards to Mosman would also create a common resort to suicide. My knee required occasional rubs along the dark chirping streets while Abhi buried his face in his phone to calculate how we could get to the Harbour Bridge just in time for sunrise. It seems that Abhi, just like the West, had developed an

---

2   Crawford 2021, 130.

obsession with numbers, to the exclusion of lived experience. Nadia Dabbagh's research on suicide in Ramallah explains how all cases were grouped numerically and neatly labelled 'mental illness'. Tatz looks at the attempted suicides of people in Indigenous communities of Australia as a result of colonial practice and explicates that 'to be perturbed, disturbed, stressed, uneasy, dis-eased, anxious, confused, aggressive, delinquent, obnoxious, is to be normal'. It is 'silly' to call it mental illness, he stresses.[3]

I ate a grape as my eyes followed a water bottle up to Abhi's mouth. Jesus' sculpted jaw yawned into the 4 am mist as I zipped up my mustard-yellow jacket. Blister Guy limped and Twenty-Three complained about the remaining hour it would take to get to the bridge – as if the additional nine of the walk didn't exist. I laid my eyes on the only fixed point, Abhi's arse, to meditate. On the first deep exhale, I remembered the morning Abhi's Toyota Camry parked to pick me up on Chalmers Street. One hand on the wheel and the other pirouetting to Arabic music he'd suggested I play, he asked about how many camels I owned and how much petrol I drank in the UAE. My counter-response in this stereotype tournament was that a cheap jasmine-scented Camry is the classic vehicle for the Indian taxi driver of the Emirates. Laughter fizzled out of his thick beard and he expressed condolences for my stolen land when he found out I'm Palestinian.

I spotted a toll booth from afar, one of the few in my lifetime that did not require a security check. No document I owned allowed me into any country comfortably – Palestine was prohibited. My Syrian Travel Document for Palestinian refugees required a visa application even to visit a toilet. I saw Syria twice and briefly. Mum holds a Jordanian passport which she, as a female, cannot pass onto her children. Less worthy than a piece of tissue, I carried it for thirty years.

Being born and bred as a non-citizen in the UAE made me feel just like Crawford does, 'the struggle against borders on a country not my own'.[4] Like so many Palestinians before me, *agora eu falo*

---

3   Tatz 2005, 119.
4   Crawford 2021, 134.

português e tenho um passaporte Brasileiro – now I speak Portuguese and have a Brazilian passport.

I ascended the Harbour Bridge and filled my lungs with Sydney. Gorging on the voluptuous city, I wondered why anyone would want to kill themselves here. The sun cracked through the skies and water danced beneath us. I stood possessed by Sydney's incantations from waves, birds and the munching of apple between Twenty-Three's teeth. I dabbed my eyes with a withered tissue I found in my Nike tights. Above me, steel – a man-made alloy created by mixing iron and carbon. Dorman Long, a British firm, designed and built the Harbour Bridge – colonisers love steeling. Parts of the bridge reminded me of the Eiffel Tower; I climbed it on two trips while visiting my sister who studied at the Sorbonne. The smell of a fresh baguette came to me and my stomach rumbled.

Abhi overexplained a miscalculation of kilometres he'd made, ending with his solution that we walk three laps, back and forth, on the bridge. Jesus found Abhi's suggestion silly and his miscalculation amateur. His smile stayed with him as he bent over with his ripped fifty-year-old physique to tie his shoelaces for the third time.

Twenty-Three hovered around him. 'I vould buy bettah shoes if I woz a triathlete.' Jesus suggested he become a triathlete first, then worry about others' shoes.

A police report on 'hotspots' explains that these 'spectacular views offer a suicidal person a helicopter view of the world while contemplating ending [one's] life'. Peering through the caged walk, I understood how 'the aquatic setting contributed to the attraction, both aesthetically and psychologically'.[5] The views were so irresistible that William James Lewis jumped less than a month after the bridge's opening in 1932. A second person used William's spot on the following day, triggering a ripple effect:

---

5   In Ross et al. 2020, 3.

Since 1935, barriers have been installed and enhanced. From footway to roadway, guards to cameras, investments poured into suicide prevention. I cringed at the unseemly cages around us and a British accent came out of me: 'If you wish to self-slaughter, kindly do it on your own premises or go to the countryside; the bridge is too lovely.'

I squinted my eyes at Crown Sydney flipping me the bird from Barangaroo, and a desire to jump into the water rushed through me. A guard eyed me as my fingers touched the fence and sweat slid into my eye, burning it shut. My breath felt shallow and Slessor's voice echoed in my ears as he called out for his dead friend. I walked along the bridge carrying Slessor's agony and Billy-Ray Belcourt's 'radical empathy for those who experience aliveness as a kind of ever-present death knell'.[6]

Abhi gobbled a muesli bar into his fifty-eight-kilogram body after he passed me pawpaw. The hunger made me consider squeezing the processed fruit lip balm into my mouth. In pre-Islamic times, Arabs killed themselves by overconsuming alcohol or starving themselves – my grumbling stomach began to empathise. They starved honourably, though, to end economic hardships and hunger, *with hunger*. That pride of refusing to eat food that was never there – sounds like something my proud father would do.

Over time, suicide became more of a taboo and Belcourt finds that 'it's routinely coated in negative affect, for it marks the loss of a life that could still be here'. Its immediacy and a person's agency are what make it harder to accept. Every other form of unnatural death is either immediate but unintended (hit by a bus) or deliberate but gradual. When it combines both, it starts to appear like a selfish act. Belcourt also highlights Leanne Betsamosake's perspective that 'suicide's not something you do to other people, it's something you do for yourself'.[7] However, in strongly tied communities, suicide brings shame, affects status and defies religious practice. It becomes something you do to your parents, their family, their reputation and can damage their social standing. There's a lot to think about before killing yourself if you are Palestinian.

6   Belcourt 2021, 132.
7   Belcourt 2021, 139.

Jesus wrapped a pink scarf around his head and dangled one of its ends on the back of his shoulder. He wore it like a true Muslim woman and deserved to be congratulated. '*Mabrook el hijab*,' I giggled at him. 'Congratulations on wearing the veil,' I translated. He nodded, smiling, and didn't find it as funny.

'Too much sun,' he said.

'Too much pink,' I replied.

I liked Islam more before I tried wearing the veil for two years. My dad cried and said a thousand *mabrooks* when I went to surprise him in his office. Pushing through the door where the scariest words of my life were written, CAPTAIN MOHAMMED CHAMMA, I appeared in front of him with a sky blue scarf. As he wept in joy, I became certain that wearing a veil, or killing yourself, is something you do to other people.

Walking into the CBD where everyone wears a suit and takes life too seriously, I recalled how a dictatorship wreaked havoc in Tunisia when Mohamed Bouazizi set himself on fire. His wares were confiscated in December 2010 for lacking a permit to sell fruits and vegetables. Receiving a public slap by a female police officer did not provoke his self-immolation, despite patriarchal integrity. It was the denied hearing at the governor's office that made the burning of his flesh more tolerable than being unable to provide for himself and his family. He died after three weeks, *Allah yerhamo* – God have mercy upon him. In a faith where suicide receives no prayers, *Al-Rabi' al-'Arabi* sprang up and millions prayed for Bouazizi. 'Farewell, Mohamed, we will avenge you. We weep for you today. We will make those who caused your death weep.' They saw his suicide as 'caused' by an outsider; it provided a cathartic release for the Arab world and did not appear selfish.

My velcroed eyelids were pulled apart when the barista announced, 'Espresso for Diana'. I brought the Sydney Uni Sports and Fitness backpack to my front and reached for a banana. I forced heat and bitterness down my throat and thought about how a café that serves bad coffee in Sydney must wear a scarlet letter. Blister Guy faltered and Twenty-Three disagreed with Jesus about cricket. A couple of times people asked if my name was real when I got to Sydney. I was clueless what this question implied until, months later, some Turks explained how they changed their names to Mark and Nicholas to get jobs. Emrah had been applying for months and only got a reply when Mark sent the email. I gathered that Diana probably felt unsuited for my olive skin, and Iman, Jameela or Abdullah might've sounded more satisfactory to Lesley.

I watched the ferries in *Warrung* – Little Child – which changed its name to Circular Quay. This total erasure evoked the *Little Boy* from the Second World War and a shudder zapped through my body. I squished the end of the banana between my lips and located Abhi stretching his calves on a bench. He seemed excited that thirteen new walkers would meet us in a few minutes.

Whenever I walk towards the Sydney Opera House, I feel a desire to throw a hat in the air as I receive the *You Have Arrived in Sydney* award. This building is all foreigners know about Australia, along with shark-eaten surfers, K-animals and some convicts historically chilling on *terra nullius*. Of course, Melbourne is the capital city and if Canberra is ever stumbled upon, the pronunciation is can-bear-ah. It takes a few weeks in Sydney for the stereotypes to get tweaked: some surfers are attacked but most are left intact, koalas cost money to be seen, kangaroos are pests and everywhere begins by acknowledging the Traditional Owners of the land, depending on which they meet, and paying respect to Elders past and present.

My fanciful moment of hat throwing was interrupted by the newcomers. Unlike what Abhi imagined, we now stood in the presence of Dementors who extracted the last bit of life out of us. It was like meeting a group of drunk teenagers after a long meditation session. Nausea simmered in my belly while posing for a photo with the iconic building. I immediately sprinted towards the Botanic Gardens afterwards and tumbled on the first green patch I found. Devouring the scent of eucalyptus on my skin, I stretched each sore limb into the grass. Beds of flannel flowers surrounded me when a small blonde girl with a blue snake lolly stared at me. I recalled the Arabic word for lolly, *bonbons*, which we borrow from the French. Images from Saleh Bakri's 2017 Palestinian film *Bonboné* flashed through my mind as I smiled at the little girl. The protagonist in the film uses the lolly wrapper to deposit sperm into, for his wife to smuggle out of the Israeli prison and use to impregnate herself with. I watched the girl hop around as the blue snake dangled from her mouth.

On the way to Rosebay Park my skin started peeling and I remembered to block the sun with lotion. A white t-shirt fashioned into a turban offered very little protection for my face and even less fashion. In a turban and spotting signs for HMAS military and naval bases, I anticipated a bomb from Israel in a flash. I didn't even realise that an 'A' was missing between the 'H' and 'M'. Sweat poured from my neck and down to my boiling feet. I bit through half a cucumber Jesus gave me in exchange for three pecans. He placed them in his mouth and tied his shoelaces. We spoke about Her Majesty's Australian Ship, Gaza and watermelons. I googled Khaled Hourani to show Jesus the artwork watermelon he illustrated in 2013. Jesus held my phone in his veiny, tawny hands and stared at the artwork entitled *Palestinian Flag*.

His brown eyes widened like a child who had discovered a hidden cookie jar and asked me when Palestinians started to carry watermelons around. It was in 1967 after the Six Day War, when it became a crime to raise the Palestinian flag. Impressed, he broadened his defined shoulders and nodded while returning the phone back to me.

Muqawama, resistance, is a word that lives in many Palestinian homes, in the *zeit w za'atar* sandwiches, the *tatreez* on clothes, poetry and song. For that, suicide would defy Palestinian resistance and be seen as an un-Palestinian form of behaviour. Many Palestinians believe suicide is what the *ajaneb*, Westerners or foreigners, do. Similarly, Tatz discovers that it is an 'alien concept' for the Australian Indigenous communities, with no 'Aboriginal language or dialect having a noun corresponding to suicide'. Both Dabbagh and Tatz believe that modernity has increased suicide rates in these communities and turned them towards 'modern' types of self-harm. The colonised were elbowed and shoved into egalitarian animal farms where some people are more equal than others. Tatz walks us through this process: 'a feeling of frustration; followed by a sense of alienation from society, [...] no longer caring about membership, loyalty, or law-abiding behaviour; and then the threat of, or actual, violence.'[8]

---

8   Tatz 2005, 19.

We stopped for Blister Guy to use the toilet and I raced Abhi to a bubbler. Humans played *Finska* in a park as a Bull Arab scrunched to produce three faeces. I thought of the few animal faeces I saw in Dubai and asked why the dog is Arab. Abhi shrugged, suggesting a racist named it because it hunts pigs. Google gave me: 'This breed requires heavy socialisation and training, or they can become aggressive.' It appears that even on dogtime.com, Arabs are marketed poorly. Palestinians often describe being treated like dogs or animals – if only they knew how some humans pick up dog faeces after their beloved pets. However, participating in political riots and protests makes them feel like 'human beings'. During the first Intifada in 1991, suicide rates dropped when society came together under a unified goal. When life resumes under oppression, hopeless and without purpose, death starts to become more attractive. Tatz describes how Indigenous youth have no fear of dying; 'rather it's the fear of living'.[9]

A woman who walked the one hundred kilometres a year before appeared by my side. She signed up for the last twenty this year. She told me her name and asked for mine with her eyes blinking separately. A side of her lip seemed bigger and tilted. She mentioned struggling with some mental health issue, maybe bipolar disorder, that affected her relationships.

'Men are shit,' she exclaimed and searched my face for consensus. I agreed, in accord with female solidarity, which was founded on this motto.

After forty minutes, I found Blister Guy smearing chutney onto his cracker. Jesus overheard me craving a green apple and whipped one out for me. What a saviour.

Being born into layers of history, flavours and languages becomes a privilege that non-white Aussies discover too late. Most of their lives are spent proving that they are whiter than their families and rejecting their tongues and spices. I am still trying to grasp what the aspiration of being white is about. With a chequered colonial history, the only remaining element is the colour white, which most white folks spend hours tanning. If the envy is about food, this may come as unfortunate news, but fairy bread was stolen from a little unicorn town

---

9   Tatz 2005, 103.

and appropriated as Australian. All unicorns were wiped out during the apartheid and in fact, it would be a lot easier for a unicorn to self-slaughter than see its fairy bread become Australian.

I eyed a falafel wrap between a hipster's fingers. He chewed a strand of his hair along with it but my stomach growled anyway. Abhi pushed our walking speed to reach Bronte Beach on the twenty-four-hour mark. Jesus questioned Abhi's insistence while Twenty-Three dismissed the deadline with a wave of his hand. 'Ve are valking anyhow, who caihs if we get dere fifteen minutes before or aftah.' DJ finished the walk in twenty-four hours and Abhi couldn't fall short – Jesus understood but his stiff ankle interfered at times.

I pulled out my phone and saw a text from dad wishing me a good walk. I teared up. In another message, my sister was unhappy about her olive oil tour in Greece, 'It's sad the Israelis get all the credit for the olive trees and oils. *C'est dégueu!*' My rusty French failed me so I sent a sticker of Queen Elizabeth squinting, and typed something about karma and the British. I threw my phone into the cheap backpack. My shoulders were getting tired.

A pound of blood blotched onto my pad while Abhi entertained the new walkers by switching between Marathi and English. Sentences came out heavy through his pale, dry lips and he quickly slipped away to join us; everything outside the five of us felt like flies on our faces. Colourless and ghostlike, he materialised next to me. The Nike app woman died at seventy-eight kilometres, so his eyes fixated on his old green trainers instead.

'*Kollo 'al fadi,*' I said and translated instantly, 'It's all for nothing.'

Parroting *'al fadi* a few times, he tapped the hand I rested on his shoulder.

The walk felt meaningless to me when scenery became repetitive and the pain in my body grew bigger than Sydney. I found living in the UAE much more challenging than the walk, though. I grew up in a mall where oxygen came through aircons and snow from a machine; where rain poured from seeded clouds, sustenance came from Burberry and the 'soul' purpose was to maintain a work visa. When all that failed, it was deportation and a return to the homeland – Palestinian diaspora never knew where that was. Every identity of mine was subject to scrutiny and security checks. I find solace in

Tatz's interpretation of Camus' 'existential suicide: ending the burden of hypocrisy, of the meaninglessness of life, of the ennui and lack of motivation to continue to exist'.[10] I often contemplated jumping from the eleventh floor overlooking a man-made lake with a barren island in its centre. My eyes, thirsty, found everything in Sydney. But something did not sit right here; something smelled funny.

I peeled the Kathmandus off my throbbing feet. They sizzled in the cold waters of Watsons Bay and the beauty of Sydney struck me again. We walked towards the South Head peninsula with Abhi's small mouth and large teeth smiling in the breeze. I thought about how easily one could slip a pencil in the gap between his incisors. My eyes delighted in the colours around me and started to fill up; that tissue in my Nike tights was beginning to evaporate but I used it anyway. Blue waters crashed against the cliff, clouds flirted with the sky and a raven swayed and moaned above us. Mahmoud Darwish reminded me that on this land, there is what makes life worth living. I fought the temptation to jump above the 130-centimetre fence. All the suicide prevention signs said to HOLD onto HOPE, there is always HELP. They said WE CARE. WE CAN HELP. DAY OR NIGHT. I looked around for the Angel of the Gap; I knew he died in 2012 but craved his biscuits and warm cup of tea.

I find solace in what I imagine the Angel's words to be: it's okay that you were born in Dubai rather than Palestine. That the Indigenous are pushed out of their homes while you choose which Victorian terrace in the Inner-West you wish to read Edward Said from; while you sip on your herbal teas as bleach, pesticides, nails, pills and glass shatter Palestinian guts; as you hang Japanese paintings with sixty-dollar wooden frames on your wall, they hang themselves on eucalyptus trees. You hang the painting because you dream of living in Japan, and you will, while they hang themselves in the words of Tatz, as a symbol of martyrdom, tyranny and tragedy. Inviting solidarity against uncaring relations, unmet needs, personal anguish and emotional payback. Maybe the biscuits would be so good that I'd believe him.

Jesus made it clear that silence was essential in the final hour but Blister Guy recited the ingredients of his ginger chutney recipe

---

10   Tatz 2005, 98.

anyway. Twenty-Three asked Abhi to list the food in the lunch pack we were receiving at Bronte. After mentioning the dessert, Abhi walked ahead of us and started to look smaller. Humans and animals chased after balls splashing into Bondi and Tamarama. Sartre told me, before I went on this walk, 'to make written notes of every aspect of my character before leaving, so that on my return I could compare what I used to be and what I have become'. I now recognise the hole that the Indigenous youth spoke to Tatz about, 'a "hole" in their lives [they] don't know [...] They suffer the label "Aborigine", yet cannot comprehend what it is in "Aborigine" that causes such antagonism or contempt'. It births a desire to part this earth as a reclamation of ownership of their Indigenous bodies, and power to control their deaths, if not their lives.

My mind and body became foreign to me amid this network of life and death, numbness stretched from hand to spleen and the last minutes of the walk were the hardest. How it changed me may not be apparent, but now I know that walking on stolen land is always unsettling. I bit into a piece of toast and melted into the Vegemite: bitter, acrid and foul like Emirati petrol – feels like home.

References

Androutsopoulou, Athena, Eugenia Rozou, and Mary Vakondiou (2020). Voices of Hope and Despair: A Narrative-Dialogical Inquiry into the Diaries, Letters, and Suicide Notes of Virginia Woolf. *Journal of Constructivist Psychology* 33(4): 367–384. https://doi.org/10.1080/10720537.2019.1615015

Belcourt, Billy-Ray (2021). *A History of My Brief Body*. St Lucia, QLD: University of Queensland Press.

Burnley, I. (1995). Socioeconomic and Spatial Differentials in Mortality and Means of Committing Suicide in New South Wales, Australia, 1985–1991. *Social Science & Medicine* 41(5): 687–698. https://doi.org/10.1016/0277-9536(94)00378-7

Crawford, Anwen (2021). *No Document*. Sydney: Giramondo Publishing.

Dabbagh, Nadia Taysir (2005). *Suicide in Palestine: Narratives of Despair*. Northampton, Mass.: Olive Branch Press.

Gilmour, Benjamin (2019). *The Gap: A Paramedic's Summer on the Edge*. Sydney: Viking Australia.

Lockley, Anne, Yee Tak Derek Cheung, Georgina Cox, Jo Robinson, Michelle Williamson, Meredith Harris, Anna Machlin, Caitlin Moffat, and Jane Pirkis (2014). Preventing Suicide at Suicide Hotspots: A Case Study from Australia. *Suicide & Life-Threatening Behavior* 44(4): 392–407. https://doi.org/10.1111/sltb.12080

O'Connor, Rory, and Jane Pirkis (2016). *The International Handbook of Suicide Prevention*. Hoboken, NJ: John Wiley & Sons.

Owens, Christabel (2016). 'Hotspots' and 'Copycats': A Plea for More Thoughtful Language about Suicide. *The Lancet. Psychiatry* 3(1): 19–20. https://doi.org/10.1016/S2215-0366(15)00492-7

Phillips, Juanita (2012). 'Angel of the Gap' Don Ritchie Dies. *ABC News*. https://www.abc.net.au/news/2012-05-14/angel-of-the-gap-dies/4010518

Ross, Victoria, Yu Wen Koo, and Kairi Kõlves (2020). A Suicide Prevention Initiative at a Jumping Site: A Mixed-methods Evaluation. *EClinicalMedicine* 19: 100265–100265. https://doi.org/10.1016/j.eclinm.2020.100265

Silly Walk Sydney (2020). *Silly Walk Sydney*. https://sillywalksydney.com/

Slessor, Kenneth (1939). Five Bells. *The Academy*. https://resource.acu.edu.au/siryan/Academy/texts/FiveBells.htm

Suicide in Australia (1999). Sydney: Wesley Mission.

Tatz, Colin (2005). *Aboriginal Suicide Is Different: A Portrait of Life and Self-destruction* (2nd ed.). Canberra: Aboriginal Studies Press.

Tumarkin, Maria (2018). *Axiomatic*. Melbourne: Brow Books.

crash

Libby Newton

this phase is long walks in comfortable/uncomfortable silence/
    conversation up & down the south coastline
sleeping in late and rising with the sun, guilt sticking to you like glue,
    thinking up ways to chew through the hours ahead
step ahead, step
ahead, checking your step count over the course of the week
checking your boobs to see if they've grown
checking your uterus to see if it's still there and not the washboard abs
    you dreamt of last night and every night since you were fifteen
fun, fit and flirty in activewear, because fitness is the passion of the
    masses
once lockdown hits

sit and scroll through indeed and seek
imagine you're a two-page-CV-one-page-cover-letter away from some
    minimum wage job a little less soulless than the last
which on second thought really was fine and (as best friend says) did
    exactly what it said on the tin
which is more than can be said of the vaccine rollout

in other cities/states, your sisters carve out their days
you phone and take turns crying & consoling, crying & consoling,
    sharing nicely like you never did as children
treading the minefield: an ex's engagement, a friend's cancelled
    kitchen tea, a work colleague's faux pas, a parent's insensitivity

this cousin leaving the closet, this cousin cooped up in the closet,
    despising the damned closet and those alan jones clones who
    police the doors, who give cause for this
slip and slide
between therapist and therapised

this phase is ending the call when they're ready and you're not
eating when you clock up x number of hours since your last meal,
    registering the stomach grumble, like
            the gasping exasperation of the dietitian you used to
                see
            the intrusive *dingdingding* of a hello kitty alarm
                clock
sheepish, shuffle to the fridge
assemble: chickpea brown rice spinach: nutritious delicious
    suspiciously
jutting out your chin
you'll eat something different when you're dead

later, watching television with your prudish parents, you cringe and
    giggle at the sex scenes because you are built in their image (your
    parents' – not the sex scenes')
chastise the sitcom couples that break up and make up ad infinitum
learn the algorithm: excitement, hesitation
obsession, copulation . . . . the prickly flamenco dance
disparity in feeling, followed by the cursed incantation (i <3 u, says A
    to B)
and the pause which says B isn't ready to hear it, might not ever be
    ready to hear it, certainly does not feel in kind, all leading to
    nauseating heartbreak and the question of whether ~~you~~ A will
    ever make it through this, in light of last time and the
    completeness
of the loss
of both the love object and oneself

[*pomegranate*
splitting,
seeds
skedaddling,
leaving the demented husk]
which you suppose is the way things go when one stupidly allows
    oneself to believe, uncritically and unconditionally, in the
    irreproachability of the love object

on screen, chaos ensues, and you make a mental note to revisit lacan's
    seminar viii
not because intellectualising the phenomenon makes it any easier, but
    because you want to impress *your* unattainable love object when
    next you meet

fuck

you need a hobby
at least then you could burn through all this unstructured time instead
    of buckling beneath its weight, taking too many showers with
    the temperature set to blistering and complaining about the
    (seasonably) cold weather
you're no elsa, it *does* bother you and always has, and although you
    weren't going to finish the sentence 'i hate winter _____' with
    'because it reminds me of never feeling good enough', when best
    friend didn't miss a beat, it really did capture the sentiment
and you thought as much
even as you held your belly and guffawed

in any case, you've decided that you're not *that* neurotic, you're really
    not
you're worldly, your head is in the news, you keep abreast of *things* and
    especially the case numbers

greeting gladys at eleven, tuning in to pressers and pathways out,
      tallying instances of panic-buying against panic-crying
feeling momentarily at peace when you watch the auslan interpreter,
      her tartan stockings and her nimble fingers, notwithstanding
      their dance spells doom
kerry chant cautioning against out-of-doors exercise groups of more
      than ten, which apparently is the real cause of the spread, and
      not unvaccinated frontline workers and packed shopping
      complexes and commuter corridors and hazy definitions of
      essential
as one might be forgiven for believing

no matter – go hunting for happenings beyond this breakdown
      lockdown stare-down dance-around political merry-go-round
open the ABC news app and read something about rhinoceroses,
      which is promising and gets a smile
fun fact: the collective noun for a group of rhinos is a crash
rhinos push a few nostalgia buttons, mostly because they're the nearest
      thing to your favourite dinosaur (triceratops, naturally), but lo –
it's the northern white and functional extinction, and no, there is no
      turning back the clock for these grassland grazers – best save
      your tears for the pillow or the shower, where they can't be seen
      or heard
just like the triceratops
and now the northern white rhino

by this point, you've done the inevitable switch to facebook/instagram
      and yes, you're going to check her profile and scroll through
              happy snaps
              tagged pics
              back to fraser island 2006

and yes, you're going to be left feeling pathetic (parched, sticky, gritty)
      for doing so

wondering why you don't just pee in your hat
or shit in your shoe
or hike the andes with a bung knee

this phase is hurtling towards unknown unknowns
the knownest known (apart, perhaps, from the liberal party's problem
    with women) is that there will always be unknown unknowns
even as you sit tight, hunker down, play olivia rodrigo loud enough to
    drown the houses and the trees and the fire trails and the suburbs
    you mapped with your feet yesterday and the day before,
    saturating the escarpment in teenage angst
even as your pulsating brain shows you a scene from armageddon
    sadder than the stampede that killed mufasa
A and B don't drive off into the sunset in this one
A and B wave to each other from balconies on separate continents and
    retreat to their sitting rooms
to play fortnite
and ugly cry

Pluto in Sagittarius

Kelly Ung

In the past two years I've become someone who is really into astrology. I'd always thought that horoscopes were a certain kind of general harmless bullshit that you would read at the end of a magazine, with a vague message that your mind connects to, imposing your own perspective and experience. To a certain extent I still believe that. I'd see horoscope compatibility generators, general vague posts on Facebook suggesting that the best cooks were Taureans (feels questionable) or that Pisceans and Aquarians spent their time daydreaming (I'm more inclined to believe this). It was always good fun to compare notes with friends about these probably questionable claims. Or to sneakily put in the details of the person you had your eye on and feel like you knew slightly more about them.

But in the last two years, I've had a little more time to consider the skies, I guess. After the first wave of COVID-19, I was suddenly unemployed, soon to be graduating from a degree I wasn't sure I wanted to pursue further, seemingly hurtling into a future that was truly uncertain. Looking at the news didn't help. It was clear that the institutions we rely on daily had failed us. The government gave vague guidelines no one seemed to understand, our education systems expected us to continue to study through global turmoil and pay the same amenities and services fees, I couldn't figure out which Centrelink support I qualified for, our healthcare workers were unsupported and left in shambles. Misinformation and confusion clouded a lot of my memories of this time. I looked to social media, to books, to movies and television – to distract, to do something else, to think about anything else. I didn't want to delve any deeper than I needed to into the endless void of 'unprecedented' pandemic despair.

It started with a few harmless likes on TikTok videos, but soon I was going down the rabbit hole of astrology. It was fun to listen to the attributes of star signs, especially when it aligned with the way I viewed myself, my friends and family. But more videos appeared from the vast algorithm of TikTok's depths. I wanted to know more, wanted to learn my friends' time of birth to quietly compare birth charts and make sense of how I came to know their personalities. I'd always known my sun sign, the one most people know, being born in late August I was a Virgo sun. But the deeper I fell into the web of astrology the more I learned – how the moon changes signs every few days, how one's Mercury sign would be close to if not the same as their sun sign because of its placement in the solar system, how Pluto enters a new sign every decade or so.

There are multiple generational planets: Uranus, Neptune and Pluto, all on the outer edges of the solar system where it takes the planets years to finish orbits and enter new signs. Uranus supposedly represents shocks within one's system and is forward-looking. Neptune connects creativity with divinity, often associated with spirituality as well as compassion. Pluto represents transformative subconscious forces, often associated with regeneration and rebirth. Pluto gives a view of what lies beneath the surface and what is part of the subconscious, so the astrological sign in Pluto imbues the generation that holds it with a constellation of attributes shared among these people that distinguishes them from the signs before and after it.

Pluto was in Scorpio from 1983 to 1995, and then moved into Sagittarius from 1995 to 2008, until it entered Capricorn where it remains until 2024. People with their Pluto in Scorpio are supposedly resilient and stubborn, free spirited and interested in power dynamics; this sign suggests pushing back against societal rules and expectations. People with Pluto in Sagittarius, like me, move past this push back and into envisioning a new future in search of adventure, looking to evolve and change, seeking out knowledge and spontaneity.

I'd always felt unsatisfied about the generational division between Millennials and Generation Z because I never knew which camp I fell into. Pluto in Sagittarius seems more definitive, it is clear when a generation stops and starts because it's written in the sky. I felt connected to the way that one's constellations at birth gave a kind of predetermination of one's way of life, the immense outcomes of a generation. In lockdown I felt the need to give into every impulse I'd previously held back on; get a tattoo, pierce my nose, read every book with this ridiculously limited, yet vast time I suddenly had. What did it matter – I had nothing to lose.

I started to understand the essence of what those horoscopes at the end of magazines were supposed to be sharing. I found myself expecting moments of change in Mercury's retrograde and handing over control to the cosmic network of stars.

* * *

I began half-heartedly bringing it up with my friends, annoying some adamant non-believers just for the fun of it. Not that I blamed them. I still don't think I necessarily believe astrology will map out my life, but I think I've let myself believe in it more lately.

Astrology has always felt like a pseudoscience that never followed any type of logic. It seemed more sensible to believe in the verifiable conventions of life, presenting themselves in hard facts.

I'd always felt as though my life would fall into place eventually. Adulthood felt like a rite of passage making you feel right in the world after the turmoil of adolescence. At some point, you'd find yourself among the strands of vague interests and hobbies, studies and jobs. The pattern of the strands becomes clearer, woven together neatly as things align. The logical progression through life.

Nothing in the last two years has felt logical.

* * *

I don't personally prescribe to the belief that everything there is to know about a person lies in understanding the time and location of their birth. But what I found comforting was the idea of predestination and patterns within a world that feels unknowable. Looking at astrology and the interpretation of one's birth chart requires introspection into your own actions and allows for the dissection of aspects of your life.

Through astrology I reflected on my own experiences in a new light. It felt as though I was given the time to properly stew in my own thoughts, the vast changes that had occurred in the tumultuous years of my early adulthood (or maybe it was a combination of my analytical Virgo sun and intense contemplation of my Scorpio moon). I'd never been a spiritual person, but maybe that was due to a lack of knowledge or a lack of time.

I understand these newfound interests are not the answer to all, I know that it's a reaction to a period of tenuous belief in the state of the world. But I guess I will continue looking to the stars, trying to have faith in something for now.

Threads

Dennis Haskell

So, the trip is over. All the cases empty,
the clothes freshly back on their hangers
and we, freshly back in the lives
which, with a bit of a grin,
we could describe as 'normal'. So, I write
to Sydney friends we had no time to meet
apologetically, promising, 'Next time ...'

And the visit's curiously involved detachment,
our splash out of the ordinary,
at times blankets my mind – unforgettable, unremarkable,
as if the trip were a thread
to seam up memories:
white, high-ceilinged houses,
a blue-green harbour,
the gentle relatives, even the fringes
of the lives we left behind
and partly brought with us.

To go back to your past life
is to meet yourself, and find
it is no longer you –
the guilt of colour, all the patches
unthreaded from the quilt.

No. 11

Angela Xu

Fractals infinitely replicate themselves on different scales. A tree, for example, creates fractal patterns, as the shape of the trunk becomes the shape of the boughs, and the branches, and the twigs, until it forms the veins of each leaf. Jackson Pollock was known to use this phenomenon in his paintings. What seems to be senseless chaos on the canvas, when looked at carefully, actually reveals fractal patterns that he created by making gravity his collaborator.

There's a Pollock in Australia, *Blue Poles*, which sits in the National Gallery of Australia in Canberra. It's also known as *Number 11, 1952*, or simply, *No. 11*. Eight poles sit within the chaos of blue, red, yellow and white, and every day visitors sit before it, wondering how a canvas that looks like it was painted by a four-year-old could be considered one of the greatest pieces of modern art. My parents took me to see it when I was ten. Of course, I was far more interested in painting my own ceramic Christmas decoration with the kids' program than looking at any painting, but as my parents explained to me the concept of fractals and pointed them out in the painting, the chaos didn't seem so aimless anymore. They traced the never-ending, repeating patterns with their fingers through the air, showing me how each fork, each turn, each wobble, is an echo of something that came before.

It towered over me at two metres tall and I remember wondering how many similar paintings had come before this one. *Number 11*, supposedly it was the eleventh he painted in 1952, but what if it was the eleventh that contained the pole motif? What if it was just an arbitrary number he assigned to the painting? How many paintings had he made before this one? How many versions of these eight poles existed in the world, in his drafts, in an abandoned storage unit that he forgot about, in reproductions, news articles and photographs? The number '11' seemed all at once more and less significant. In a system of infinite repetition, how could we even label and quantify every single version?

The next month, I turned eleven, and the question of fractals again came to visit. My parents gave me a photo album and told me to store my memories in there, every birthday and Christmas I wanted to remember, every person that meant something to me, every version of myself that I wanted to keep alive in rough, handwoven pages. I stuck in photos of myself as a young child, pressed leaves from a vacation to Orange, tickets from movies I went to with friends, drawings from art class. When the pieces of your life are laid out on paper, it's impossible not to wonder which is the real you. Whether it's who you are when you're with friends or when you're with family. Whether it's who you are when you're young or you're old. Clippings of mere moments cannot possibly do justice to a whole life lived, but they prompt the question of what life you're living.

As I got older, I kept saving things in my album. For a while, only photos were saved and stuck in, until my family and friends grew tired of taking photos for every little thing we did together. Then, it was tickets and brochures, as I became enamoured with the idea of being someone who was always *doing* something. And for the last couple of years, it has been nothing, as the notion of meticulously capturing and saving everything started to bore me. The book now bulges at the front, bursting with glossed photos and dog-eared tickets, while the back lays empty, grounding the album in the inevitable reality of a childhood fading.

* * *

I visited *Blue Poles* again today. On my bucket list of things to do in Canberra before I moved away for university, this was my last stop. It wasn't the most obvious, after seeing friends and family, eating at my favourite café and feeding ducks near my primary school. It wasn't until late afternoon that I decided to go. An hour before closing, I slunk my way through the dispersing crowd and sat in front of the painting, unravelling the coloured strands and tracing the route of each fractal system. Some ended after a while, coming to an abrupt stop after travelling across the canvas, culminating in droplets that held onto the motion. Some were eclipsed by another strand and remained hidden behind layers of paint. Others simply disappeared from view, having reached the edges of the canvas. I like to think that they never end; that even though they have disappeared for us, they continue their self-repetition.

'Are you ready?'

Mum's voice pulls me out of my reverie.

'Almost, ten minutes.'

I look around my room for the last time, the bare walls and desk shying away from my gaze as though I were a stranger. As I reach into my pocket for my phone, the ticket from this afternoon flutters to the ground, flashing red, white and black. I pick it up, my eyes meeting the photo album sitting almost expectantly on the bookshelf. Reluctantly, I slip the crinkling ticket into the back of the album, before unfurling its front cover.

Fractals infinitely replicate themselves on different scales. Page to page, a different version of myself is captured, from my age and appearance to my handwriting and what I've kept from that time of my life. Each version slightly different, but still recognisable as me. That's the thing about fractals, their replication is never perfect. Some versions are slightly ruffled, some glimmer and glow, while others hold a tinge of sadness. I see some lived a life of adventure; travelling, hiking and experiencing everything they could. Others seemed to hardly do anything out of the ordinary, as the realities of school, work and life chased at their heels.

How many versions of myself have existed, how many have walked this earth, appeared in photographs, in memories, in the eyes of others? Which version was I? Perhaps, like *Blue Poles*, I was number eleven, a polished version, but nowhere near the maturity captured by decades of living.

The album closes with a ceremonial puff and I nestle it in the mess of my suitcase before fighting the zip closed.

As long as I am a fractal system, maybe it doesn't matter which version of myself I was. As long as I can still recognise the remnants of me that my album conserves, as long as I can trace the route of my replication, as long as I have a name that says more than *Number 11, 1952.*

My door gives a reluctant squeak and swings open.

'Ready.'

Yggdrasil

Allen Chan

they prosecuted my phone,
confiscated the blueprints
of my day and constructed
a temple from its symbols.
they crisscrossed its images,
scissoring the edges against each other
until one became
enmeshed within another.

a suspended (state of retrieval).
they took the combinations of
faecal-laced lockers, swiping
through fingerprints to
look and see how many times
I had been left on read,
a diagnosis of blue ticks.
they labeled each
double text – an allotment
of miscommunication.
they had no prescription for my
wounds, they knew
my scars were
for others to graft.

they tried to link – the usage
of emojis with the invisible chamber that
pulled the strings.
but they never would be able to get
a (peach and eggplant) emoji to
equal a heart.

they counted the pixels in my smile,
placing it on a protractor until
satisfied with the degree.

they felt certain, my words, my
witness.

they were unmoved
by missing evidence, the lack
testified the need.
they charged my phone
as an accessory
to love.

Thoughts of a Student Sitting in a Zoom Breakout Room

Angela Xu

You know that opening theme from the second season of the
      Muppets?
the whole gang – Kermit, Miss Piggy, everyone – is tucked away
in their own bedazzled arch as a ceaselessly catchy tune blares

this is kind of like that, except I'm Kermit
and everyone else is dead
(muted)
(cameras off)

and my bedazzled arch is not bedazzled
it's just an arch

we were supposed to be discussing the prescribed readings of the week

how the impact of phosphate mining in the Pacific was part of the
      social, political and environmental dynamics of the islands, and
      how exploiting the mining benefitted Australia and New Zealand
      and helped them become powerful international agents in
      Oceania

or something like that

my bedazzled (not bedazzled) arch reveals my penguin pyjamas

slyly peeking out from beneath my hoodie
five pairs of gumball eyes and seven pairs of penguin feet

they stare at four black rectangles
white names etched in
and an ever-telling slashed red microphone in the bottom left corner

uhm, so
does anyone have any ideas?

I take a sip of green tea
hoping that its bitterness will drown out my own

four slashed microphones stare back at me
taunting me
as if challenging me to speak first

I uh,
thought that the readings really showed how the islands were socially and
politically reliant on the environment, so the mining kind of destroyed
everything by making the environment unable to sustain agriculture
or traditional living anymore

and uhm,
it kind of shows how like, the uhm, islands after being exploited for mining
are further exploited by Australia by being incentivised to become
refugee detention centres through like government aid packages and
stuff, cause they need that aid to help their environment and economy
recover

I look down at my notes
maybe within the scribbles denoting the tensions of Pacific
        exploitation and colonisation

there's something that will distract me from the awkwardness
that pricks me with each second passing by

prick
prick
prick

silence, in reality, is not really silence
a breath
a sniffle
the rustle of a sleeve
the scratching of a head
composes the symphony that is life

but here
silence is silence

there's an anechoic chamber in Minnesota
where you can hear the sound of your lungs sometimes
and the longest anyone can last is 45 minutes

breakout room ending in
10
9
should I leave now or stay until it's over
8
7
6
the longest I could last in the chamber was 5
4
3
2
1

New Journalists for the Digital Media Age

Melissa Snook

> That's journalism; a news analysis is journalism; an editorial is journalism. The chief difference between these and what Oliver does, if anything, is that he's entertaining, so that, when he spends fifteen minutes arguing the stakes of net neutrality, people actually pay attention and even act on it. If that makes it 'not journalism,' then it's journalism that has the problem.
>
> James Poniewozik, *TIME Magazine*

From their early beginnings in vaudeville, comedians have traditionally taken the role of entertainers. The purpose of the comedian has always been to generate a humorous response in the listener through such things as joke telling and observational humour. However, beginning in the mid-twentieth century, the role of the comedian as joke teller began to combine with the task of social commentary. Humour in the US came to focus more on satirical observation of American culture and politics, often making fun of, or highlighting a problem in society. In 1972, Maxwell McCombs and Donald Shaw argued that mass media outlets such as television were central to the understanding of politics.[1] A growing viewership of late-night comedy shows – *The Daily Show, The Colbert Report* and *Last Week Tonight* – has emerged alongside the traditional television network broadcast. With the rise in popularity of comedians such as Jon Stewart, Stephen Colbert and John Oliver in this genre, we are also beginning to see an increase

---

1   McCombs and Donald Shaw 1972, 176.

in trust between the comedian and the listener regarding political topics. Pew Research Center studies following major elections over the last twenty years have demonstrated a shift towards comedy shows in how the younger generation (for the purpose of this study, I am referring to 18–29) are gaining their knowledge and understanding of political issues. I argue that amidst claims of whether late-night shows constitute journalism, comedians are cleverly using journalistic techniques to have a significant impact on the political knowledge of young Americans compared to traditional news broadcasts. Essentially, I will demonstrate that young adults, particularly left-leaning democrats, are abandoning traditional news networks in favour of late-night comedy shows.

In an interview with American journalist Jorge Ramos, comedian John Oliver strongly denied the claim that he was a journalist.[2] Like Oliver, a number of late-night comedy hosts have made the same clarification. They argue that as comedians, news comes secondary to the joke.[3] However, the characteristics of these late-night comedy shows draw stark parallels with traditional broadcast journalism.

Is late-night comedy 'broadcast journalism'?

Whether comedians can be counted as journalists has been a controversial debate over the past decade. Jon Stewart, former host of *The Daily Show*, saw the beginning of this transition of late-night comedy shows from tabloid entertainment to hard hitting, contemporary exposés on political and social issues in America.[4] Since Stewart, a number of late-night hosts have followed in the same tradition; from Stephen Colbert to John Oliver to Stewart's *The Daily Show* successor Trevor Noah. Let us first consider the different arguments proposed in the debate on the equivalency of late-night comedy shows with broadcast journalism.

---

2   FUSION 2015.
3   Robinson 2015.
4   Peabody Awards 2015.

They use the same mediums of content presentation

Frank Barnas and Ted White note that interviews have always been an important and efficient part of broadcast journalism, better than online research for attaining information, and their use offers insightful opinions from witnesses to experts.[5]

Late-night comedy shows also use this method of knowledge creation. Typically, the host of comedy shows use interviews for entertainment purposes: interviewing the star of the latest film release, for example. With the rising presence of news segments in late-night shows, comedians have begun to shift the function of the interview from tabloid guests to political guests.

John Oliver's *Last Week Tonight* is dedicated to reporting the latest news of the week in a comedic fashion. Like most news broadcasts, the show follows the anchorman-behind-the-desk aesthetic. Every now and then, Oliver conducts a special news broadcast where he takes on a controversial political or social issue, and interviews an expert or someone of importance to the topic. Among Oliver's most notable guests include Stephen Hawking and Edward Snowden. Let's take one of these examples and see how comedians use the interview process to better educate the public.

In April 2015, HBO aired an episode of *Last Week Tonight* where Oliver travelled to Russia to interview American former National Security Agency (NSA) employee and controversial whistle-blower Edward Snowden for a segment on government surveillance.[6] For the average American, government surveillance and the role and abilities of the NSA are difficult concepts to grasp. However, John Oliver took this issue and constructed the interview in a way that the average American would understand, although in a slightly unorthodox fashion.[7] Instead of listening to Snowden explain government surveillance, Oliver claims that he only cares whether the government can see his 'dick pic'.[8] While this may be inappropriate for a formal interview, the back and forth discussion on whether the government could in fact see a 'dick

---

5   Barnas and White 2013.
6   Last Week Tonight 2015.
7   Last Week Tonight 2015.
8   Just in case you were wondering, they can.

pic' is extremely funny and forces an answer about the complexities of the overarching issue. This leaves the viewer with a pretty decent understanding of how government surveillance works.

Interviews are also used in late-night comedy shows for political issues. During the 2004 primaries, Jon Stewart interviewed a few prominent political figures including John McCain, Bill Clinton and John Kerry, on important issues like the war in Iraq.[9]

Significant effort goes into fact checking and research

John Oliver has remained adamant that he is not a journalist.[10] While his show does perform some of the functions of broadcast news, including fact checking and research, Oliver argues that these aspects of his research, writing and reporting are necessary for the joke:

> We are making jokes about the news and sometimes we need to research things deeply to understand them, but it's always in service of a joke. If you make jokes about animals, that does not make you a zoologist. We certainly hold ourselves to a high standard and fact-check everything, but the correct term for what we do is *comedy*.[11]

Regardless of the presentation of the content, the effort of research and fact checking that would go into each segment of the show is astounding, especially for a comedy late-night program.

It's comedy, not journalism: news is secondary to the joke

Probably the main argument made by comedians when asked whether they are journalists is that comedy and journalism are two separate things.[12] The main objective of the late-night shows are to make people laugh, whether the content is focused on politics, religion or tabloids.

---

9   National Annenberg Election Survey 2004.
10   FUSION 2015.
11   Poniewozik 2014.
12   FUSION 2015.

It's not objective reporting

This is an interesting argument. While comedians do not practice journalistic objectivity, it can be argued that neither does traditional media news outlets. Throughout coverage of the 2016 presidential election and during former President Trump's term in office, Fox News had been strongly right-wing in its position, presentation and judgement of the news, as will be discussed in the second section of this article.[13]

It is true that late-night comedy shows tend to be more left-leaning and anti-republican. During the 2016 elections, Saturday Night Live (SNL) created a satirical parody of the debates between Donald Trump and Hillary Clinton.[14] The segment mocked Trump ruthlessly: making fun of his constant attacks at Clinton, the way he says 'China' and the ridiculousness of his ideas and beliefs.[15]

It is both

Rather than calling late-night shows either journalism or comedy, I would argue that these shows draw on journalistic techniques to appear trustworthy and as a source of knowledge. Geoffrey Baym, author of *From Cronkite to Colbert: The Evolution of Broadcast News,* discusses the potential of this third position that is often ignored.[16] Late-night comedy shows, rather than one or the other, are instead a *fusion of both news and entertainment.*[17] This puts the shows in a unique position, able to discuss and report news and issues in a format that keeps people entertained while increasing knowledge amongst its consumers.

Due to its bipartisan structure of news and entertainment, late-night shows are able to ignore certain conventions that traditional media broadcasters are subject to. One such convention dictates the content of quotes.[18] In traditional broadcast media, quotes are often cut

---

13 Fang 2018.
14 The Liberty Daily 2016.
15 The Liberty Daily 2016.
16 Baym 2009, 104.
17 Baym 2009, 104.
18 Baym 2009, 106.

to fit an eight to twelve second bracket and all nuances of speech are excluded.[19]

Traditional vs unconventional election coverage

One of the biggest news blunders of the past two decades was the reporting of the Florida vote in the 2000 election. During the election night coverage, a number of news broadcasters made crucial mistakes that turned election media coverage into a joke.[20] Major news stations Fox, CNN, ABC, CBS, NBC and MSNBC were all quick to call Florida's poll results, resulting in a premature concession call and an early election winner.[21] While these news broadcasters were scrambling to find the truth, and as a consequence severely confusing the public, Jon Stewart was revolutionising late-night comedy and political news.[22] Not only was Stewart reporting on the election with correspondents at the Republican and Democratic conventions – something quite unheard of for comedy shows previous to this election – Stewart began a segment titled *Indecision 2000.*[23] Jon Stewart was keeping the public informed while also mocking traditional news networks.[24]

The 2016 election between Hillary Clinton and Donald Trump was surrounded by controversy, with news media on both sides of the political spectrum targeting the candidates. John Oliver reported repeatedly on the election campaign.[25] In an episode just after the election, it's clear that Oliver was not satisfied with the result.[26] His report was full of disbelief, mockery of media reports and facts used to try and discredit the President-elect.[27] However, his reporting was

---

19   Baym 2009, 106.
20   Marks and Bill Carter 2000.
21   Marks and Carter 2000.
22   Yahr 2015.
23   Yahr 2015.
24   Yahr 2015.
25   DeVore 2016.
26   Last Week Tonight 2016a.
27   Last Week Tonight 2016a.

not completely biased. In another episode during the campaign, Oliver takes shots at both Clinton and Trump.[28]

What did the coverage look like? During the primaries, media coverage by traditional news broadcasters focused more on poll results and projections, while only eleven percent of coverage was focused on the candidate's policies.[29] During this period, Trump received the majority of coverage and was cast in a relatively positive light in comparison to coverage of Republicans Marco Rubio and Ted Cruz.[30] In comparison, while Hillary Clinton received more coverage than Bernie Sanders, the majority of the coverage of democratic candidates was negative.[31] What these statistics show is a greater focus on scandal reporting, such as the issues of Clinton's emails and Trump's taxes. Further statistics from news reporting during the Republican and Democratic conventions show a similar trend. News coverage of Trump focused on the campaign in general and other unspecified issues while his policies were only discussed thirteen percent of the time, and his qualifications and leadership were mentioned only three percent of the time.[32] The research also shows that when his policies were discussed, eighty-six percent of that coverage was negative.[33] In similar fashion, news coverage of Hillary Clinton at the general election shows even worse results. Policies and issues were only mentioned in four percent of media coverage while the state of her campaign was given the most airtime.[34]

It is clear from both the 2000 and 2016 elections that traditional and unconventional media both have their positive and negative aspects. During the 2000 election, *The Daily Show* served as a place to find political information, while the latest election saw media on both ends of the political spectrum focus on the controversies rather than the policies.

---

28 Last Week Tonight 2016b.
29 Patterson 2016a.
30 Patterson 2016a.
31 Patterson 2016a.
32 Patterson 2016b.
33 Patterson 2016b.
34 Patterson 2016b.

In comedy we trust

One of the most important factors of any news broadcast, for it to gain any level of success, is that there must be a significant level of trust between the news host and the audience.

In the 2015 TIME magazine's '100 most influential people', comedy greats such as Lorne Michaels, Amy Schumer, Kevin Hart and John Oliver were listed alongside prominent figures such as Hillary Clinton, Barack Obama and Ruth Bader Ginsberg.[35] In the same year, Jon Stewart's *The Daily Show* won the highly coveted Peabody Awards – an annual awards program highlighting the best and most influential in broacast media.[36] The award recognised *The Daily Show* as:

> A different animal, an evolutionary leap. In an era of politicised, echo-chamber news channels and traditional-journalism timidity, *The Daily Show with Jon Stewart* didn't simply mine the day's news for jokes. It spoke truth to power and withering sarcasm to hypocrisy, taking on the news media as well as the news makers, and thus became a trusted source of news for citizens united in their disappointment and disgust with politics and cable news ... Stewart deconstructed real news reports, covered elections and conducted interviews that made powerful politicians fume and squirm.[37]

The hypodermic needle theory, or magic bullet theory, proposed that consumers of mass media are highly susceptible to messages and opinions.[38] What this means for television news programs is that there is a certain level of trust between news broadcasters and their audiences. As we have seen with the prominence of late-night shows, this level of journalistic trust is also being applied to comedy hosts. Jon Stewart, throughout his long career at *The Daily Show*, demonstrated this level of trust between host and viewer, as someone who spoke the

---

35   TIME 2015.
36   Peabody 2015.
37   Peabody 2015.
38   Fourie 2001, 294.

truth and kept people informed on the latest and biggest news. During the recording of his final episode with the show, fan-made posters of Stewart's face with the caption 'The Daily Show . . . In Jon We Trust' were passed out to fellow audience members. Similarly, another poster from a political rally held in Washington DC had Stewart's face on it and the words 'In comedy we trust'.

In his book, Jeffrey Jones put forth the idea of 'entertaining politics', the idea that television is finding new and creative ways to report on political news.[39] This contemporary form of news broadcast is engaging with its audiences in a way that traditional forms are unable to, as he states:

> Audiences are receptive to, if not also hungry for, political programming that is meaningful and engaging to them – programming that connects with their interests and concerns, provides new ways of thinking about politics, criticises that which needs scrutiny, and speaks to them through accessible pleasurable means.[40]

Late-night comedy shows also play a role in educating the public on political issues. According to scholars McClennen and Maisel, satire functions as 'public pedagogy', in that it 'teaches the public about vital issues central to the health of our democracy'.[41]

But how does this make late-night comedy shows better than traditional broadcast media? I discussed earlier the argument of bias in news reporting and that news broadcasters such as Fox are right leaning. Natalie Stroud argues that people choose their news source based on similar values.[42] For example, a conservative republican is more likely to watch Fox.[43] Statistics from the National Annenberg Election Survey found that of those young adults that watched *The Daily Show* one or more days during that week, fifteen percent were

---

39   Jones 2010, 15.
40   Jones 2010, 15.
41   McClennen and Maisel 2016, 31.
42   Stroud 2008, 342.
43   Stroud 2008, 350.

Republican compared to forty percent Democrat, and eighteen percent conservative compared to forty-three percent liberal.[44] I believe the younger generation are abandoning old school news outlets out of frustration. With Fox reporting on issues such as the 'Emoji Cheeseburger Crisis' or 'Are UFO's Real', this is no surprise.[45] David Buckingham argues that 'television news is largely failing to fulfil these responsibilities, particularly among young people'.[46] What Buckingham is suggesting is that young liberals are turning to alternative means of news because traditional media is not contributing to a properly informed population.

In our current climate of on-demand media, news broadcasting is turning to the internet.[47] What we see starting to occur is the transition of debate from television to digital media such as YouTube.[48] John Oliver contemplated this idea, saying 'If YouTube *is* the future of political discourse, perhaps it's time to embrace it'.[49] As Baym points out, Comedy Central places all their content of *The Daily Show* and *The Colbert Report* online for anyone to access.[50] Not only is late-night comedy creating public spaces for political discussion, but it is also making that discussion available on a 24/7 basis. The popularity of these shows rises through digital mediums. John Oliver's segments on Trump and government surveillance currently have, as of September 2021, thirty-four million and thirty-two million views respectively.[51] With the ability to then engage with the content on YouTube, there is a participatory factor introduced to the news that doesn't translate well into traditional media broadcast.

The entertainment aspect of news broadcasts on comedic shows is not a hindrance, but an encouragement to viewers who would not normally take notice of long, complex news topics. Unlike his counterparts, Oliver's show features segments that can go for over ten

---

44 National Annenberg Election Survey 2004.
45 Fang 2018.
46 Buckingham 2002, vii.
47 Baym 2009, 146-7.
48 Baym 2009, 146-7.
49 Baym 2009, 146.
50 Baym 2009,147.
51 Last Week Tonight 2016, Last Week Tonight 2015.

minutes long.[52] For a country of people whose attention span is only eight seconds, it is a testament to his role as a journalist and comedian that Oliver has the success and influence that he does.[53]

It is late-night comedy shows such as *The Daily Show* and *Last Week Tonight* that go a long way in better educating the population on current political issues. In a study conducted by the University of Delaware Center for Political Communication, a survey found that late-night show audiences were better informed on net neutrality than those of traditional news broadcasters such as Fox and CNN.[54]

Throughout this chapter, I have suggested that young adults are abandoning traditional media networks. The research and statistics on political news over the last decade or so have shown the emergence of this particular narrative. In a 2000 study, it was found that twenty-four percent of young adults turned to comedy shows and unconventional media regularly for election news.[55] The 2004 election shows similar results. While only six percent of Americans get campaign news from comedy shows, this statistic increases to twenty-one percent among the younger generation.[56] The more important question though, is whether these forms of news broadcast impact on young adult knowledge of campaigns and elections? In a 2004 Pew study, it was found that late-night shows were significantly effective in providing current and new information.[57]

In the National Annenberg study, it was found that amongst young adults who were asked six questions relating to the 2004 election, of those that watched *The Daily Show*, five percent got zero correct, while thirty-four percent got five or six correct and forty-one percent got three or four correct.[58] Compare this to those that did not watch late-night shows: only fifteen percent got five or six correct.[59] Lastly, statistics from 2012 show a similar trend. In particular, audiences of

52   Last Week Tonight 2015.
53   McSpadden 2015.
54   Center for Political Communication 2014.
55   Pew Research Center 2018.
56   Pew Research Center 2004.
57   Pew Research Center 2004.
58   National Annenberg Election Survey 2004.
59   National Annenberg Election Survey 2004.

The Colbert Report and *The Daily Show* were often better informed than those of Fox or CNN, for example.[60] These statistics from the last twenty years show a positive upward trajectory of the younger generation gaining knowledge from alternative news means compared to older audiences of traditional news broadcasters.

Why are young adults turning to late-night comedy for news? I hinted earlier that traditional media is not meeting the needs and interests of the younger generation. While I do still believe this is true, I think a more plausible explanation is that entertainment and politics work better together for young adults. One school student said:

> I think he [Jon Stewart] just kinda added a little satire to it [the news]. So that you can take the same thing that you are tired of hearing about and think about it a little differently and kind of humorously. But at the same time he gives you the facts – but for every fact he gives you, he gives you something kinda funny to think about it as well.[61]

Not only does late-night comedy have impact, but also it keeps the younger generation interested and up to date with the latest news and events.

Conclusion

As all the evidence suggests, there is a decline in both content quality and information retention of audiences for traditional forms of news broadcasting. While late-night comedy shows might not be considered journalistic broadcasting, there is merit in using a journalistic style of joke-telling that both entertains and informs their younger audience.

In a 2010 interview, Jon Stewart said:

> We don't do anything but make the connections . . . We're just going off your own instinct of, 'What are the connections to this

---

60   Pew Research Center 2012.
61   Rottinghaus, Bird, Ridout and Self 2008, 286.

that make sense?' And this really is true: We don't fact-check [and] look at context because of any journalistic criteria that has to be met; we do that because jokes don't work when they're lies. We fact-check so when we tell a joke, it hits you at sort of a gut level – not because we have a journalistic integrity, [but because] hopefully we have a comedic integrity that we don't want to violate.[62]

And yet the year before, the public voted Jon Stewart as their most trusted news host. So are comedians and late-night comedy shows journalists? I'll leave that for you to decide.

References

Barnas, Frank, and Ted White (2013). *Broadcast News Writing, Reporting and Producing.* New York and London: Taylor and Francis Group.

Baym, Geoffrey (2009). *From Cronkite to Colbert: The Evolution of Broadcast News.* Oxford: Oxford University Press.

Buckingham, David (2002). *The Making of Citizens: Young People, News and Politics.* London and New York: Routledge.

Center for Political Communication (2014, 10 November). *National Survey Shows Public Overwhelmingly Opposes Internet "Fast Lanes".* https://timedotcom.files.wordpress.com/2015/03/ud-cpc-natagenda2014pr_2014netneutrality.pdf.

DeVore, Jackie (2016, 7 November). *John Oliver's Election Recap – 2016.* YouTube Video, 1:52. https://www.youtube.com/watch?v=ER3W5hfvC14.

Fang, Marina (2018, 13 January). Fox News Defends Trump's 'Shithole' Comments as Just the Way Normal People Talk. *Huffington Post.* https://www.huffingtonpost.com.au/entry/fox-news-trump-shithole_us_5a58aaa4e4b0720dc4c64a73.

Fourie, Pieter Jacobus (2001). *Media Studies: Institutions, Theories and Issues.* Lansdowne: Juta Education.

FUSION (2015, 12 May). *John Oliver to Jorge Ramos: 'I'm not a journalist'.* YouTube Video, 8:34. https://www.youtube.com/watch?v=117TPkXGVCo.

Jones, Jeffrey (2010). *Entertaining Politics: Satiric Television and Political Engagement.* Lanham: Rowman & Littlefield Publishers.

---

62   Fresh Air 2010.

Last Week Tonight (2015, 5 April). *Government Surveillance: Last Week Tonight with John Oliver (HBO)*. YouTube Video, 33:13. https://www.youtube.com/watch?v=XEVlyP4_11M&t=2s.

Last Week Tonight (2016a, 13 November). *Donald Trump: Last Week Tonight with John Oliver (HBO)*. YouTube Video, 21:53. https://www.youtube.com/watch?v=DnpO_RTSNmQ.

Last Week Tonight (2016b, 13 November). *President-Elect Trump: Last Week Tonight with John Oliver (HBO)*. YouTube Video, 29:00. https://www.youtube.com/watch?v=-rSDUsMwakI&t=194s.

Last Week Tonight (2016c, 25 September). *Scandals: Last Week Tonight with John Oliver (HBO)*. YouTube Video, 21:15. https://www.youtube.com/watch?v=h1Lfd1aB9YI.

Marks, Peter and Bill Carter. (2000, 9 November). The 2000 Elections: The Network Predictions; Media Rethink an Urge to Say Who's First. *The New York Times*. https://www.nytimes.com/2000/11/09/us/2000-elections-network-predictions-media-rethink-urge-say-who-s-first.html.

McClennen, Sophia and Remy Maisel (2016). *Is Satire Saving Our Nation? Mockery and American Politics*. New York: Palgrave Macmillan.

McCombs, Maxwell and Donald Shaw (1972). The Agenda-Setting Function of Mass Media. *The Public Opinion Quarterly* 36(2): 176–187.

McSpadden, Kevin (2015, 14 May). You Know Have a Shorter Attention Span Than a Goldfish. *TIME*. http://time.com/3858309/attention-spans-goldfish/.

National Annenberg Election Survey (2004). *Daily Show Viewers Knowledgeable About Presidential Campaign, National Annenberg Election Survey Shows*. https://cdn.annenbergpublicpolicycenter.org/wp-content/uploads/2004_03_late-night-knowledge-2_9-21_pr2.pdf.

Patterson. Thomas E. (2016a, July). *News Coverage of the 2016 Presidential Primaries: Horse Race Reporting Has Consequences*. https://shorensteincenter.org/wp-content/uploads/2016/07/Election-2016-Primary-Media-Coverage.pdf.

Patterson, Thomas E. (2016b, September). *News Coverage of the 2016 National Conventions: Negative News, Lacking Context*. https://shorensteincenter.org/wp-content/uploads/2016/09/2016-Convention-News-Coverage.pdf?x78124.

Patterson, Thomas E. (2016c, December). *News Coverage of the 2016 General Election: How the Press Failed the Voters*. https://shorensteincenter.org/wp-content/uploads/2016/12/2016-General-Election-News-Coverage-1.pdf?x78124.

Peabody Awards (2015, 31 August). *Jon Stewart – The Daily Show: Indecision 2000 – 2000 Peabody Award Acceptance Speech.* YouTube Video, 3:48. https://www.youtube.com/watch?v=OkywunmMRP4&t=124s.

Peabody Awards (2018). Institutional Award: The Daily Show with Jon Stewart. *Peabody.* http://www.peabodyawards.com/award-profile/the-daily-show-with-jon-stewart.

Pew Research Center (2000, February 5). *The Tough Job of Communicating with Voters.* http://www.people-press.org/2000/02/05/the-tough-job-of-communicating-with-voters/.

Pew Research Center (2004, 11 January). *Cable and Internet Loom Large in Fragmented Political News Universe.* http://www.people-press.org/2004/01/11/cable-and-internet-loom-large-in-fragmented-political-news-universe/.

Pew Research Center (2012, 27 September). *Section 4: Demographics and Political Views of news Audiences.* https://pewrsr.ch/3fP4LcX/.

Poniewozik, James (2014, 17 November). Unfortunately, John Oliver, You Are A Journalist. *TIME.* http://time.com/3589285/unfortunately-john-oliver-you-are-a-journalist/.

Robinson, Joanna (2015, 13 May). John Oliver Rejects the Notion that He's a Respected Journalist. *Vanity Fair.* https://www.vanityfair.com/hollywood/2015/05/john-oliver-not-a-journalist.

Rottinghaus, Brandon, Kenton Bird, Travis Ridout and Rebecca Self (2008). 'It's Better Than Being Informed': College-Aged Viewers of *The Daily Show.* In Baumgartner, Jody C. and Jonathan S. Morris (eds). *Laughing Matters: Humor and American Politics in the Media Age,* 279–294. New York and London: Routledge.

Stroud, Natalie Jomini (2008). Media Use and Political Predispositions: Revisiting the Concept of Selective Exposure. *Political Behaviour* 30(3): 341–366.

The Liberty Daily (2016, 2 October). *Alec Baldwin and SNL Nail Portraying the First 2016 Presidential Debate.* YouTube Video, 9:31. https://www.youtube.com/watch?v=Ukt2j4p_tv4.

TIME (2015). The 100 Most Influential People. *TIME.* http://time.com/collection/2015-time-100/.

Yahr, Emily (2015, 5 August). How 'Indecision 2000' Changed Everything for Jon Stewart and 'The Daily Show'. *Washington Post.* https://wapo.st/3qRMMsT

Self-deconstruction

Tahira Kale

I am tethered to the different masks I wear, they are all distinct from
    one another.
Hypocritical to wear even one
I think too fast and forget to breathe slow.
Every day I wake up and stare at the array of alluring masks and say:
'who should I be today?'
I slither my way through the day, counting the slick lies that I spread
    in return for another's smile.
The vivid-coloured skies turn to a thick smog
when the pins on my face fall.
Green mist blurs my vision,
as I live in a fallacy of my own construction.

Phone Friends

Cherie Baird

I have friends who live in my phone.
The best of the lot lives in Lille, really,
but it seems safer
to trivialise our friendship this way
when we've never met.

I call her *my French friend* and
my mother frowns as if
at a child dreaming up companions.
I wonder what my friend calls me,
whether she avoids the cross-cultural implications of my name.
She texts me at 5 pm and scolds me
when I reply instantly,
urges me to sleep.
It's 1 am here, after all.

My occasional-adoptive-mum lives in Boston.
Happily child-free, she reassures me that
I'm intelligent and kind, that I'll do great things.
Sometimes on bad days
I buy her a coffee: I like knowing
I've made at least someone smile.

Another friend lives in Lithuania
with a bundle of children and a travelling husband.

We write each other stories to pass the time;
she dreams up poems about
angels and demons in bookstores.
She makes me feel fearless, adventurous.
Like I could grow into the capacity
of my actual age, no longer just aspiring toward
the abstract hopes once thrust upon a bright child.

There are hundreds of us, loosely
falling together like lost souls
shivering in the night.
I recognise usernames and cartoon renderings,
country flags and favourite emojis.
We share images and stories,
give virtual hope and hugs that auto-play.
One friend has chronic pain;
another cares for her brother full time;
one lives with a roommate and two dogs post-divorce;
another teaches at university and watches *Jeopardy!*
with a grandmother who asks every night,
'Whatever happened to Alex Trebek?'

I marvel at my Polish friend's bedroom makeover
and my Swedish friend's first book.
I cry when my Texan friend reunites
with their twin flame,
and grin when my Melbourne friend suggests
we could play board games in person.
My mother doesn't just frown this time,
she wonders where along the way
I unlearnt *don't talk to strangers.*
I struggle to explain that *these aren't strangers*:
I've known them for four years.
Our lives are more deeply entwined

than mine is with the crowd of familiar faces
I greet politely every week
as we pass each other by.

My friends encourage me to walk through fears,
wish me luck with crossed fingers and
hold out a hand in the lonesome small hours.
Congratulate my wins;
share the grief of my losses.
I know their faces and their stories,
their work and their passions,
their favourite characters, worst days,
awkward encounters, spontaneous hairstyles,
friends' problems, pets' names . . .
Why on earth should it matter
if we've never met?

Incognito Mode or: How I Learned to Stop Worrying and Love the Net

Michael Kowalczyk-Barker

How I craved the desire for human interaction. And how I despised what I wanted most: that basic human need for technological manipulation. To unlink and unplug had been a painful process, but nowhere near as unbearable as living with the physical consequences of my attempted circumvention of the rules. The left side of my face still twitched, and a dull pain still resided near my temples, occasionally rising to that of an unpleasant roar. Yet most of the symptoms had receded. Only the guilt and misery remained at the forefront of my mind. That, and a strong determination not to return. To reject the information highway that was placed in my mind from a young age, and that I relied upon for knowledge, memory and thought. It's too bad there is no other way. The human brain is the only peripheral still compatible. To surf the Net was to drown, and I was tired of drowning.

The waiting area was filled with unfortunates like myself, some in the same state, some much worse. Those that returned were beaming, bright and whole, and often stopped to share words of wisdom and comfort to those that were yet to be seen. None of them returned like me. It was disconcerting to see this alien display of face-to-face interaction. Uncomfortable, I stared instead at the poster across the room: How To Think Properly, Stupid. The poster displayed an early human, twenty-first century perhaps, hunched over a primitive home computer setup with a complete look of befuddlement. Standing over this archaeo-primate was one of our doctor-programmers explaining the finer points of information retrieval via early search engines, much to the growing confusion of the being in question. Humorous; but also sad. My ancestors would have struggled like this. *Perhaps we shouldn't make fun of our predecessors*, I thought. *Perhaps I shouldn't have done what I did.*

'They will see you now,' the receptionist said to me, her face changing almost instantaneously from a look of polite boredom to near-genuine reassurance. *Too quick*, I thought, as I walked past her into the office, *to be natural*. God knows how many upgrades she has had. Oh hell, God wouldn't know. He was unplugged.

* * *

I attempted to gather my thoughts before the eventual questioning as I sat in the bleak enclosure. But the office was not free from distractions. A desk scattered with artefacts lined one wall. The other was smothered with an iScreen projecting a mountain scene; slow flowing, crystal clear streams that wrapped around little mounds of conifers while large, snow-capped peaks dominated the horizon. Presented in such high definition that it made my eyes water. I stared in amazement. I had never seen nature up close like this before.

'I often like to take walks in here among the mountains. Or perhaps the forests or fields, depending on my mood. It is a good reminder of our connectedness with nature, and how we truly are a part of the natural world. Now then, please relax into the ergonomic ecstasy of the memory foam and let's discuss your intra-cranial neural port and the firmware update issues you are currently experiencing, shall we?'

I hadn't even heard them approach: the cyber-therapist or his associate. Couldn't even feel them. Not anymore. All part of the consumer-seller mode functionality of their programming I assumed. He looked at me like a disappointed father; she looked at him. So it began.

One small diagnostic later and I was ready to blurt out my transgressions.

'Hmmm … recurring pain across the temples, remnants of partial facial paralysis. Stallone syndrome?' the doctor chuckled to his associate, fully aware of the offence such comments gave to the near-natural muscle-heads that worshipped at the Altar of Balboa. Pop Faith, I slyly observed, was often mocked by its most ardent and envious admirers (one of my last free thoughts, it would turn out). 'Dips in processing power, kernel memory unaffected, incompatible

... oh.' He stopped. My thoughts collided; excuses swimming in a sea of panic surely reflected in my increased heart rate and breathing.

Oh God, I thought. *He knows. Of course he knows.*

'Perhaps another mishap with the ongoing NBN rollout?' the assistant murmured to her colleague helpfully.

'No,' he said, staring at the charts with an authority well beyond his peers, 'this was self-inflicted.'

'My boy,' he turned to me with a look of stern reproach, 'have you been using AdBlock?'

My neck whipped as my head snapped to attention (an autonomic response honed by years of caffeine abuse).

'No,' I replied forcefully and shrilly. 'I would never!'

'Be honest,' he commanded, 'and what you say will not be recorded on your permanent ledger.' There was no point in lying anymore. He had conducted a simple diagnostic. My mind was an open book!

'Perhaps ... this one time –' I began, only to be promptly interrupted.

'You are aware,' he said in monotone, 'that the user agreement of the latest neural firmware update states, in section 15, subsection 12, that software of the advertisement blocking, application suppressing, separate-neural inducing or multiple re-routing type can lead to incompatibility with the latest update, resulting in potential neural, psychological or physical complications. Are you not?'

'Well –'

'Of course you are,' he interjected. 'You have selected "Yes" to the Terms and Conditions. Marked. Dated. Time stamped. Would you like to have a look?'

'No,' I replied, defeated.

Silent judgement. Titters of disapproval. Clocks ticking by the microsecond.

All I had was my resolve.

I broke.

'It's just the Ads ... they were everywhere! I couldn't think without comparing, couldn't sleep without bidding, couldn't eat without noticing what I was missing out on. A few microtransactions here and there and suddenly my time and money were being wasted without end. I didn't know where I was half the time. I felt ill; I needed out! Do you know what it's like to live a life of endless consumption without even a hint of self-betterment?' Tears streamed as I stammered these reasons and more to the techno-sapiens, hoping they would understand.

They did not.

The woman had fashioned a compassionate smile as she began her assurances to the crying child in front of her.

'There are Apps for all that!' she said giddily. 'All reasonably priced!'

I looked stunned at the saccharine expression in front of me.

'Remember, an App a day keeps personal failure at bay!' she finished on a sing-song high.

I attempted a response, gave up, and turned to the doctor-coder with one last attempt at interpersonal understanding. My voice broke through the new-wave of tears, 'I just couldn't take it anymore!'

He moved to me with a grace and techno-fluidity that must no doubt have required dozens of programmers' countless hours to achieve. His voice, a pitch and tone so soothing it allayed my fears and massaged my false beliefs.

'My son,' he said, eyes full of calm concern and a flash of empathy that was almost human. 'Advertisements are a natural part of life. Like births and funerals, they are inevitable. We *will* help you through it.' He turned to his associate. 'But first, we should do something for the pain.'

And so they did.

* * *

Neurochemically it was nothing special, but to me it was everything. The relief from suffering was more than welcome, but it was a brief glimpse of the network that I had left behind that gave me the greatest pleasure. The quick connection to download the patch that ended my suffering had given me a vision of the glories and achievements; the forums, platforms and games; the news, opinions and validation that had always filled the emptiness and replaced it with purpose. That land of information, education, competition and achievement. The

World as I knew it. And despite my best attempts to hold on to that determination to resist, I wanted more.

The thought-engineer noticed my sudden change in disposition. Before I could even formulate an idea he had begun a soliloquy of great import.

'You see,' his voice dropped to a synthesised baritone, 'we are social creatures. Like fish in a school, birds in a flock, insects in a hive, so too are we drawn to form networks. At a distance of course.'

I nodded meekly. The pain was gone, and I just wanted another taste.

'You wanted to be a part of something bigger than yourself. You yearned for it.'

I wanted to shake my head at these clichés, but instead I continued nodding.

'And now you are weighing up the choice between a life of knowledge, communication and closeness, and one without.'

I could feel the self-loathing growing, and I knew the solution. A microsecond of connection was all I needed. Nothing more.

'There is a whole world out there, and you are shutting yourself off from it.'

I know, I know. Or at least I thought I did. I tried to remember why I even came here in the first place. But it was hard. So very hard. And I just wanted one more taste.

As I sat in agonised contemplation, he moved to pick up an antique off his desk with a gentleness generally reserved for something of immense value. A holy artefact that he was holding up to his face with a look of reverence, as he mused in a tone of profound contemplation: 'What is a phone without being Smart? What is the mind without being Connected?'

A silent round of applause from his associate. His point made, he turned to me, obviously satisfied with this conclusion. I wanted to say something witty. A scathing comeback, or at the very least a well reasoned argument supported by a plethora of facts. But instead I was screaming internally, and I had no idea what I was screaming about. I had been reduced to noise.

'Why do you resist?'

The question startled me and temporarily calmed the internal storm. I began to reach for the list of reasons I had come in with, the ones I would use to convince them not to reconnect me but to allow my separation from society. But they sounded feeble when compared to the glories I had just experienced, and I was in no state for a debate among equals. Nevertheless, I pushed on.

'Well for one,' I stammered, 'I don't like Ads.' The cyber-profiler raised one eyebrow questioningly. 'I mean, it's not that I oppose the impulsive consumerism that is the basis of our great society,' I backpedalled, 'or the great politico-influencers that have made it all possible – Praise Be Upon Them.'

He nodded approvingly, though his eyes probed deeply, searching for any potential reasons I could have to oppose the global *raison d'être*, and destroy them pre-emptively. 'But I *am* afraid of viruses, and malware. They're often found in Ad links,' I concluded, in a tone of assurance that convinced me that yes, in fact, this *was* a valid concern. A concern not shared by those in the room apparently, those with more experience in these matters than I.

'A common view among those with your disposition,' he said (I did my best to hide the fact that this comment hurt me deeply). 'But one that can be dealt with easily. We have anti-malware more malicious than the malware it fights to protect you from.'

'But what about hackers?' I broke into his spiel. 'They can use the Ads to control your mind and your thoughts, or so I heard. I don't want my mind to be something that anyone can edit.'

'Relax,' he assured me with a gesture of absent-minded thoughtfulness. 'We have fail-safes to prevent such a thing from happening. Failing that, I'm sure someone will edit it back.'

So I pushed on, and drowned a little bit more. Each point raised dragging me further and further out to sea.

'Your concerns are baseless,' he abruptly cut my next point short, my list still half unsaid. My mouth stopped mid argument; I knew that it was ultimately futile. It was the equivalent of launching pebbles at a concrete wall in order to break through, expecting sheer force of will to do the job that the laws of physics could not. Besides, how would I work, be paid, or order food? Most businesses did not allow in-person purchases. Perhaps I could stay on the older networks. But they were phasing those out. I was trapped. If there was a forest to run off to, I would go there and try my luck in the wild. But a hologram doesn't count though, does it?

'Besides,' he looked at me questioningly, and not without a hint of concern, 'what alternative do you have?'

'I can always disconnect,' I said, doubting the notion that such a thing was practical or even possible.

'Could you now?' he scoffed. 'Perhaps *you* could survive outside the Net, but what about your parents?' He glanced at my charts. 'They are of retirement age. Do you think *they* could survive with one less person crowdfunding their retirement?'

'Well,' I rebuked, 'I could send them money by mail, or a cheque, or . . .' I trailed off, knowing full well how stupid these ideas were before they even left my mouth. It was unlikely they had access to such archaic means of transfer, and even if they did, it would take days to reach them. Maybe even weeks! Too late to have any real impact.

'Are you worried about the sun? Is that what it is? Are you worried it will knock all your thoughts into the aether?' he snorted in derision as the assistant subsequently chuckled, a staggered response no doubt part of the play.

'I'm not one of those flare-heads!' I responded in outrage, my pulse rising along with my desire to leave. But the mocking was only beginning.

'Are you worried that you'll die if the signal drops below four bars?' he sniggered. 'That you'll forget your password?!'

They burst into laughter.

I had been insulted, derided and scolded enough for one day, I concluded. I was going to leave and vowed to take a relaxation course when I got home, or perhaps listen to some soothing music. Then I realised I was unplugged, and everything I needed was gone. Not permanently of course.

The laughter died.

'It looks agitated,' the nurse-assistant said, gliding over to me on techno-organic motors. 'Perhaps another small dose for the pain?'

'No, I am fine,' I said through grinding teeth and the slow discomfort building in my temples. 'Just fine. Although, perhaps,'

I started as she was turning away, 'a small connection? Just for a microsecond. Enough for another patch.'

'Of course,' she replied with a snap-frozen grin.

* * *

I sat enraptured as he listed off the benefits of the new update. Some of them I knew intimately; some were completely foreign to me. *I guess I should have read that user agreement after all*, I thought, chuckling to myself.

'. . . in fact, they have multiple drop points across every segregation zone, so you don't even have to move a muscle. Not to mention elevated multi-task functions. I can simultaneously order three Anti-Glare Foils for the price of two whilst voicing my concerns in the current socio-celebrity landscape,' he finished breathlessly.

It was a stunning presentation indeed, and I was still savouring the last bits of data dancing across my temporal lobe before worming their way further in. The iScreen bathed the room in dazzling displays, and I must admit I often had to remind myself to blink my eyelids and hold my tongue.

'Of course, our ancestors were also obsessed with the outmoded notions of 'romantic' and 'physical' love! So much so that it was one of the first facets of society to move entirely online, as confusing as that may seem. But what better way to know someone honestly than through their own words and pictures. You will not find a more accurate and truthful representation, not in-person, I can guarantee you that. And with our latest patches and socio-representational software you can do even *more* than that!' he winked.

He must have sensed the last remnants of my hesitation however, for he reached deep into my psychological makeup and drew forth a notion so powerful it was impossible to resist. 'What about your thoughts, your ideas?' he whispered close. 'Do you want those bottled up inside, or do you want the world to know?'

I sat; pondered. Truly the denizens of my favourite forums would be enlivened with what I had to offer. Friends and family would marvel at my witty insights into the human condition, and my posts about topics ranging from the mundane to the political would be met with the amount of Likes the world had never seen! Who am I to deny this to others? To be so selfish? To give opinions in person with the speed of a snail seemed laughable in comparison. Yet there was still one concern, one snag that was slowly unravelling the hard algorithmic-physician's work. I leaned in close, my voice reaching a quiet barely perceptible to the human ear.

'But can I use a … VPN?' I asked. A sly grin. A knowing glance. But no answer.

This was it.

I was baited, hooked and drawn in. I wiped the appropriate amount of drool that had gathered during the presentation, and went to give my final say in the matter. Yet he was not done. For my sake or his own, he continued.

'Look!' he shouted as the iScreen filled the room with an awe-inspiring sight: a grey-brown sphere covered in a dusting of lights, like a Xmas bauble of the finest manufacture. The colours shimmered in the clouds, dancing and mixing to produce spectacular streaks and crescents, glittering rainbows and delightful showers of every colour combination imaginable. The lights of the stations and satellites that orbited just added to the effect; a constant shimmer and glow. Our ancestors called the Earth a marble. I doubted that anyone could come up with a more fitting name for our home.

'Do you see our world?' he continued. 'Our little brown ball? Our home? Are not the monuments of humanity visible to all? The soaring billboards, the bright lights advertising the finest wares and services? Our system is covered in it, and beyond that. Look!' he exclaimed as the room filled with a series of interconnected lights and pulses. 'Beyond our star, through the gates and into the web-ways of space, we have the Universe!' His voice crescendoed into a squeal his vocal processors could not control nor conceal. 'Can you *imagine* if we could cover all of that with Advertisements?!'

I nodded rapidly in unequivocal agreement, clapping so hard I could hear skin split around the palms (she clapped along with me). I was unconcerned about the damage such action would cause my bio-organic components. I would replace them later. And besides, he had more to say.

For the wonders did not stop at merely explaining the future of humanity and its workings in the universe.

'Besides, there is always Incognito Mode! We will not look at your history. I Promise!' he boasted with a pride and pomp only acquired through years of meticulous sycophancy.

Mouth agape, I marvelled at the idea of my sordid history being invisible to all, and wondered why I hadn't activated it sooner. I began to ponder whether my friends and family were doing the same. I made a mental note to message them later; an in-person visit seemed unnecessarily extravagant. This is the World of the Net we live in after all, not some barbaric pre-history of in-room interaction (excepting the operating room of course – a place of unparalleled holistic healing and re-education bar none).

I was ready to give my verdict until I met his gaze, and the last vestiges of happiness departed my thoughts to leave room for the cold emptiness. They shook their heads in unison, and he held up the chart. My scans; my transgressions.

'And yet you have sinned,' he stated plainly. 'Do you deny it?'

'No,' I replied meekly, wishing I could throw myself down before them. Wishing I could move.

He reached down with an air of gentleness usually reserved for the enlightened.

'Nevertheless,' he spoke, his eyes as calm and clear as the implants would allow. 'We are not here to judge you on what you have done, we are only asking you to consider carefully what you would like to do next.'

Oh mercy, I thought as the tears returned. *Warm happiness.*

'Yes,' I said. 'Please bring me back.'

'It would be our pleasure,' they replied.

As I leaned into the chair and the plug leaned into me, the techno-priest offered some last words of sagely sales-pitch: 'It's never too late to select Buy Now, even if the bidding is over. Aside from being an integral part of any entrance exam, achievements and trophies are essential reflections of our entrepreneurial and competitive nature. Oh, and remember to remove the Ads from your eyes before you cross the road. Many unfortunate accidents happen that way. Well, I think that is all,' he tapped the chair, my head; it was all the same. As he was walking away he shifted stances; modes; configurations. His assistant noticed, and bowed her head in a sign of respect.

'There is one thing, however,' he said as he turned back, an aura of seriousness bathing his moulded features. What he said next would impact my life immeasurably from this day forward to my final disconnection. Words of wisdom so profound and yet so well known that I found myself caught unwittingly in the deeper meaning of it all. It would remove my fears and doubts for years to come, and always provide a path for me to follow.

'Remember,' he said, 'to always Like, Comment and Subscribe.'

I was stunned. It was as if God himself had come down from Mount Olympus and given me the karmic secrets to good life, endless happiness and prosperity. *I will*, I mouthed back, breathless. Then he changed, and I knew that I had made the right choice, for I had Friended him. We shared a special bond.

'Ping you later!' he said in a cheer while flashing his perfected dentitude.

'Not unless I ping you first!' I replied, finger-guns blazing. He laughed. She giggled. I smiled. We were all smiling. Then the darkness came, and I allowed myself to be taken. 'Oh, but one more thing,' I whispered out, slowly fading into the reboot cycle. I was so distant that the concept of me seemed purely theoretical. I struggled to maintain what I needed to say. What I wanted to say from the beginning. 'You called me a boy, a son, but I'm not a –'

'Quiet,' it whispered.

And then the World came back to me.

* * *

I left the office with a sense of satisfaction and fulfilment that I could never have acquired offline. A sense of connectedness and being that made my threats of separation seem like a childish tantrum spurned by a pointless rebellion (like leaving a warm home purely to spite well-meaning parents). That, and a strong desire to purchase things. The door closed behind me, hiding a small cubicle, a chair and an intra-neural plug. I dared not look back. There was no time to dwell on it. No time to contemplate. From now on I was only looking forward;

diving in. Surfing, at best. And yet there was a flicker of understanding and a feeling of familiarity that I dared not interrogate further. A small ember of recognition that I doused immediately. The time for doubt and pain was gone. I was whole now, and wholly happy.

I walked to the receptionist's desk as I mentally rearranged that most important to me – recent posts, checkout lists, swiping right on anything that moved. It was all instinctive, even the novel experiences. I also attempted to retrieve my earlier thoughts in case they still had any use, but found it a complicated and somewhat futile affair. Luckily for me, I also found that I didn't care. The recurring pain that had plagued me was but a fantasy, and my earlier fears must have surely been nothing more than the hysterical exaggerations of a doubting mind. *Yes*, I assured myself, *all was as it should be.* My only worry now was the occasional dead spot and the subsequent fear of being alone. How foolish I must have been to think that separation was what I wanted! How naïve!

I gently pushed the advertisements out of my field of vision (being particularly fascinated with the none-too-subtle links for 'AdControl – Perfectly Compatible!', an App for temperance called iChoice, and of course iScreen – *we all scream for iScreen!*) as I walked into the now almost empty waiting room of the rehabilitation clinic. I politely thanked the receptionist. They responded in kind. Radiant and full of vigour, I strode past that delightful poster and on my way to new familiarities. Yet one poor devil remained, one I could see but not sense and could not help but approach. Tucked away in the corner, it dabbed at its eyes as its body shook in regular rhythms. Poor wretch in need of comfort. Its eyelids would not close and its hands moved without purpose. I looked up the symptoms immediately, and knew the transgression that had been committed to allow such a response: repeated access attempts to forbidden sites via onion router. This one flew too close to the sun. Nevertheless I approached dutifully and charitably as I lent out my hand.

It backed away. Pavlovian avoidance. Understandable in most circumstances, but this situation was different. This was too important to avoid. Emulating the smile and good cheer of my new Friend I attempted the ancient art of conversation, hoping to entice the being into a state of cooperation. The unplugged loved to talk; to confess (all top ten Psychology Now articles said so!). Mustering all the empathy I could allow (while simultaneously ordering three Anti-Glare Foils for the price of two), I reached down with an air of gentleness usually reserved for the enlightened.

'My son,' I began in a massaging tone, 'why did you do this?' It looked up with a gaping emptiness reminiscent of the subject in the poster. Then comprehension returned, and it began to talk.

'It was all too much,' it said in a squeak. 'I couldn't concentrate, I couldn't sleep. The time … I couldn't tell what it was. What I was doing. And the money –' it cut short in a hoarse rasping while it attempted to wipe its eyes and cough out the last of its phlegm. If it could cry anymore, it would, but bio-lacrimal glands had limits. It needed upgrades if it wished to continue.

'I wanted to know *why*!' it gasped finally. 'But they wouldn't let me. So I tried to find out in any way I could. I didn't think –' It stopped in mid-speech as it was racked by another cough. Then it regained itself as the convulsions lessened, and a new resolve had grown within the being that was once (and will be again) one of my kind. 'I will disconnect,' it said finally. 'There is nothing, and I repeat nothing, that will ever make me go back. I don't care if I lose it all. Once they fix me, I will not return,' it finished in a whisper of determination.

I patted its shoulder as I scanned its face. Within seconds I knew all about it. Its friends, family, history, goals, achievements, failures, embarrassments, successes. And its desires. Without even the need to connect I reached deep into its psychological makeup and drew forth a notion so powerful it was impossible to resist. Who needs pebbles to break down walls when you have the laws of physics on your side?

With these words I allowed it to break free of its doubts, its pain and its mistaken ideas of liberation. With these words I allowed it to take the next few steps into the office, and to my Friend, the great restorer. With these words I allowed it to finally rejoin humanity.

I whispered into its ear:

'What about your thoughts, your ideas? Do you want those bottled up inside, or do you want the world to know?'

Net Worth

Tom Evans

The hallway leading to the entrance is quiet now, each body moves cautiously, filing along the plush rug that has been rolled out in front of them. A strained leather belt, one hole too tight, the squeaking of leather boots polished to a blinding shine the night before. I watch from my usual spot as one person reaches to their chest and clears their throat, and another sprays an overpriced perfume – sounds and smells that are all too sickeningly familiar to me.

With each step the narrow passageway seems to rise in temperature, piercing white lights cast sharp shadows off the slowly advancing bodies. Sweat covers the fake-tanned and melanin-injected skin of the procession, but no quality suit or skincare can hide the balding patches covered with gelled-back hair. Breaths quicken, ragged with the fruit-flavoured water vapour inhaled moments before.

They can see the large wooden door ahead, as the low tremor heard when entering the building now rises to a loud hum. Nothing moves save for beads of sweat and wispy hairs, the hands of some of the participants jitter from the waning caffeine in their bloodstream. Men in white wigs stare down from their vantage points, perched in window frames on both sides of the corridor.

A subtle nudge ripples up the line to the person at the front, who then reaches out to grab onto the cold brass doorknob, his salmon pink shirt pulls back to expose his forearm with a large metal watch and indiscreet tattoo. He blushes, coughing as he readjusts his sleeve and opens the door.

The mechanical bodies begin to wind up now, shoulders pulled back, belts centred, hair pushed behind ears. A bright light from inside floods the corridor along with an explosion of sound. Faces with previously unreadable expressions now become plastered with wide smiles, shiny white teeth reflecting the artificial light onto the faded wallpaper as each body begins to file into the room.

* * *

Leading the charge is Matthew, his back starts to twinge slightly from pulling his shoulders back so far. He reaches straight for a silver platter and grabs a cheap plastic flute half-filled with sparkling wine. Raising it to his dry lips he feels the sickly sweet liquid slide down his throat, and a cool sensation washes over his body.

Matthew is fairly new to these types of events, but he already knows what the deal is. A second-year student studying a degree in commerce, he's certain he has a better chance than most of the people here. There is something at stake here tonight, as there always seems to be when he is wearing his favourite Paco Rabanne perfume. This time it is his reputation.

It's not surprising that there are people here he already knows – classmates, high-school friends, college brothers. Even a few girls he has taken out on dates before, although they were never good enough for him. There's William from his finance tutorial off to the side, hands dancing in the air in front of him like a conductor, but his graceful movements don't seem to have the audience in front of him transfixed. Ben is also nearby, his booming voice always turns the heads of those who think they're missing out on something, and instead just find an ex-prop private school boy with distinct sweat patches showing under a carelessly ironed blue dress shirt.

Matthew is unsure where to start, whether to play it safe in numbers and stick with William and Ben or go for it solo. From the corner of his eye, he sees a golden sign, and is unable to make out the embossed lettering that is beckoning him over. He answers with a measured and purposeful stride towards his first target.

'Hi there! I'm Sarah from Best Consulting Group. Let me know if I can help you with anything.'

Best Consulting Group. Matthew is aware of this firm, having heard rumours of its lucrative bonuses and heartfelt gift hampers that let the employees know they aren't just another number.

'Hello, I'm Matthew,' he says confidently in reply. 'I'm a second-year finance student with a top ten percent average mark. I was also dux of my high school ... selective of course.'

Matthew sways on his feet, conscious of his delivery – a slight inflection on the words in the wrong place. Was he succinct enough? Did he smile too much, or not enough?

Sarah grins, nodding mechanically as the rest of her body remains still. Matthew swears for a moment that in her bulging brown eyes she looks scared.

'Impressive,' she says in reply. 'That's certainly the calibre of applicant we expect at Best Consulting Group. So, what are some of your career aspirations. And why *you*, Matthew?'

He can only smile inwardly at this question. He recites his answer every day, rehearsing to his reflection in the mirror in between his morning shower and his five-step cleansing routine.

'I am extremely passionate about creating shareholder value. Ever since I was young, I've always dreamed of a corner office, a healthy salary and the opportunity to create *shareholder value*.'

Sarah seems more animated now, her pencilled eyebrows rising.

'Wow. I've got to be honest with you, Matthew. That is one of the most genuine, most inspiring answers I have ever heard from a student wanting to work at Best Consulting Group.'

Matthew stands tall now, and it's only natural that Sarah reaches out to shake his hand.

'Sarah Ra, I'm part of the sponsor team for this event and it's a pleasure to meet you. You're more than welcome to add me on LinkedIn at any time, please feel free to endorse my Microsoft Word skills – I'm rated as proficient, you know.' He smirks in reply, of course he will endorse her Microsoft Word skills on LinkedIn, but only if she endorses his Microsoft Excel skills. It's not his first choice of workplace, but he's getting a good vibe. That is until Sarah begins to clap, slowly but loudly, nodding her head in rhythm. Matthew opens his mouth to say something, but Sarah then begins to laugh, reaching behind her to retrieve a show bag before handing it to Matthew.

Weird, he thinks, *cool name but odd person*. At least he has a shiny new BPA-free plastic bottle to show off in tomorrow's finance class.

And with Sarah still clapping and laughing away, Matthew decides to make his exit to the next stall.

'G'day there, mate! How are you this evening? I'm sure you know who we are.'

Matthew barely has time to flatten his hair and make sure his shirt is properly tucked in before gazing at the impeccably dressed man before him. A perfectly tailored navy suit and a crisp white shirt match flawlessly with his chestnut leather belt and boots. His name tag reads 'MIKE' in bold letters, handwritten but with perfectly straight lines.

Matthew looks up at the silver sign above Mike, the embossed and foiled letters are unmistakable, *Very Best Consulting Group*.

Incredible, he thinks. A boutique firm with the sort of reputation as the Very Best Consulting Group would usually not even bother showing up at an event like this. And yet, here stands Mike in all his glory. Now this is a company Matthew could see himself working at.

'Hi mate, I'm Matthew. I'm a second-year finance student with a top ten percent average mark. I was also dux of my high school, selective of course.'

'Not bad, not bad at all,' Mike says in reply. Matthew is thrown, usually this elevator pitch has them on their knees from the outset.

'I'm Mike by the way. Mike Ra.'

Strange, Matthew could have sworn the previous person had a similar last name, but she is nothing to him now, not with the Very Best Consulting Group in front of him.

'Look, I'm just going to go ahead and say it. My passion in life is to create shareholder value. And not only that, I'm also a great problem solver and critical thinker.'

A gasp, Mike stands there with his eyes wide and mouth open.

'Mate, you are kidding,' Mike says as he steps closer towards Matthew, scanning him up and down. 'Passionate about creating shareholder value *and* a critical thinker? Next you're going to tell me you're an excellent team player too.'

'Actually,' Matthew says raising his voice, shoulders pinned back as his stomach flexes against his leather belt, 'I was captain of my rugby team and I'm treasurer of the Finance Society too.'

'Jesus, mate! What the hell are you even doing here? Wait a second …' Mike reaches inside his suit jacket to pull out his phone. 'Scan my

QR code now for my profile, and as soon as you get home, remind me to put your name forward as our latest intern at Very Best Consulting Group.'

He can't believe it. Matthew knew he had the credentials needed to work for a company like Very Best Consulting Group, but he thought he would at least have to prove his worth by doing their online psychometric tests first. Well, just as long as it didn't include any of those useless empathy tests he was terrible at – who has time to care about anyone but themselves these days?

'It would be my pleasure,' Matthew says, reaching out his hand to shake Mike's.

'Mate, please help me,' Mike says in reply, his eyes darting from side to side.

'I'm sorry, what did you say?' Matthew replies, confused.

This must be part of the hiring process – he'd heard of these top firms doing things differently, and the hiring process was no different. This was most likely conflict resolution, he needed to pretend he cared about others and look for any opportunity to create shareholder value.

'Oh, my bad! I meant to say, pleased to meet you – it's been a long day. They don't give you much time off here at the Very Best Consulting Group.'

Mike laughs nervously to himself, wiping at his left nostril as if something was there.

'Yeah ... no worries, Mike. I'll send you a message later.'

Mike continues to laugh, bending over to retrieve a show bag for Matthew before beginning to clap, just like Sarah did moments before. Perhaps Best Consulting Group and Very Best Consulting Group weren't the right fit for him after all, this was turning out to be a strange night indeed.

The stale atmosphere in the hall mixes with the cold air pumping out from the air-conditioners and the cheap perfume that struggles to mask the distinct smell of body odour. Scanning the crowd, Matthew can only see an ocean of navy and charcoal, bland skirts and suit pants.

'Matthew!' He turns around to a slap on the shoulder from Ben. 'What a sight for sore eyes.'

'Jeez, Ben. Looks like they'll let anyone in here these days.'

Ben bellows his raucous laugh before wrapping his arm around Matthew.

'Yeah, and this unwell man is looking for some girls to woo and grad roles to secure. What talent on show tonight, eh? And I'm not talking about the companies here. I wonder if these ladies know what college I go to?'

Matthew can only laugh in reply, wary that Ben's sweaty arm has tainted the suit jacket he spent hours ironing this morning. 'What do you reckon about the companies here tonight? They seem alright, I guess,' says Matthew.

'Mate, they're fucking bonkers, I'll tell you that much. It's like most of these recruiters have seen a ghost. Been hearing some really weird shit.'

'Me too,' Matthew admits, clenching his jaw and looking up towards the polished white ceiling. 'To be honest, I reckon it's just a test. There are always scouts looking out for new recruits, just like those ones at the assessment centres.'

'I don't know man, I'm a bit off all this fanfare tonight. The old man has me a job secured at his firm anyway. I'm just here with the lads before we all go out and get on it later,' Ben replies confidently as he now mimics a crazed person trying to clear a blocked nose and swings his jaw from side-to-side.

'Anyway mate, enjoy this freak show. I'm off to try my luck with some of the girls near the entrance. Hopefully I make it out alive and don't get bored to death. Remember, your network is your net worth!' Ben laughs to himself, punching Matthew's arm as he wanders away.

So maybe this is all indeed a test. Tonight is invite only, vetted based on your marks and how many societies you are in – the stakes are high. Perhaps Sarah and Mike are in on this together. Looking down at his metal watch, Matthew realises time is running out to make his way to the main stage, the real reason why he came here tonight instead of rewatching *The Big Short* or *The Wolf of Wall Street*, the two greatest films of all time.

The Very Very Best Consulting Group. Just the name itself makes Matthew feel all warm inside. What beauty, what grandeur. Many nights has he dreamed of the untold amount of shareholder value he could create from his desk on the hallowed floors of that fine establishment.

The company stall is unlike all the others – simple wooden constructions with a sign along the top. This is a large, red canvas tent centre-stage that completely overshadows the stalls below. Adorning the entrance to the Very Very Best Consulting Group are two large candles perched on polished bronze stands.

Matthew is unsure if they are real, but it doesn't matter. This is the lengths the cream of the crop go to, the secrets one finds inside this tent are all that matter to him. No longer would he need to feign community work, societal contributions, or even be nice to group members. It was time to take a step towards his future, and his hands were shaking with excitement at the prospect.

Pushing aside the curtain draped over the entrance, he steps inside.

The dimly lit room is filled around its perimeter with hooded figures, each wearing extravagant red gowns that cover their faces and bodies. Matthew isn't surprised by any of this. The Very Very Best Consulting Group is a fraternity, a brotherhood. To be in its ranks is to walk among giants.

'Step forward to the altar, if you are worthy,' echoes a voice from one of the cloaked figures, but it seems as if they are all uttering these words at once.

Matthew can now make out the altar at the back of the tent as his eyes adjust to the candlelight. A slab of black marble calls to him as he considers the logistics of moving a massive slab of marble onto the stage just for this event. But then again, this is the Very Very Best Consulting Group, they can do anything.

'Place your hand on the altar of Ra and speak your truth.'

This is his moment, the moment he has been building up to since he was five years old and he told his parents to stop lying to him about Santa and wasting their time with toys and instead get him shares and connections for his portfolio.

With a deep breath and a final adjustment of his comb-over, he begins.

'My name is Matthew and I'm a second-year finance student with a top ten percent average mark. I was also dux of my high school, selective of course.'

The altar begins to tremble under his hand as the cloaked figures move to encircle him.

'I am passionate about creating shareholder value, it's all I've ever wanted to do since I was young. It's what defines me as a person.'

The whole tent is trembling now, each cloaked figure begins to chant something Matthew can't make out as they move even closer around him.

'The skills I possess include problem solving, critical thinking and …' Matthew pauses as the chant rises to a crescendo. He feels his body shaking and the flame that was flickering inside him grow stronger.

'And one day I dream of working to the best of my ability for the Very Very Best Consulting Group, managing shareholder value efficiently and effectively.'

Matthew is overcome with emotion as he collapses over the altar. Never in his life has he spoken with such passion, such poise. He can feel his eyes well up, but he refuses to show weakness.

The chanting from the hooded figures dies down and the sounds from outside the tent soften.

'Henceforth, you will be known as intern number 2487. This honour of an unpaid internship has been bestowed upon you with Ra as our witness.'

Lifting his head, Matthew stares at the cloaked figures in disbelief, smiling in joy.

'Rise, intern 2487. Join us on the stage as we induct you into our ranks.'

One of the hooded figures grabs Matthew from behind with cold lifeless hands and lifts him up, leading him outside the tent. Now, the hooded figure stands beside him at the lectern on the stage.

'To be in the Very Very Best Consulting Group, you need to be the very very best,' he whispers into Matthew's ear, 'and this means making hard decisions to trim the fat, to ensure a constantly evolving firm that minimises loses and maximises profits.'

Matthew nods in reply, of course he knows profit over people is the best way forward.

'So, intern 2487. Say the word in the name of Ra and we shall begin.'

There is a murmur from the crowd of people who have gathered near the stage. Several people now begin to move slowly towards the exit. Others simply stay motionless in their positions, confused.

A loud bang reverberates around the hall. Some of the hooded figures have moved to close the doors of the fire escape and the main entrance he walked through not too long ago.

Matthew pulls his shoulders back even more than before, struggling to breathe normally.

'Yeah, let's do it.'

As the last word escapes from his mouth, the screams begin to fill the hall as hooded figures and recruiters begin to draw weapons: calculators, metal rulers, even paper weights. Whatever company-branded merchandise is on hand is now being used to bludgeon, slice and stab recruiters and students in the hall.

Matthew spots William backed up into a corner, blood dripping onto his Egyptian cotton shirt. *What a shame*, he thinks to himself, *what a waste of such a nice shirt*. Matthew wasn't really that close to the guy anyway. Once he'd softened him up with some beers and got the nomination for treasurer, he hadn't really had anything else to do with him.

In the crowd he also spots Sarah and Mike violently slashing out at second-year students and fellow recruiters. Sarah catches Matthew staring blankly at her and stops to wave at him before swinging a metal ruler across the throat of a woman she has pinned to the ground.

For a moment, Matthew begins to feel something strange in his stomach, like he is going to be sick. He turns away briefly to regain his composure.

After calming himself down, Matthew turns back to see that most of the entertainment is now over. Screams are reduced to whimpers as the remaining attendees brush bloodied hair and chunks of skin off their trousers and jackets.

* * *

The procession led by Matthew and the hooded figure beside him now begins to file down the stage and onto the bloodied floor below.

I watch them all walk past silently ignoring me. I clutch my mop and bucket and wear a blank expression on my face.

'Fucking lunatics,' I say under my breath as I watch Matthew step directly over the body of his mate Ben, which is slumped next to the hallway – poor guy, he nearly made it out before the main event.

Now, like always, it is up to me to clean up all this mess on my own.

After being horrified the first few times, I've come to accept just how fucked up all this is and get on with it. The pay is good too, which is a bonus. I wouldn't want to think what those creepy old white men would do if I upset them in any way and decided I'm done cleaning up mutilated students.

That reminds me to check the portraits in the hallway for any bloodstains, they can be hard to spot after the tiredness I feel from dragging bodies to the dumpster.

It's always some guy like Matthew who thinks he's the main character and ends up kicking things off at events like these. I could tell just by the way he walked in that he was going to be the one to do it. What were the chances that the two people he talked to were part of that Ra group?

Now that's a story for another time, those happy clappers. Anyway, I'm off to clean up the remains of another finance networking event. At least it wasn't one of the marketing network events – I don't think I could stomach cleaning up one of those right now.

The Suit

Djuna Hallsworth

Long ago, the trousers had two sets of clean creases that ran from just below the waistband to the lower seam on each leg. One set was stitched into the sides of the fabric and created a shapely, tapered silhouette; the other was pressed into the garment with a steaming iron for no apparent reason. Once a week, the trousers were deposited at the dry cleaners conveniently located en-route between the townhouse and the bus stop, meaning The Suit did not have to deviate much from the usual morning routine. On occasion, though, it was necessary to make a brief appearance at the post office several blocks away. This happened when the postal officer who did the rounds in The Suit's suburb had chosen to leave a scribbled card in the mailbox, instead of the parcel itself. The card informed The Suit of when the parcel would be available for collection, which was between Monday and Friday, 9 am and 5 pm; essentially, times that The Suit would, without fail, be working. There was quite possibly nothing more infuriating than paying a postage fee to have an item delivered to your home only to find yourself queuing with old-age pensioners and parents who spoke excessively loudly and slowly to their five-year-old children at 8.58 am. All of this just to retrieve what was undeniably *yours*.

The last item The Suit had ordered through an online store was a fabric mask to cover one's nose and mouth. It had been highly recommended that people should start wearing them, regardless of their level of natural immunity and usual hygiene practices. The Suit was in two minds about the message that wearing such a mask – which, admittedly, was largely cosmetic and certainly not medical-grade – would send. Would it be a confession of poor habits? As if one could not be trusted to press the button on public transportation and then refrain from putting the same hand into one's mouth? Or would it be a badge of sorts, identifying The Suit as a proud member of the disease resistance? The Suit resigned to following the public health messages and purchased a plain grey mask late one night, ensuring the delivery person understood that they had the authority to leave the parcel outside the home should The Suit not be there to receive it. Surely it was counterintuitive to purchase what was effectively a barrier between oneself and the general public, only to have to brave a retail shop over-populated with people who still salivated on envelopes to seal them.

The purchase of the mask was made one year ago. Around the same time, The Suit had deposited the trousers at the dry cleaners for the last time, the day before the small enterprise closed its doors indefinitely. The trousers, so far as The Suit knew, were preserved in a wide plastic sheath, complete with crisp creases and a powdery smell of synthetic lilac. *I paid for someone to iron creases into my clothes,* The Suit thought. *I gave money to someone to wipe my benchtop and shower screen; I paid a premium for food from a fridge in a café that I could easily have made at home; I paid someone to tell me how much money I earned and how I could pay less tax; and I paid strangers to drive me in their cars instead of taking the bus. And if I wanted to talk to someone about how utterly incomprehensible I find all of this now, I could pay them to listen.*

The Suit cast this thought aside and resumed slicing vegetables into thin sticks. Carrots had been marked down to fifty cents a bag and The Suit had bought five bags. Carrots were an excellent source of vitamins, though which vitamins, precisely, The Suit did not know. They could also be used in dishes of both the sweet and savoury variety, and could also be snacked on between meals. The Suit could prepare a carrot and garlic dip in which to dip carrot sticks. This was an amusing thought and The Suit had laughed out loud, much to the alarm of nearby people in the supermarket. Carrying them home was a good form of exercise, given that five kilos of carrots in addition to rolled oats, almond milk, lentils and a kilo of onions would be a substantial amount to carry on the 1.8 kilometres walk home. *What an extremely successful day!* The Suit reflected, paying a total of $9.45 for the groceries. Walking was still free, but who knew when that might change.

The truth was that The Suit needed a job. It was either that or commit larceny, but this was not the ideal choice of the two options. Aside from tax evasion, The Suit had not committed any illegal acts and preferred not to start now. Since the recession, the public had lost trust in the stock market. *It took them long enough,* The Suit thought. People did not want strangers to trade pretend money and pretend assets on their behalf anymore. They wanted to grow their own food in balcony gardens and share one stepladder between a whole floor of apartments. *There's a revolution coming!* The Suit's mother had said, shortly before she died of the disease. She had been old and had several chronic health conditions. The news had implied – because people like her were going to die sooner or later anyway – that they might as well die sooner and free up hospital beds. *They're not wrong,* The Suit reflected somberly at the time. But she was right about the revolution, and she wasn't even afraid. The Suit's mother had been a bold and forward-thinking woman. She was disappointed that her only child had chased money instead of inner peace. Recessions, like bushfires and supermoons, seemed to be more and more frequent and there was nothing The Suit feared more than being jobless and homeless. Why have less when one could have more? The Suit had always been sure to send expensive and luxurious presents for Mother's Day to illustrate some of the joys of having an excessive amount of wealth.

The Suit had been looking for a job for nearly ten months. Every Saturday, after reading the financial news and completing the cryptic crossword, The Suit would skim the classifieds in search of job openings. Those that did not provide details of the role or organisation could be immediately dismissed, as with any that promised income of 'up to $3k a week,' or used exclamation marks. The Suit would not be a delivery driver – it was far too dangerous and paid far too little – and absolutely drew the line at any kind of work that involved displaying the body for the pleasure of others. This did not leave many openings. Sometimes an advertisement might appear for a role in construction or as an in-home care worker, neither of which The Suit felt qualified for or confident enough to attempt. The decision to buy discounted carrots was not entirely voluntary. The nested egg that The Suit had been sitting on for the last year was beginning to dwindle. Mortgage repayments needed to be made and credit card bills were overdue.

Electricity and internet had increased in price and so had many other basic services, such as hairdressers, plumbers and mechanics. Oddly, it had become rare to pay for parking anymore but that was because the cost of petrol and servicing made it simply untenable for most people to have a car. The state supplied vehicles to people who needed them, like police officers, paramedics and personal friends of the Prime Minister.

Even before, The Suit had preferred to take public transport or a taxi instead of owning a car – it allowed for the opportunity to multitask in a way that driving did not. Now, walking was really the only choice, given the sharp increase in the price of bus fares, but The Suit did not mind. It was safer to walk because the chances of contracting the disease were greatly reduced in the open air, and walking passed the time. The Suit might walk eight kilometres to the house of a friend who was hosting a dinner gathering, and then eight kilometres back. In the past, a trip of this length would certainly be taken in a taxi. Looking back on it, this seemed downright ludicrous, because The Suit paid for a gym membership. How laughable to limit one's exercise to time spent in a gym, and to refuse exercise outside of it.

Once the carrots were finely chopped and placed into a pot of simmering water on the stove, The Suit settled down on the two-person sofa that really only sat one person comfortably and tore the top off of the Workforce Active pamphlet that persons who were registered as unemployed received from their local council. The pamphlet detailed all the available work opportunities in the surrounding suburbs – at least all the above-board and union-approved ones. Since the recession, recruitment had become centralised so that unemployment figures and public benefits could be documented and managed by each tier of the government. There were so few jobs since the disease had swept across the country that the criteria for hiring people was overhauled, in the name of fairness and equity. With very few exceptions companies were not permitted to conduct their own recruitment and hiring processes and only individual employers and a select range of small businesses could do so, as could persons that were seeking help for a short contract. Such openings were advertised in the local newspaper or on bulletin boards in grocery stores.

The Suit remembered a time from childhood when these advertising formats were commonplace. It was inexplicable that they had returned. The future was, apparently, far more mundane than anyone had imagined. Analogue communication was, the government had argued, the only way to ensure democratic and systematic access to relevant information. Swarms of academics and historians had retaliated with lengthy arguments that contradicted this claim, but, now that their professions were no longer considered essential, their authority as society's voice of reason dwindled. Fiction had surpassed non-fiction as the content of choice for most. The collective desire for escapism had reached an all-time high and it was common for people to fabricate more desirable stories to embellish their existence rather than report the banal and disappointing truth.

More often than not, The Suit ended up turning Workforce Active into an inspired collage artwork, rearranging the phrases and faces to form amusing, albeit sometimes disturbing, posters. This fortnight's edition had a feature article on interviewing.

Do you feel like you're wasting time in unsuccessful interviews? You're not alone. Seventy-eight percent of jobseekers are frustrated by their lack of results following failed interviews. They don't know what they are doing wrong. But we do. It could be as simple as a limp handshake or a seed in your front tooth, but the fact is, you are not performing at the level expected by prospective employers. Seventy-eight percent of employers told us that they have had to let new recruits go before the end of their probation period because of poor hygiene, unruly appearance or odd behaviour. The data is clear: seventy-eight percent of this country's unemployed population is untrained in the fine art of social etiquette. The solution? Government-supported training in self-presentation and modern manners.

The Suit scoffed and leaned over to pick up a pair of scissors that lay on the coffee table. If the number really was that high – and it wasn't, but even if it were – that must mean the vast majority were correct, and it was the employers whose standards needed to change. The pot on the stove made a satisfying splashing sound as the water turned to steam.

Certainly, basic respect and courtesy must be considered as valuable traits, but surely they were not more valuable than the skills required to perform the main duties of the role? The Suit retrieved a glue stick from the desk drawer. If the government was going to pay to cultivate particular skillsets, there must be attributes more useful than politeness.

The finished poster read:

> Do you feel like wasting time? The fine art of a limp handshake is simple. The government is wrong. The modern population is seventy-eight percent odd, but don't know they are.

Below the text was an image of a cloud of air freshener with a torso, making the OK sign with its fingers. The Suit chuckled and affixed some tack to the back of the paper before sticking it to the lounge room wall with the other creations.

The following day was Friday, but it didn't really make any difference to The Suit, because each day was much the same as the next. Fridays meant the rubbish bins were being emptied. The Suit had fleetingly considered being a sanitation assistant, given that this was an essential job, and this kind of work would be needed for the indefinite future, or at least until the local parks were converted back to landfill sites. Because this notion had been entertained before the number in the bank account had dropped to below four figures – before the situation was desperate – The Suit quickly dismissed it.

On this Friday morning, The Suit was enjoying pre-soaked oats and a hot tea with almond milk when the telephone rang. This was highly unusual, and The Suit considered letting it go to voicemail before realising it could be the government. The only people that rang anymore were the government.

It was the government. They said they had the ideal job for The Suit, and did 12.45 pm work for a video interview. One couldn't really say no to the government, so The Suit said yes, even though speaking to a computer screen would be extremely uncomfortable and, if the Workforce Active data was to be believed, ultimately pointless. A video call, however, was better than filling out a form and the fact that The Suit had been approached personally boded well for the chances of success. The trouble was, The Suit reflected, sipping now-tepid tea, that the job could be very undesirable.

'Have you heard of the census?' the woman from the government asked at 12.52 pm. She pronounced 'census' like 'sensors' and it took The Suit a moment to understand.

'Yes. Doesn't everybody participate in the census?' The Suit replied, wondering if there were any adult citizens who did not know what the census was, despite taking part in it.

'Exactly!' the woman beamed. 'It's a very paramount government activity, but some people don't appreciate just how paramount.'

The Suit winced at the use of 'paramount'.

'Perhaps you recall being visited by a census agent?' she continued.

'A long time ago, certainly,' The Suit admitted, reflecting that the last census took place online.

'Not everyone has internet anymore,' the woman said, as if she could read The Suit's mind. 'So, we need to employ census agents to ensure the accuracy and comprehensivity . . . comprehendibility . . . the comprehensiveness of the data. It's paramount.'

'Right.'

'It pays very well and there is the opportunity to become employed with the Department of Information Security afterwards, if you perform well.'

If I perform well?

'Do I have the job?' The Suit asked without thinking.

'Do you want it?' the woman responded hopefully.

The Suit thought for a moment. A job was available, and it paid well. In fact, there hadn't even been an interview: no questions, no screening. The job belonged to The Suit before the interview had even begun.

'Can I say no?'

'I don't think you should,' the woman said in a lower voice. 'It wouldn't look good. You would seem resistant to assistance. We call it RTA. It's not a good thing.'

The Suit considered that carrots probably would not be on special again next week.

'Okay then. I'll say yes.'

'That's wonderful!' the woman exclaimed. 'Training commences in two weeks and is paid. Do you have a bike?'

'Not anymore.'

'We will arrange one for you.'

'Do I get to keep it?' The Suit asked, thinking of all the one kilogram bags of vegetables that might be on offer in the coming weeks and how a bike would make transporting them home so much easier.

'For as long as you are employed with the Department,' the woman said, typing at her keyboard as she spoke. 'I have also arranged for the induction manual to be sent to you. If you have any questions call Ron, he can answer most of them.'

The Suit assumed Ron's number was in the induction manual that was being sent out. The prospect of ringing somebody was not attractive, but if the manual was comprehensive there would be no need for this.

Two weeks passed slowly, and no vegetables were on offer: only oranges and bananas. These were not useful because they could not be used in savoury dishes. The Suit was looking forward to the paid training sessions, especially the 'being paid' part. The bicycle could be collected the day before, from the local council offices. The Suit wondered how many other people would be in the training cohort and what backgrounds they might have. Might they also be ex-Suits?

Available to collect with the bicycle was a thick spiral-bound book that turned out to be the induction manual. The Suit cycled home feeling jubilant. The manual would make a nice change from the radio plays that were being re-aired to save on royalty costs, and which The Suit had already heard. The manual featured all kinds of interesting demographic information about the city, including some amusing statistics. Did The Suit know that forty-five percent of citizens believed they weren't being paid enough for their work, but that seventy percent of these respondents resided in four of the six most expensive suburbs? That warranted a chuckle.

Only forty percent of people believe they are 'politically active' but eighty percent voted in the last federal election: what does this mean for the integrity of our electoral system?

The Suit flicked to the section that featured the details of the position.

> Your job is simple, yet crucial, to the future planning of the nation. Without the data, we cannot know what our citizens are thinking, and we cannot know how they will respond to change, be it good or bad. Your job is simple: ask them.

The Suit wished that a job as a copywriter or editor had become available in the Department of Information Security, as whoever currently held this role did not appear to deserve it. *Do they think I am a bit simple as well?* The Suit wondered. *My job is not to ask them, it is to drop off a survey and pick it up again when it is complete.* This was how the census had worked when The Suit was a child. Presumably, as everything else had regressed back to the 1990s, the upcoming census would be no different.

> You, along with a team of thousands of agents across the country, will find out what makes our people tick, and provide the government with the information it needs to protect and secure our nation's stability in uncertain times.

The Suit flipped a few pages, feeling that the glorified description was covering the truth of the situation: what was actually required? The job was straightforward and paid well. What was the catch?

> Your first day: No doubt you will be nervous, because talking to strangers can be daunting! Just remember, they might not have spoken to anyone outside of their family for a long time, so you will be a light in the dark, so to speak. It's important to dress well and look clean (please attend the free Modern Manners program available at your local community centre if you are unsure). When you sit on their sofa or chair, be sure to use your hygi-mat, which you will be provided with before your first day. Do not accept any food or beverage while you are in the house; you may bring your own flask as consuming tea/coffee together could help with rapport-building. Familiarise yourself with the questions before you start so that they do not come as a

surprise. You need to ask all the questions and record an answer in every space. If the respondent refuses to answer a question, make a note of this and inform your supervisor (questions in Part 6: Intimacy and Relationships and Part 8: Toilet Habits can prove the most challenging, along with Part 10.2: Taxes and Declarations. Prepare a contingency plan for these sections).

The Suit read and re-read this section, then flipped back a page to see if the preceding information provided any helpful context. This was unexpected. The census was a survey that people filled in on their own, in their own time. It took a long time – maybe an hour or two – but that was why the agents came back a few weeks later to collect it. In the past, that was what had happened. But the information under the 'Helpful Hints' and 'What to Expect' sections were suggesting that the job was something quite different to what The Suit had been expecting. This was not desirable. The Suit called Ron.

'This is Ron.'

'Hello, you don't know me,' The Suit began. 'But I work, or I will work, for the census, or on the census, or anywa–'

'Let me stop you there,' Ron cut in. 'You've signed a contract, you know. You can't pull out now.'

The Suit paused.

'How did you . . .?'

'You can't, it's a breach of contract and you'd be fined,' Ron's voice was firm but in a way that sounded like he was putting it on.

'But I don't necessarily want to . . . I mean, I just want to clarify what the job entails.'

There was silence on the line, aside from a faint crackling.

'Hello?'

'You want to keep the job?' Ron asked slowly.

'I suppose so. I'm just confused. Why am I going into people's houses? Why do I need a flask?'

Ron laughed and when he spoke again his voice sounded higher than it had before.

'You don't need a flask, but the days are long, so I recommend it. And you don't have to go inside but I find papers can blow around if you sit outside, and noise can make it hard to hear in some areas.'

'I don't follow,' The Suit responded, but this was not entirely true. It was clear enough. This was not a paper survey, it was an interview, and The Suit needed to ask questions and record answers to 132 questions.

'Which part?'

'I thought I just needed to drop the papers off and come back to pick them up later.'

'Ahh. No,' Ron said. 'That's not how it works anymore. You need to ask the questions, so that we know people are understanding them. People are also less likely to lie if they are addressing another person, compared to if they are writing in a booklet.'

'Okay. But why not do it over video call, or even a phone call?'

'Wouldn't work,' Ron replied confidently. 'We thought about it but not everyone has internet.'

'But phones?' The Suit was perplexed, but knew Ron couldn't really do anything about the situation. The census format had been confirmed.

'Look, I get what you're saying but . . . I'll tell you something, but you can't tell anyone, and you didn't hear it from me.'

'Okay?'

Ron cleared his throat, and The Suit heard the distant sound of a door shutting.

'This census, it has a double purpose. Maybe even a triple purpose.'

The Suit paused, not daring to say anything that might cause Ron to change his mind about divulging this secret.

'So, yes, we need to gather demographic data, like normal, but you'll find at training tomorrow that you will also be looking for "non-verbal cues".' He stressed this phrase as if it were a completely new concept that The Suit was unlikely to have ever come across.

'That's why we want you to be there in-person, so you can observe.'

This seemed simple enough so far and was not the bombshell The Suit had been anticipating.

'But the other thing is,' Ron continued, 'that a lot of people haven't left their houses in a very long time. Maybe a year.'

The Suit swallowed. This seemed plausible.

'So . . . the government, or we, are also thinking that it might be good if people, you know, talk to other people. But they don't want to, or they think they don't want to.'

Ron was starting to trip over his words. The Suit interjected: 'People are isolated, is that it, Ron? You want us to go and talk to them?'

'Not me, personally, but yeah, the government.'

There was a longer pause this time.

'It's not a bad idea,' The Suit conceded. Ron exhaled loudly in a blatant sign of relief.

'Yeah. Yeah, it's not bad,' Ron replied, sounding like he hadn't really thought about it much before. 'A lot of people don't want to go into other people's houses because of, you know, the disease and stuff, but also they don't want to talk to strangers. We had to increase the salary for this job a lot. People just wouldn't do it otherwise.'

'Even though they'd be marked as RTA?' The Suit asked, smiling.

Ron laughed out loud. 'Yeah, even though they would.'

After the phone call with Ron, The Suit sat on the sofa for a while before starting on dinner. Dinner was going to be the same as breakfast: porridge with a banana. The Suit reached for a notebook and pen from the coffee table and made a list of all the things that seemed intimidating about the job now that the truth of it had been revealed. When that was done, The Suit wondered what to pack for lunch for the first day of training, and what to wear.

Once There Was and Once There Wasn't

Danial Yazdani

Welcome to the land of the liminal,
the nation of the in-between.
You have heard of us, seen us, felt us too,
but we are far from what we seem.

Ancient sites are ready to crumble
on the outskirts of our urbanised cities.
I'd like you to consider – and I will not stumble –
the remainder of our immortal pities.

Gas and noise, and trash and steam,
cloud the judgement of our people's eyes.
They are kind and hospitable, unexpectedly bearable,
but take one look beneath the surface,
and to no surprise awaits a discovery
of this and that, of this and that, of this –

Why can't I seem to join my words,
to articulate the functionings of this society?
To look past the blood, sweat and tears of the herds
of people lining up behind hospital doors
in a state that lacks democratic propriety –
I cannot.

Yeki bood, yeki nabood,
Gheyraz Khoda, heech kas nabood.

Vast geographic terrains,
aromas and spices concealing the pain,
the smell of poverty and the lower class,
further hidden beneath the full stomachs and
gas coming out of the master's arse(s).

To sit in solemn silence,
and to pray, and pray, and pray it will get
better.
But no.
No God or higher being can distil such filth from the matter.
It's every man for himself at the moment,
we cannot possibly stand together.

Once there was, and once there wasn't.
There was no one but one God.

A standard set by those seated in power,
slowly, but subtly, erasing the narratives that make them cower.
Making an effort to wipe them from the minds of the people,
wanting them both to sordidly sour.

One falls, one stands, rarely one may extend a hand,
but the word 'unless' and *'kashki'* twists the tips of our tongues,
as if it wishes to stand.

To raise its voice, *their* voice, to cry out loud,
Vive la révolution! *Afarin!* One unanimous shout that can rattle the
     roots of the ground.
Perhaps this will shed away the skin of liminality

and the stagnation of a nation,
bound by the chains and shackles, and backwardness,
of those teasing their, *our*, patience.

Yeki bood, yeki nabood,
all dying to be understood,
Gheyraz Khoda heech kas nabood,
returning to the lost glory that stood.
Kasi ra midani?
Holding the legacy of a history,
Ke cheezhayee ke manda ra nejad bedehad?
as famous as Persepolis, and the country's existence as a mysteriously
        unfulfilled
Prophecy.

National Scandal

Tori Wills

I.

Shawn sits with his family on the couch in the TV room; all lined up like the Simpsons at the end of the opening credits. This is his nightly routine: he comes home from work, showers while his wife prepares dinner, eats, and then the whole family sits together to watch their shows. A celebrity talk show comes on after *The Big Bang Theory*. The host's monologue is about that awful actor running for Governor of Texas and the photos of him two-timing with the nanny. There's a joke about how the girl got her unusual last name that makes Shawn snort chardonnay out of his nose. Cynthia gives him a scolding look, but he recognises the press of her lips as holding back a smirk. The kids look between their parents, eyes wide with the knowledge that something from the secret world of grown-ups has been communicated, just then, on live TV. When Kyle asks what a gag reflex is, Shawn tells him 'it's, um, another way to say laughter, you know, because it's your natural reflex when you hear a great gag. Two pairs of little brows frown with derision: 'I don't get it', 'How is that funny?'

II.

Sierra flops down on her sister's bed (Savannah shouldn't make it up all nice and neat if she doesn't want her on it) and opens YouTube on her phone. There's a new video in her subscriptions: TrulyMaddieDeeply posted 'I WENT TO SCHOOL WITH TESSA POKORNY (Chase Alexander mistress)!!! + GIVEAWAY :P'. *Heck yes*, she thinks as she taps the small image of Maddie's scandalised but still pretty face.

Chase Alexander is someone from the news or movies or something, right? Maddie is probably her favourite YouTuber right now, because she seems super sweet and has such good fashion sense and Sierra felt real bad for her when she revealed her ex had hacked into her account to make those racist tweets. She had seemed so relatable in the video where she explained what he'd done, sobbing on her bedroom floor. Sierra had seen Savannah in the exact same position when her first boyfriend had dumped her. After Maddie's video, Sierra watches 'Bethany Alexander Talks Heartbreak and Her New Movie', 'BREAKING: Alexander Exits Texas Governor's Race', 'Who is Tessa Pokorny? What we know so far' and 'Chase Alexander Files Charges Against Pokorny's Husband: Exclusive'. Savannah comes home from school and shoves Sierra off her bed. From her own bunk, Sierra stares at the brown spots on the ceiling, twisting her phone around between her fingers. She promises herself that when she's older she'll be good, like Bethany and Maddie, only date nice guys, never take naked pictures and never ever cheat.

III.

Joe stretches out on the couch, feet pushing the yet-to-be-sorted mail pile into the important mail pile on the Malmsta coffee table. Images from the TV flash and light up his naked body. There's a news bulletin between shows. Normally he'd get up to piss or check he isn't missing anything good on another channel, but the remote is on the TV stand and he's putting off the moment he'll have to peel his skin painfully from the leather. He watches that babysitter slut push her way through a writhing mass of reporters up the steps of some courthouse, flanked by power-high bodyguards. She's wearing a sombre navy skirt suit, soft makeup and a tiny cross on a fine gold necklace. *Deceptive bitch. She isn't fooling anybody.* Joe has seen the grainy footage of her sprawled out on a hotel bed, putting on a show in the shower, on her knees in front of the politician, begging for it. If he was her husband, he'd have hit her too. Joe misses most of *Family Guy*, head thrown back against the couch cushions as he fantasises about other means of punishment.

IV.

Maddie repositions the latte so that the headline about the court case will be visible in the shot. She moves through a series of tried-and-true poses while Maria snaps away, cooing encouragement. 'Gorgeous! Hand on your chin, look thoughtful.' After a few minutes, Maddie waves the camera away, mindful of their coffees getting cold. She knows all too well the strain being a content creator can have on relationships and is practising positive boundary setting. So, yes, while Sunday brunch with her bestie is valuable content, that TED Talk said to limit productive 'on' time to a set period, then switch to 'off' mode. Maddie places her phone face down and turns all her attention to Maria. She asks about Maria's work, nodding along as Maria complains about the toxic office atmosphere, her passive aggressive colleagues. She asks about Maria's fiancé Scott, who is apparently chasing the story with Tessa. 'Oh my gosh, I wish I'd known before I did my video!' There's the old discomfort when Maria says she hasn't seen it. Drowning in work, she says, though Maddie suspects Maria just doesn't get the whole vlogging thing, thinks its childish. The conversation falters, which it never used to. They seem to have less and less in common. But gossip is always reliable, so Maddie seizes on Tessa, how crazy it is that someone they knew slept with a movie star. Except Maria barely remembers Tessa. She'd been focused on grades while Maddie obsessed over the school's intricate social hierarchy, its relevance dissolving like coffee foam as soon as they graduated. They chat about the affair, the fallout, Bethany Alexander's new look, the new governor. Eventually the awkward silence returns. So sorry, Maria says, but she's got a work friend's bridal shower to get to. They should totally do this again sometime. Maybe in a month or two when Maria's less busy?

V.

Heather scrolls through her Twitter feed and pours out another two fingers of Baileys. #Pokorny is trending, and Heather savours the images of the girl fending off press and escaping the courthouse the way she savours another mouthful of creamy liqueur. She doesn't know if the fine and eighteen months' probation are standard for hindering prosecution, but it seems lenient. She pours over some more videos. With her hair up, Pokorny looks like Maria from Marketing. Heather knows Maria runs a secret group chat with some of the other girls in the office, probably Cynthia and Sara, and that they joke about her on there. She's noticed their shared looks whenever Maria asks about the online dating. The other night Heather dreamt she was in the witness stand, recounting Maria's crimes against her. But then she was also the judge who got to send Maria to jail, and then Heather was also a celebrity being interviewed on one of those TV talk shows. The audience were appalled by her hardships, delighted by her cutting remarks. Heather lets the Baileys linger on her tongue. There's a link to some blog post titled 'What the Alexander-Pokorny Scandal Tells Us about Slutshaming' making the rounds. The author's profile shows a chubby woman with a blue buzz cut. *i'll tell you what it tells us,* Heather types into her direct messages, *she's a slut and she should be ashamed. your just defending her because you wish it was you she went down on. give it up lez bitch no one wants a whale.*

VI.

Ash burns his tongue on 7-Eleven coffee as he fiddles with the dashboard monitor. His diet these last few weeks has consisted mostly of coffee and Red Bull, plus the occasional assembly-line burrito or Snickers whenever he started to feel dizzy. Fuck, he's gonna have to do a juice cleanse or something once the trial is over and they're called back to Houston. The first few days Ash thought he was destined to have a breakdown, cramped up in the news van all night, sealed in with Pete's farts. But actually, it's been a blast. Lecturers and superiors at KPTC always hinted at the wild, tight-knit atmosphere of being stuck on a story with a bunch of other reporters for weeks at a time, fighting with rival muckrakers over literal trash, playing hurry up and wait trying to get new footage of the family. Ash had always assumed it was some pathetic attempt to sex up the tedium of entry-level grunt work. This is his first run and he honestly hasn't felt this high since his sophomore year MDMA phase. Carla and Pete, Scott and Ezra from WSB, Serena and the rest of the rival 6ABC crew – they don't look down their noses at Ash like those college assholes did. They respect him as one of their own. They feel like actual friends. Sitting in the passenger seat while Pete dozes, Ash watches the dawn emerge slowly behind the Pokorny family home and silently thanks their stooge daughter for marrying that dumbfuck sorry-excuse-for-a-blackmailer, and then having the audacity to fuck the husband of America's Sweetheart.

VII.

You spend the first six months on the couch in your parents' living room. You know you shouldn't watch those same programs that hounded you for months chase after the next poor schmuck caught doing something dumb or taboo or mildly illegal. You know it's unhealthy and hypocritical, but you can't find the energy to care. Finally, the vans out the front drive off, hunting the next scandal. Then the late-night hosts stop mentioning your name, and, after what seems like an age, the death threats slow to a trickle. You start to think about the future. It upsets your parents but filling out the paperwork for a name change feels like your only option. You have half a sociology major, put on ice when Jack's company fell victim to the recession and you had to look for a second job. You log into your old university email and send out some queries. You set up a meeting with a divorce lawyer, and when your mom's constant hints start to get to you, you set up therapy appointments too. You take up running, binge *Buffy*, go through a nail art phase, get a library card and catch up on all those bestsellers you've been meaning to read. You go on a date with the guy from the inquiries desk, although he breaks it off once he realises who you are. You swap the Ravishing Ruby hair dye for Cocoa Macchiato, closer to your natural shade and more discreet. You set up one of those dating apps, and tick 'Men and Women', something you would never have done a few years ago. With your new name, you manage to get a job copying data from one spreadsheet to another. You enrol in distance education, prioritise your studies for the first time in your life, and graduate. One day, years later, you spot your own face in the sidebar of a news item: 'Remember these celebrities? Where they are now will shock you!'. You chuckle, bemused but hardly shocked when you click through and find you aren't even mentioned in the article.

Neighbours

Hannah Roux

In church my pew is next to yours,
I drink a cup of wine with you
and share a loaf of bread, us two,
and think of what you'd think of me.

Here '*me*' means sexuality –
not lies, or crying poetry
or chlorine rinsed from my wet hair
or blinking at what singers wear
or all my many countless sins.

'*Me*' means parts of me I hide
like shells, like oyster-flesh inside
the heart of me that bends and sways
like sweet clematis in the breeze
toward a pair of singing trees.

Her hand in mine, his eyes on me
both felt like singing in the heart –
or hair that's blue with a side-part,
or lashes brushing bright high cheeks,
or smiles and tangling of our feet.

I stand, my neighbour stands, we sing
and our two voices rise, like dust,
as one to heaven; must I trust –
whatever it is you'd think of me –
that God thinks something else of us?

Will & Grace vs Trump

Queer Representation in Popular Television

Melissa Snook

After a long eleven years, the nineties hit sitcom *Will and Grace* returned to screens in 2017. When it first aired in 1998, the flamboyant New York lawyer, Will Truman, was the first queer male protagonist to appear on American television screens.[1] Coming from a time when LGBTQIA+ issues were a highly controversial political and social topic, the appearance of central queer identifying characters on network television was a huge step forward for LGBTQIA+ representation. According to *The Guardian*, in 2012 the current US President Joe Biden said that *Will and Grace* 'did more to educate the American public [on LGBTQIA+ issues] than almost anything anybody has ever done so far'.[2] Popular culture tries to assure the public that queer people deal with the same issues and have the same everyday lives as straight people. Aaron Nyerges, lecturer in American Studies at the University of Sydney, says shows like *Will and Grace* are important for 'giving a space of representation,' particularly for those 'who feel underrepresented in mainstream media'.[3] In response to Biden's claim, Nyerges says, 'there's a kind of educational factor in popular culture and it does a lot for advocacy and the politics of representation'.[4]

As this suggests, popular culture performs a very important function in society. Within our favourite shows we are able to explore controversial issues, and *Will and Grace* is no exception. Through the 'remediation of its own past,' says Nyerges, 'television turns back on itself and becomes conscious of itself as a form of representation'.[5] The

---

1   Hart 2016.
2   Mulkerrins 2018.
3   Nyerges 2018.
4   Nyerges 2018.

current instability of politics and social life in America has fostered a recognition of responsibility within popular culture writers, particularly that of *Will and Grace*, to explore issues of acceptance and sexuality. Unlike its predecessor, the reboot isn't able to exist within an 'everyday-life' format anymore. It has a responsibility to its LGBTQIA+ community to critique current issues and present a united front against homophobia.

The revival of *Will and Grace* coinciding with the 2016 election of businessman Donald Trump as President was no accident. Eric McCormack (Will Truman) says the reboot 'started from a pure need to say something, on behalf of Hillary and on behalf of sanity'.[6] It is important in times like these, that popular culture and television writers not shy away from confronting difficult subjects, and instead put them centre stage where they have the ability to reach and impact wider audiences. As Nyerges says, 'Consumers and users of social media are absorbing the messages of network television'.[7] With growing tensions between the LGBTQIA+ community and former President Trump during his presidency, the message of sexual acceptance and gay rights was necessary in that moment for the American public. Messages of tolerance and happiness as a right to all Americans regardless of sexual orientation unite us all against the bigotry of the country's former leader.

The reboot took the old, hilarious show thousands of people loved, and took that audience marching straight to Washington DC. From the very first episode there is a strong sense of contempt towards the government, taking shot after shot against former President Trump. While Jack McFarland (Will's friend) is cosying up with a secret service agent, and Will is flirting with an attractive congressman with objectionable policies, Grace Adler is tasked with redecorating the Oval Office. While she eventually decides not to take the job, she does leave one special piece of memorabilia behind: the iconic red MAGA (Make America Great Again) cap. However, she does make one change to the hat, with it saying 'Make America Gay Again'

---

5   Nyerges 2018.
6   Mulkerrins 2018.
7   Nyerges 2018.

instead. This queer play on the slogan is repeated again in episode fourteen when Karen Walker, socialite and friend of Jack and Grace, tries to order a MAGA cake and is refused by the baker. Conceding to the request, the baker instead writes 'IM A GAY' on the cake. Pointing out the Supreme Court case where a gay couple was refused when asking for a wedding cake, Nyerges says 'it's a fairly clever play on the whole homophobia in cake-making debate and religious exception to making a cake for a gay couple . . . it has to capitulate to the demand of making a MAGA cake in order to be consistent . . . even if you're homophobic, you should still make a cake for a gay couple'.[8] 'There's something fun about the scrambling of MAGA and IM A GAY and the general word play that's involved in both political sloganeering and camp queer humour,' says Nyerges, 'There's a nice queering of the slogan that's going on'.[9]

Anti-Trump sentiment aside, the show's strongest political statement from the reboot is its treatment of gay rights and culture. In October 2017, just over two months after Donald Trump announced a ban on transgender people serving in the military, NBC aired 'Grandpa Jack'. The episode follows Jack finding out he has a gay grandson (Skip) who is struggling with his identity and his parents' expectations. This episode perfectly represents the importance of the show for its current audience. Its focus on sexuality, though briefly discussed in the original series, transforms the reboot into a place of representation and a safe space for the LGBTQIA+ community to express themselves against the anti-gay Republican government at that time. Sent to a conversion camp to 'straighten' him out, Jack shows up to talk Skip through the difficult time. Though entertaining, camp 'Straighten Arrow' is a concerning representation of the conservative views towards LGBTQIA+ sexuality, particularly amongst youth (there is a framed picture of former vice-president Mike Pence hanging on the wall. In an article from *The New Yorker* Trump reportedly said, 'Don't ask that guy [Mike Pence] – he wants to hang them all!' when asked about LGBTQIA+ rights[10]). The motto of the fictional camp is 'It's not

---

8   Nyerges 2018.
9   Nyerges 2018.
10   Mayer 2017.

always best to be yourself'. In an emotional heart to heart between Jack and Skip, he reminds his grandson 'You are exactly who you're supposed to be'.[11]

It's difficult to definitively say that popular culture has a direct impact on society and public opinion on issues such as gay rights. 'It's really impossible to predict how its messages may be received,' says Nyerges, 'It's an unpredictable method for pop culture to do educational work', yet it does go a long way in 'nurturing tolerance'.[12] The rising popularity of queer shows does give a sense that people are becoming more accepting of the LGBTQIA+ community. The 2018 Netflix reboot of *Queer Eye*, for example, is as emotional as it is fabulous. Part of its charm is recognising that these five gay men are each special individuals who have such loving and giving hearts. The journey of each person (usually very religious) in learning about the struggles of the LGBTQIA+ community and coming to accept the Fab Five resonates with the public. The emotional and overwhelmingly positive response to the show, as well as *Will and Grace*, has pushed popular culture against the negativity of the current political climate towards a space of acceptance and tolerance.

According to the 2016–2017 study of LGBTQIA+ representation in media by GLAAD (Gay & Lesbian Alliance Against Defamation), only 4.8 percent of characters on primetime TV identify as part of the queer community.[13] It's a little sad to think that this is the best result to date. Despite these statistics, shows like *Will and Grace* are continuing to highlight LGBTQIA+ issues. Not alone in its mission, more and more television programs are including gay, lesbian, bisexual and transgender characters. From *Orange is the New Black* to *Queer Eye* to *Unbreakable Kimmy Schmidt*, American TV is becoming a powerhouse of complex, strong LGBTQIA+ characters. One by one, each character is changing the way we see and think about sexuality and the LGBTQIA+ community.

---

11   *Will and Grace* 2017.
12   Nyerges 2018.
13   GLAAD 2017.

References

GLAAD (2017). *Where We Are on TV '16-'17: GLAAD's Annual Report on LGBTQ Inclusion*. https://glaad.org/files/WWAT/ WWAT_GLAAD_2016-2017.pdf

Hart, Kylo-Patrick R. (2016). We're Here, We're Queer – nd We're Better than You: The Representational Superiority of Gay Men to Heterosexuals on Queer Eye for the Straight Guy. In Hart, Kylo-Patrick R. (ed.). *Queer TV in the 21st Century: Essays on Broadcasting from Taboo to Acceptance:* 62–76. North Carolina: McFarland & Company Inc. Publishers.

Mayer, Jane (2017, 16 October). The Danger of President Pence. *The New Yorker.* https://www.newyorker.com/magazine/2017/10/23/ the-danger-of-president-pence.

Mulkerrins, Jane (2018, 20 January). 'We had death threats': The Defiant Return of *Will & Grace. The Guardian.* https://www.theguardian.com/culture/2018/ jan/20/we-had-death-threats-the-defiant-return-of-will-grace.

Nyerges, Aaron (2018). Personal communication.

Will and Grace (2017). 'Grandpa Jack'.

Train Lines

Ellen Burke

A few years ago, my sister and I caught the train to Northern Sydney to have dinner with our extended family. She had just moved to the city to go to university, and I had just returned from travelling overseas. It was late summer, the night was deliciously cool without being cold, and we chatted amicably on the way there. I recall feeling ever so slightly superior as the older sister considering I knew enough about Central Station to get us to the right platform easily. I was excited to guide my sister through the city I had come to know. I chose seats for us on the top level of the carriage, and when we crossed under the arch of the bridge I gazed hungrily out at the sunset over the harbour.

We ate dinner and caught up with our cousins as night fell. When finished, we waved goodbye and returned to the train station, lit yellow under the night sky. The train pulled in and we dropped onto window seats facing each other in a bay of six. The train was quiet at first but eventually the carriage filled, and a middle-aged man sat next to us. He sat in the direction of the train's travel, facing me and next to my sister with his leather briefcase slumped on the seat between them. He was about forty, older than us but younger than our parents, and was dressed in a suit jacket and shirt, but no tie.

He started talking to us – well, to me. The more he spoke, the closer my sister pressed herself to the window of the train. He had been at a work event he said, hence his late train journey. We talked about disconnection. That despite being physically close, no one on trains ever speaks to each other, instead we are glued to our phones. I didn't mind talking to him. Having just returned from travelling, my sentimentality was heightened. This man had a complex life full of thoughts and desires which, for a brief moment, I was privy to. Sometimes he would address my sister, or gesture towards her, but her frown would only deepen. Our stop approached. When I disclosed this, the man began to tell me I was special, not like other people, and he wanted to continue our conversation, wanted my phone number. Smiling, I politely declined. My sister got up and surged to the train door. I followed.

When we stepped onto the busy platform she hissed at me, 'What were you doing? Couldn't you smell the alcohol on his breath?' I gaped at her; I hadn't smelt anything. I'd probably been poised to tell her off for being so rude to him, but now I was speechless. She was fuming, set to explode. She couldn't believe that I, her older sister, had put us in a position of danger. She continued to burn my ear as we descended from the platform.

And then we heard a yell from above us. Looking up, we saw the man from the train leaning over the railing, calling for us to wait. Terror jumped up my throat. We ran, leaping down the stairs into the throng of strangers. I couldn't have been more grateful to be among them. I kept glancing behind us as we hurried along the corridors, but I didn't see him again.

The cool night air rushed to greet us as we emerged from the station. My sister's rage was again palpable, her mouth pressed into a thin line, her eyes refusing to meet mine. I didn't need to be told again. I think I apologised. But also, maybe I didn't – I couldn't shake the feeling that he wasn't a threat. Whose interpretation of the man was correct? Did he mean us harm, or did he just want a moment of human connection? I still now don't know which one of us was right.

When reflecting on how COVID-19 has changed the networks around us, I remembered this story and realised that an interaction like this would be impossible in our pandemic-stricken world. Two networks, distinct yet both fundamental, have been altered. Train networks are crucial to cities, and the virus has impacted upon them in subtle yet significant ways. Train carriages were interesting environments to begin with, and now COVID-19 has affected the atmospheres of carriages, altering the way we sit and interact with others as we travel across our cities. The scope and depth of our social networks has also changed. For many people, I suspect, the pandemic has shortened and strengthened our network of friends and family. Meeting strangers on trains has been the last thing on my mind lately as Sydney's winter lockdown worsens. I've avoided people like the plague (after all, they may have it) and concentrated on maintaining my existing relationships. COVID-19 has changed so much of our lives, and it remains to be seen which changes are permanent.

Trains are unique environments, intermediaries between public and private space. We pay our fares, expect them to be tidy and quiet, and yet they are government run and open to all – well, all who can afford them, use stairs, navigate the ticket machines and the like. You can nevertheless find yourself in a carriage with an uncommon mix of people: school and tertiary students, office workers, tradespeople, tourists, the elderly. Conversations between people can drift through carriages, often in languages other than English. For the most part though, people sit in silence staring at their phones, as the man and I noted that night. We are not free to relax fully, as we would privately, yet nor are we in a usual public setting. The public–private boundaries are slippery, as train time is 'neither leisure nor work time,'[1] and has

---

1   Berry and Hamilton 2020, 112.

its own unique set of social rules. Research has looked at how mobile phones have transformed the nature of train-spaces, further blurring the public–private divide. The private leaks in through half-heard phone calls, or half-glimpsed Instagram feeds. Work lives creep in through emails and texts. I have often wondered, especially since my encounter with the man, if mobile phones have reduced the possibilities of communication with strangers. In one of my favourite films, *Before Sunrise* (1995), two young characters meet on a train in Europe and a romance blooms. I remember seeing the film and being struck with nostalgia for a time I haven't known as an adult. Who could I have met if I didn't spend so much time bent over my phone? I could have expanded my own personal networks by reaching out to those that utilise the same train networks as me, and yet instead I am pulled into my existing internet webs. It seems a shame.

COVID-19 has affected how train networks function, and I would argue they have further reduced the possibility of human-to-human interactions. For most of the pandemic, the prevailing public health protection mantra has been 'social distancing'. On trains, this has manifested in carriage number limits and, in Sydney, those now familiar green plastic stickers directing us to 'sit here'. In the first stages of the pandemic though, these measures were not necessary as the number of people catching trains dropped by up to eighty-five percent in Australian capital cities.[2] Think for a moment how eerie that is – empty trains rattling through the city, carrying only those deemed essential, whilst we waited to see if the numbers would rise or fall. Who would have thought this could happen? When people did brave trains in our first lockdown, atmospheres were tense and hostile, with initially increased incidents of verbal abuse towards train workers.[3] As cities re-opened, we slowly boarded trains again to work, study and socialise, but clad in face masks and more wary of our fellow passengers than ever before.

I would say that tension in train carriages has lingered beyond lockdowns. We are far less likely now to strike up a conversation with a stranger. In a pre-COVID world, when someone sat next to me in a

---

2   Naweed, Jackson and Read 2021, 438–444.
3   Naweed, Jackson and Read 2021, 439.

train I accepted it, with a little disgruntlement. But in a post-COVID world, when someone sits near me, I react like my sister did the evening we met the man: I push myself into the plastic wall to keep the gap between us as wide as possible. Should someone board the train with a runny nose, the tension tightens. I braved the train to visit my parents last year, and about an hour into the journey someone with the sniffles sat behind me. My mask felt useless. Eventually I moved carriages when it seemed they were not to depart anytime soon. Face masks have become a standard part of life on public transport, and they of course limit even our polite interactions, unless you have perfected smiling with your eyes. Perhaps this is unsurprising, but I believe it is concerning. With talk of the negative mental health effects of lockdowns,[4] it seems sad to me that trains have become sites of anxiety, and that the possibility of human connection has been stifled.

When I think back to the encounter, I realise that another reason it would not happen today is because my relationship with my sister has strengthened. As we have gotten older, we have come to better respect our differences, and hence get along better. The pandemic has also played its part. As lockdown stopped us socialising, my interactions were limited to people I felt comfortable on the phone with. I found myself calling and texting my family the most. Because I know them so well, I don't need to rely on facial expressions or body language to gauge how they are or how they perceive me. With most other people, after a few rounds of texting I forget their real voice and often end up misinterpreting or disengaging with their messages, truth be told. When lockdown lifted, I valued socialising with friends more than ever, but also found it exhausting. Not being overly confident in group settings to start with, I feel as if COVID-19 has sent me backwards in sociability. But when I'm with my family, we can sink into comfortable silences punctuated with superficial yet delightful conversations about what to have for dinner. It's not all rosy of course, the lack of usual social filters can lead to tactless comments and conflicts. But overall, I feel lucky and grateful for the case my family provides. The importance of them in my shrinking social network has become clear.

---

4   Martin 2021.

In May this year my sister and I found ourselves travelling north on the train again for a family dinner, albeit a much smaller one than the night we met the man. I couldn't help but compare journeys. This time we flipped the chairs so we sat in a three-seat bay, keeping the seat between us empty so no one could squeeze in next to us. We wore masks. We chatted, relishing the chance to do so, and around us the other passengers were quiet. I am even more grateful for that time now as I write this in Sydney's extending lockdown. It has been a long time since I thought about making conversation with strangers on trains, but not very long at all since I thought about making conversation with friends and family.

Train lines link our cities together, gifting mobility and granting access to regions of the city otherwise unknown. I started writing this thinking that I could write about social and train networks separately, but really they are intertwined. We use trains to keep our social networks alive. Trains are also sites for social engagement, although now in a much-altered environment. Since COVID-19, the possibility of interaction with strangers is limited by masks, social distancing and heightened wariness. Yet, by the same token, the connections we do have with people have become more valuable. When on trains now I am not disappointed at myself for putting my head down and texting, instead I am grateful that I still have people to text.

References

Berry, Marsha, and Margaret Hamilton (2010). Changing Urban Space: Mobile Phones on Trains. *Mobilities* 5(1): 111–129.

Martin, Sarah. (2021, 14 July). Covid's Mental Health Toll: One in Five Australians Report High Levels of Psychological Distress. *The Guardian.* https://tinyurl.com/3ebdzhfv

Naweed, Anjum, Janet E. Jackson, and Gemma J.M. Read (2021). Ghost Trains: Australian Rail in the Early Stages of the Global COVID-19 Pandemic. *Human Factors and Ergonomics in Manufacturing & Service Industries* 31: 438–444.

Challenges

Sally Chik

'It'll be a challenging role'
a friend says,
I try to forget
what happened,
no one
        remembers

when my manager laughed
when he put his hands on me
        and I pulled away,
        'He's flirting with you'
when he asked me to feed him
        by hand
        as he fed on my humiliation
when he asked for a coffee
        and told me to
        get in his car,
when I said no and he said
        'I thought you were special'
        I stuttered and he said
        'You hurt my feelings'
when he wheedles a lunch date
        to make it up to him
        'I'm only teasing'

It has been years
and I say no now
I retweet #MeToo
to a network that barely cares
I can joke around
I have enough challenges
when he finds me in empty rooms
      and I hear the laughter

when no one asked
      I didn't tell

when he took me to a boys' lunch
      where they all joked about
      sex and brothels
      he winked at me
      'Let's buy some toys'
      they all cracked up,
      clapping
when I laughed when they said
      that I wouldn't understand

when I challenge myself
      why didn't you say anything?
He was powerful
and he had powerful friends
when, anyway,
      he was only joking

Great Feeling Wants a Container
Thoughts on Home and Space

Claudia Ware

On the day P left her marriage, we bolted from the theatre and walked down Boundary Street in search of a divorce-kebab. It was a fitting way to end the day. Us: exhausted, blissed out on the heavy warmth of a greasy meal. P: grief-ridden, me: along for the ride. By some stroke of luck, we'd found ourselves working on the same project at the state theatre company up north, old friends-turned-colleagues. By greater luck, and perhaps providence, we found ourselves living on the same street. For nearly three months, we relished the domesticity of daily friendship, the intimacy of tracking with someone day in day out, of having nothing to catch up on and therefore everything to say. It was a Monday when we ordered our divorce-kebabs; an early curtain call, an earlier-than-usual bedtime. The sky stretched, bruised blue above our heads, autumn wind tickling with the edges of winter. I snapped a photo of P on my phone – 'the night you left your husband,' I said, 'one for the grandkids'. In the photo, P clutches her divorce-kebab with two hands as if it might escape. She is all gums and teeth, eyes sloped in smile, wide and terrified.

'The house,' she said, reality leaning on her, 'where am I going to go? I need to leave that house.'

As the season rolled on, P and I fascinated ourselves with houses. In the dim blue of the wings, we whispered our tenancy dreams until the cue-light blinked orange, then green: *go*. P searched for a three-bedder sanctuary, I looked for a studio, *a room of [my] own*.

* * *

I recently read a poem by Jeffery Skinner, which suggested that poetry is useful because strong feelings need a *container*.

I was taken by this and sent it to my poet-friend, B. He never responded, so I imagine he did not see what I saw or feel what I felt. Just as a quatrain might form a stanza, a stanza forms a room: *a container*. After all, that's what 'stanza' means – room, chamber, lodging or stopping place. A room for the poetic, a chamber for feeling, a *container* for imagination.

* * *

P and I had the same move-in date for our respective stanzas. 26 June. While I packed boxes, she divided assets, fighting for pieces of a house that were home to her: a grandfather's desk, a family heirloom, a father's parting gift. The spare room in my parent's house was explosive with my own 'assets', things I'd collected over the years and, for some reason or other, hung onto.

One morning P sent me text message with a poem she'd written. It included the lines:

The division of assets
Tells me what parts of my soul
You felt entitled to

Things – I often think this – are never just *things*. They are the grout of home, sites of memory, aspiration and personhood. A *thing* is a clamorous husk.

Even when one is no longer attached to things, it's still something to have been attached to them; because it was always for reasons which other people didn't grasp.
Proust, *Cities of the Plain* (1927)

* * *

On the day I moved into my apartment, I sat on the cold timber floorboards surrounded by my *things*; boxes of books, my piano (Florence), our family's old music cabinet, my great-grandmother Alice's Victorian-era hatbox, the chair I reupholstered with my mother, a family portrait from the nineties. It wouldn't have felt right, moving to a new place without these things to cover the walls and floors and shelves. Besides, you cannot shed the skin of the past by moving to a new home (oh lordy, I've tried this), if anything, you only dangle it further behind you, having loosened its purchase on your soul.

There was one box I was reluctant to unpack. It sat on the passenger seat of my car for a fortnight, tightly bound, winking. The box contained memorabilia from my early twenties – a time of great pain, confusion and embarrassment. A time dominated by the colour blue. I didn't want to see Her, the woman in the box. I did not resonate with Her anymore, or, at least, I didn't want to. Most of all, I had no desire to re-live her pain.

When I did open Her box, I was surprised by the sheer volume of letters and cards – mostly from my immediate family. Handwritten notes were a significant trope of my upbringing. On special occasions, the emphasis was always on the note, not the gift. The phrase *cards are personal* was (and still is) delivered accusingly to anyone who dare read a note not addressed to them. Our cards were a written excavation of everything we felt and appreciated about the recipient. I had no notion that other families didn't share our tradition until I left home and continued to write letters of this nature to friends who were surprised, and at times embarrassed, by my *cards are personal* tendencies.

I knew my father and I exchanged letters during my years in Perth, but I had forgotten just how many he sent.

Dear Claudette, they began.

Don't be fooled into thinking the world isn't wonderful – it is. You are.

My parents were grappling with the woman I'd become, attempting to reconcile themselves with the girl they'd raised and the cloud of blue that had taken her hostage.

I hope and pray that you become entirely yourself.

I didn't know what 'myself' was, nor where to begin finding her.

In another of my father's letters, he writes about *seasons* and suggests I *listen to 'Turn! Turn! Turn!' by The Byrds.*

At the bottom of Her box, I found a letter written in child-like handwriting from my first attempt at a boyfriend (the one with 'ChicksFootyBeer' tattooed on his foot). There was no date, but I sensed the letter was written the week I first tasted infidelity. The word 'secrid' appeared seven times.

Secrid – *like something foul and acidic.*

It took a moment to unpick his misspelling.

Sacred.

Sounded about right.

There was very little he considered sacred.

Least of all my body.

Least of all my soul.

Though to be fair, I'm not sure I had a great sense of *sacred* myself. Looking back, fingers over eyes, I see a young woman utterly, despairingly lacking in self-possession.

Stay classy, my father signed off.

If only I did.

* * *

Soul. Is it too histrionic, too sticky and *woo woo* to talk about 'souls' – whatever that may mean? The word makes me cringe, but as someone with an appetite for the sentimental, it is somewhat unavoidable. After all, isn't it the soul that makes a person a person, not just a body? If the body houses the soul, then the soul cradles the person.

A few months ago, my brother and I drove out to say goodbye to our beautiful Nana Gladys, aged ninety-four. But as I held her hand, kissed her cheek and told her how much I loved her, I felt I was saying goodbye to the body, the house – the occupant had long since disappeared. Her embers had cooled.

A house then is also a kind of body. Just as our 'soul' clings to organs and bones and blood, we attach ourselves to walls, floors and *things.*

Our homes bear psychological weight. They are forms of self-portraiture, landscapes of the psyche. Bachelard's work is a passionate exploration of homes and spaces and an invitation to think figuratively about these ideas. In one chapter, he recalls an exhibition organised by French-Jewish psychiatrist Françoise Minkowska, who studied drawings of houses done by children during the Second World War. She found that children who had not endured hardship during the war drew houses that were well lit, proportional, and robust. For them, the house was a safe, sacred space. Conversely, Jewish children who had suffered during the German occupation drew 'motionless houses' – they were cold, angular and ill-proportioned, with sparse landscapes and sentinel-like trees guarding the building. For these children, the house was more *secrid* than sacred.

The Bachelardian house is, at its best, a site of immense intimacy. I am hospitable to this idea. It runs contrary to the macroness of contemporary life, the exteriority with which we broadcast our voices, thoughts, and identity through the World Wide Web. For Bachelard, it is in the privacy of the house that daydreams take place. And what, then, is the virtue of daydreaming (if not simply for the sheer pleasure of idleness)? I might suggest that art – broadly speaking – offers us fodder for dreaming, and that daydreaming is the personalisation of that fodder. Daydreaming is the root of *becoming*, a means by which to consider the possibilities of oneself. To daydream is to acclimatise to one's acoustics, to offer the wisdom of imagination to the rigour of knowledge.

Bachelard attributes maternalistic qualities to the home. Here, I am less hospitable. I understand what he's getting at – the house is protective, sheltering, nurturing – qualities we most readily attribute to women, and in particular, mothers. But it smacks of Coventry Patmore's 'Angel of the House'. In her most recent 'living autobiography' *Real Estate* (2021), Deborah Levy offers a more gender-neutral way of thinking about the home, referring to these places as simply spaces for living.

Spaces for living – I'm on board with this.

* * *

Since leaving the family home at eighteen, I've lived in six different share houses with twenty-three different housemates. I grew up in a family of seven; we shared bedrooms, bathrooms, corridors – we shared *spaces for living*.

I consider myself a hospitable person. I don't always get it right, but I'm comfortable with co-existence and find it relatively easy to synchronise with the rhythms of those around me – *What do you need me to be? I'm flexible, supple, malleable. How do you need me to be?* People stain me the way turmeric stains the benchtop yellow. I've been a someone to somebody many times over – a daughter, a friend, a sister, a colleague, a teacher, a lover, a housemate, a stranger-turned-housemate-turned-sister, a friend-turned- housemate-turned-stranger. Existing in relation to others, accommodating difference, is cosy and good. (I also wonder if it is slightly gendered – most woman I know are highly skilled at facilitating the moods, lifestyles and experiences of others, often denying their own in the process.) But flexibility without personal clarity is self-betrayal. I've learnt this the hard way.

At twenty-seven, I decided to live on my own – bold, given my proclivity for co-existence. I knew there'd be times when I would feel the sting of loneliness and miss the familial atmosphere of the share house, but I was eager for the crystallisation living alone might offer: *Who am I when no one is around? What are my tides, my cadences?*

I do feel strongly that we are meant to live in communities with others. My friends and I sometimes muse about starting a commune, and I regularly threaten my siblings with the idea of a geriatric share house come 2070. But there is value to be found in the company that solitude affords – at least for a season.

* * *

The day I moved into my one-bedder, Sydney went into lockdown. *Trial by fire.* I shuffled from room to room, rearranging my things, chasing patches of winter sun. I found my local coffee shop, they learnt my name, I played Florence, I lay in bed at dawn to watch the sky turn champagne, I waited for the thin lozenge of sun to claw through my south-east window at 7.35 am before losing its grip, heading north, I watched the light drop low in the late afternoon, smashed peach spun with heavy blue. Most of all, I acclimatised to myself, and watched the space become an extension of me.

* * *

Lately, I've been disciplined at tending to my houseplants. I'm no green thumb, but my friend A gave me a monstera as a housewarming gift, and I'm desperate to keep her alive. I dust her broad green leaves and notice a new one, tightly furled within the stalk of another, all lime and supple, just waiting to uncurl her fingers, waiting patiently to stretch up toward the ceiling and grow into this *space for living*.

I call P from my one-bedroom stanza. Across the line, I hear J, her youngest daughter thumping books off the shelf while M, the elder, watches *Play School*. P has been writing poems (good ones) and is daydreaming about pink bed linen. We talk about pink, about what a good colour it is, about how she deserves divorce-linen in her new home. P thinks she is going to buy them, and I say yes.

The Ends of our Lines Snapped

Karen Davids

May all mothers, lovers, parents, ancestors, friends and foes that impact you, walk with your memory into future endeavours, shaping each milestone with more wisdom.

I do not want to hear the reality

> One … must find one day that all he gains is lost/In a flood of tears, a conscience racked with pain.
> > Dante Alighieri, *The Divine Comedy, Vol. 1 (Hell), Canto 1.*
> > (Clive James' translation, 2013).

I do not want to hear the reality
feel the loss of sanctity
just to hear your voice
one last time.

We have broken, lost contact, the ends of our lines snapped.
Unearthly aliens now hover
no longer one.

The pain.
The picture of shame.
The heavy weight of regret spikes its thorns with intent.

I regress into precarity
wondering if my thoughts are any
form of clarity.

I scuttle back into my muddied rock
endlessly pacing,
painting,
portraying my quandaries into words ...
patiently resting.

Until the next wave of melancholy kindness
forgives.

An endless cycle of barbarity,
a vacuous cavity beneath our feet
carries our hearts into eternity.
But together?
Forever?

A fragile decision
rests on the revision of tragedies,
awoken by our broken call,
our epic fall.

It befalls the hands of the
divine, the sorcerer of all our sanctimonious
crimes – revealing the secret
chimes of trodden hearts; both
yours and mine.

We shed the sorrows of our past in a
prevailing illuminous tale – yet re-brushed to conceal the
bruises and blemishes.

A beauty carved with an artistic flair,
constructed and crafted like a golden offer to those we adore.
Hiding the many mishaps and misfortunes that stitch our hearts

apart.

Mercy is no secret.
It is the root of retreat; both
Yours and mine.

We mistreat our vulnerable, quivering and rebelling
hearts with an unjustified and cowardly
gasp. Unable to accept
the season of decay at our doorstep.

Without a sense of space, we dissipate into memory's
oblivious allure, unable to capture and conquer the forgiving horizon
that will befall with a melodious call.

Summoned to the waiting room.
Ready for the bang of the piercing bell
to echo in an echoless space.

We are not idle; simply misplaced.

I transgress in the ultimate act of progression

Not ready to lose you.
A call, plea for reprieve, a moment to
breathe from the stitches you continue to sew into
my heart.

You birthed me, broke me, redefined me
and left me alone, shivering in the stagnant
cold.

Acceptance comes in seasons
without reason – for its power ages like you,
only with more strength.

As if it has gained its muscles from your
perishing body to guide me through the years of
forecasted unrest brought on by your slow
Death.

How shall I relinquish the pain?

A piece of wisdom I cannot find inside.
You were my wisdom and now that's flickered into ageing dust
subtly sprinkled into particles invisible to the naked eye –
and unfathomable to the conscious mind.

Wept, wet, fret and forsaken.
In disbelief of withering freckled hands.

Reliving the pain until the relived pain
knows no more than those
withering freckled hands before.

The hands of my mother
reach in a momentous collective sea,
guiding my restless limbs that are finally freed
from the fear of immobility.

'Transgress', they say, remote from the horrors
looming in the mumbled dried hay.
Withering grass whereby we sit and pray,
together?

I kneel in forgiveness
for though such an act will hail the spirits
and prevail a sweltering sense of reprieve.

I muster up the courage to transgress the rules of decline,
yet in a differed state from initially defined.
No longer tightly holding onto the memory of your
withering mind.

Alas, I transgress in the ultimate act of progression.

The greatest of minds in the atlas of the seas
can see my heart of gold that merely hopes to hold
onto what is at once
left.

I seek a remedy; a destiny with you.
I will find you again
one day in another life.

Thank you for birthing, bathing, backing me –
teaching and teaming up with me.
A soul now lost but
never forgotten.

In every faithful memory, configuration of love,
you stand there with your own story,
your own freckled, frail and fair beauty.

I stand with you invariably
alive, withered or lost.

Mum you always were and always will be
a dear heart.

Shackled, shimmering and sun-kissed cheeks

Her vivacious gaze
mirrors the enthusiasm
for succeeding days.

Her faint smile marks an
escape from the
dried petals of the past.

Her sweet cheeks reflect a tasteful desire
for forgiveness, light and undiscovered
golden glimpses of faith.

Her shackled, shimmering and sun-kissed cheeks
reveal rosy days.

A zesty aroma oozes from an unveiling
seeking spirit,
courageous and careful in her steps.

She hears rich chirps of blossoming life
tunnel and crescendo from kelp forests,
densely vegetated wilderness and
sprouting branches scattered

in eerie pockets of her
healing mind.

Moulded by nature's gentle grasp and intuitive scent.
Each fine, frizzled and freckled
shaded leaf twinkles with a scent of childish joy.

Threaded stories of her past
spin intricately interwoven wheels of passion,
enmeshed, laced and lined with
delicacy – utter fragility.

Her palms search with an unquenchable thirst
for a burst of holy grail,
the myriad holy sails that gravitate towards
her shackled, shimmering and sun-kissed –
indeed, absolutely missed sweet cheeks
that reveal rosy days once again.

An existence unfathomably rich yet unforetold.
Ready to be remoulded, remastered and re-awakened
with a spirit unmatched by past lights,
flights that soared with a certain gentleness.

A sweet lullaby

> All the circling thus unloosed/Reflected light, which my eyes
> dwelt upon/And saw the way those swirling tints produced/A
> painted likeness that my eyes fixed on.
> > Dante Alighieri, *The Divine Comedy, Vol. 3 (Paradiso),*
> > *Canto 33.* (Clive James' translation, 2013).

A melody angelic in its grasp
is propelled towards her mask,
and with one kiss
disintegrates days of recession and transgression
that for far too long
silenced her heart's intent.

A godly switch towards freedom she did not
anticipate and frame in the visions came
during the days she was hypnotised by sorrowful regret.

At once, she is hypnotised by the sun's bravery and the
earth's multifarious rotations; laterally lacing
through turbid valleys with
bespoke rays of light,
an army of awakened beetles
and beautiful baby daffodils.

She rests at once.
A rare and finite sight.

She feels joy.

A joy yet to mature into
a ripe lullaby, sang with courage
despite the bruises that once, perhaps always will
puncture her heart.

Indeed, a fantasy awaits
persistently equates
her drenched tears against years of
love to come.

Her steps are followed
by a band of harpists, violinists and
an applause of gracious steps,
a sweet appetite for simply the best
days of delight that shall trickle in her sight.

She curiously leans in to listen to the whispers of the shore,
patiently waiting for her time to be called.

Bedtime Stories from Lockdown

Xian Ho

It was nearly midnight. She lay in her bed, headphones pulled over her ears, decidedly drowning out the world with music. It had been one of those days. She stared at the ceiling, softly illuminated by a candle whose flickering threw undulating shadows about the room.

She sensed something change. She didn't know how. Perhaps she had spent so much time in her familiar sanctum, she was attuned to its slightest change. She sat up, turning to find her dad standing in the doorway. She expected him to start shouting.

Why was she awake? Did she know how late it was? Was she trying to ruin her eyes? Go to sleep!

Instead, he padded softly across the carpet, wrapped his arms around her, and pressed their foreheads together like she was two years old again.

'Are you okay?' he whispered. He didn't shout. He didn't tell her she wasn't okay. He didn't put words into her mouth or assume something was wrong. He simply asked.

'I'm just stressed about getting all my work done,' she managed. The excuse was as easy as breathing – an old faithful one. He didn't move.

'Is that all?' he asked softly. And that was all it took. Her breathing became uneven. Her whole body shook as the tears slipped out in the darkness. She couldn't get enough air into her lungs without letting out the tell-tale sobbing sounds. He kissed her on the forehead. He hadn't done that in years.

'I don't know,' she whispered.

'I appreciate that you don't know. But if you did know –' An old joke. She laughed despite herself, but it sounded watery and thin. She hiccupped.

'Sometimes I get like this,' she admitted. 'I feel sad, and I don't know why.'

He squeezed her one last time, then sat back on the bed and took her hand in his. It was soft, strong and warm. It was a father's hand. They looked at each other, considered one another in the semi-darkness.

'It's hard,' he said. 'It's depressing. You need to see your friends, but you can't see your friends. Do you talk to them?'

They talked for a long time, in a way they hadn't in years. Quietly. Gently. He listened. She listened. And they heard each other. He told her how he coped with the present and his plans for the future. She told him about her friends and her hobbies.

He didn't leave again until he was sure that, this time, she was okay. He squeezed her hand, the one he hadn't let go, one last time. Then he stood up. He didn't tell her to go to sleep. He didn't tell her to blow out the candles. He didn't tell her she was doing anything wrong.

'Thank you for checking if I was okay,' she said, as he opened the door to go.

'Of course,' he said.

Then he was gone.

I didn't say I love you, she thought. *Why didn't I say I love you?*

Until she realised, she had. And so had he.

Just not in so many words.

Thank You

James Max Puterflam

Thank you to my mother, the embodiment of compassion, without
   whom I would not exist.
Compassion was shown from my very conception.
Through your body, you nurtured my growth.
Through the pain of my gestation and of my birth, all was done with
   compassion.
Without it, I would not have been possible.
Even after becoming physically separate, still I depended on you.
Feeding, bathing and nurturing, day after day, night after night.
Without your compassion death was certain.

Thank you to my father, the embodiment of skill and method from
   whom I have learnt about the ways of the world.
How to survive in society, to make oneself of value and worth, not
   only for others but for oneself.
You always emphasised the importance of learning and education.
Despite my dullness and lack of natural ability, you encouraged and
   supported me tirelessly.
If you could not teach me, you provided another to do so.
You provided unlimited opportunities and support, not only for
   myself, but for my mother and siblings.
Without your guidance I would be as dumb as a beast.

Thank you to my educators, the transferers of knowledge and
   facilitators of learning.

You developed my intellect and laid a sturdy foundation.
Like well-nourished soil from which interests and pursuits could
blossom.
Despite a short attention span and lack of determination, none of you
gave up, but rather persisted and encouraged me.
Simply filling my cup, as much as it could hold.
With the foundation established, eventually the joy of learning and
subsequently that of teaching developed.
Fascinated I remain by the interconnectedness of knowledge, like the
links in a chain, knowledge unbreakably binding the teacher to
student, again and again, on and so on.

Thank you to my foremost spiritual teacher and others of the kind.
All of you I chose, unlike those previously mentioned.
In you I receive that which is priceless.
That which expands and stabilises the mind.
That which explains the most important to know.
That which extinguishes the wildest of fires.
That which serves as a life buoy in the roughest of seas.
That which defends like an unbreakable shield, an impenetrable
refuge, well fortified and protected.
That which illuminates like a candle in the dark.
That which has inexhaustible qualities yet is identified by no one.
That which reveals the truth of phenomena.
That which points to the nature of the mind.
Like Mother and Father, no amount of thanks is ever enough.

Thank you to loved ones and genuine friends, the companions with
whom I endure through this all.
Practising kindness is made easy by you.
Learning from strengths and improving on weaknesses.
You remind me of the nature of things.
Unlimited expressions on scales of extremes.

Despite sharing paths and experiences alike, time prevents us from
tasting it all.
Through each other we can learn that which one life has not the time
to encounter.
Irrespective of different experiences, habits and views.
United we remain by the unstained pureness of experience.

Thank you to my enemies and those with views different than my
own.
You further remind me of the unlimited nature of this universe.
Through you I learn to tolerate and accept.
Without such learning no peace will I find.
You spin my mind around like a vortex, a whirlpool.
In distress and malaise, I erroneously divide myself from you, the
'other'.
A division which serves only a relative importance.
Through this mental creation, a mental sparring emerges.
A battle fought in my mind, against my mind.
Simply put, the self-constructed 'Me' reacts to the self-constructed
'You'.
Like someone arguing with their reflection in the mirror.
Both seen as mind and duality is resolved.
How wonderful enemies are that they provide us the opportunity!

Thank you to my selfish desires that are unlimited and endless.
You remind me that no contentment or satisfaction comes so long as
you exist.
Like holding a hand close to a fire, or a speck of dust settling on the
eye.
Impossible to ignore unless it's removed.
Since the beginning, my selfish desires have brought so little joy, and
any joy brought has long since departed.
Furthermore, they are tiresome and bothersome, arising anew as soon
as they are attained.

Without an end and ceaselessly tormenting, I ask the question, why
    continue to desire if the reward lasts not longer than the day?
On the contrary, all my unselfish desires provide untainted joy for
    both myself as well as others.
May unselfish desire emanate endlessly from all my activities.
May they remain my only desire.

Thank you to obstacles, those big and small.
It is through obstacles and challenges that progress is made.
How else can growth be known if not for a presented opportunity?
A bird will never fly unless it leaps from the nest.
One knows not their intellect unless they are sat before a test.
A cheetah knows not its speed unless it engages in chase.
Without looking in the mirror how could one recognise their face?
Without such obstacles I would remain begrudgingly complacent and
    lazy.
It is through you that thirst can be quenched, hunger satisfied and
    pain relieved.
Overcome temporarily, and one day forever.
May all obstacles crumble before me.

Thank you to suffering, the cause of stress and anxiety.
I thank you for how you have affected me and others.
By experiencing you I am not motivated by possessions or by
    pleasures.
Suffering I see in the rich and the poor, in the famous and the
    unknown, in the intellectuals and the dumb, in the foreign and
    the native, in the beautiful and the ugly.
All this suffering experienced in my mind and the mind of others.
Unknown and hidden you have evaded identification for far too long.
But due to your persistence you have since been found and can now be
    eradicated.
May I see the causes of suffering and bring its downfall swiftly and
    permanently.

Thank you to the mind, the creator of all.
The creator of heaven and the creator of hell.
The creator of hallucination and the creator of illumination.
The creator of all existing, while remaining as nothing.
My friend and foe, supporter and tormentor.
All exists as you do, and without you, none of it would be
  worth mentioning.
You have never been concerned with yes or no, happy or sad, good or
  bad.
Present, knowing, illuminating and the holder of everything.
Like space itself, and how the sky holds the clouds.
You have held everything, and experienced everything.
Everything arises with you; I cannot be more certain of anything than
  this.
It all happens now, untainted by the previous moment.
Not remaining in the past or escaping to the future.
Flowing as a diamond river, nothing stops it, not even slumber.
Uninterrupted from last night through to this morning.
Then again, from this morning until we reach tonight.
Becoming everything and yet remaining as nothing.

Thank you all, everything and nothing.

A Day in the Life of a LONER

Grace Cheng

Connecting with scripture, talking to God

I am awoken by a muted buzzing sound. It hums intermittently and my synapses work to relay this news to my brain. It is no longer night but a new day. I squint at the light that permeates through the curtains in my room. My top and bottom lashes meet each other as my eyes blink open. While I struggle to emerge from under my covers, my two hands neatly interlock; one sits naturally over the other. I sincerely thank my mighty maker for the oxygen in my lungs, the beating of my heart, and I tell Him of how He has all my heart and adoration. He is the sole reason I live both physically and consciously. Full meaning in life and complete joy only exist through Him, although some may disagree and label me deranged. I perceive one to be a fool to reject something so true and so wonderful. I grab a floral-patterned, perfectly bound book: the Holy Scripture, it is about the Triune God. This book defines me, I am free from vanity and worldly expectations because of it. I am defined by the most divine. I smooth my fingers across the silk-like pages of this God-breathed book, it feeds my soul, it makes me new. His words, they are a lamp to my feet and a light to my path. I connect with my maker and His son who justified me and perfected my faith in Him.

Connecting with nature

I brush my hands against the shrubbery that sit on the perimeter of this homey warm terracotta-bricked house – it is my way of greeting them. A middle-aged man walks toward me, I grin hesitantly from a few metres away. If I had a choice, I would personally prefer grinning at dogs and children because they have purer hearts and fewer responsibilities. I run across a peculiar house that possesses the obvious characteristics of an East Asian home. Strangely, I notice a clinical squaring off of the hedges that surround the house, it is so neatly squared that it feels disingenuous. Even worse, right behind the hedges is a row of artificial-looking roses. Next to this house is another peculiar home, an Anglo home, whose entrance, oddly, has an excessive amount of wild ferns and philodendrons sprouting in all directions. There are glimpses of birds of paradise flowers in the corner. This feels deceitful too. The Asian home's clinical squaring off of the hedges seem to me like an act of a rich migrant's inauthentic assimilation into the Western society in which they reside. The Anglo home is overtly tropical, reflecting a false narrative that the owners are well travelled. I wonder – why do we always pretend to be something we aren't? As these thoughts ruminate in my head, I become aware of how mad I may sound. This is probably why it's best to not always think aloud.

Connecting with oneself

I run past two young trendy girls who look about my age, they are in their early twenties. I nosily overhear one of the girls recounting to her friend the details of her and Jono's dispute, which took place last weekend. They both effortlessly don nineties style hoodies and colourful yet muted leggings, with matching scrunchies to complete their athleisure ensemble. They look like friendly models featured in an ad for a current and sustainable activewear brand. Somewhere in my consciousness I am jealous of how they look so connected to one another, in their taste in fashion and their relational connection. Studies show that people in close proximity are viewed as more aesthetically appealing; this is known as the group attractiveness theory. That might be true, but the reality is, I am a loner, and I simply can't live consciously without being with my own thoughts. I can't hear my heartbeat over the sound of another person's voice. If it counts for anything – I think I am most attractive when I am alone.

Connecting with someone to love

My bones ache, my soul is drained, work is trying, but this part of the day is the most challenging. Once the sun goes down, it is a dreaded, yet excitable time. A dreaded time because once I get into bed, I recognise my lack of a love life. It is as though the appearance of the moon signals our fleshly bodies to yearn for someone's embrace. Yet it is an excitable time because I am free to do absolutely nothing, this time of my day is my own. I swipe my brick-sized mobile device – and then proceeds a cruel process of heartless shopping for men. What would our ancestors say? Would they look down on us with pity for our existence and angrily exchange words of disdain? What would our literary ancestors have to say? Would they mark this as dystopian, if Orwell predicted this pandemic of human interaction? My warm-blooded heart feels minute sparks of connection to you. I zoom into your second photo and try to visualise the texture of your skin. Meeting digitally just means that I know you liked me despite my voice, despite my imperfect skin and my less than articulate timbre and you liked me for my strange curation of self.

I am leaning caringly against your wide chest as I reminisce about the time I met you. I spot you; you are a three dimensional person. Why is that surprising? Somewhere in the corners of my consciousness I imagined you to be a walking and talking pixelated hologram. You are handsomely slouched against a pillar outside HOYTS. Our eyes lock and I wave. How did you recognise my tired, pale, average appearance? I comfort myself and think this is not too different from how normal people meet. It's essentially the same thing; guy meets girl, they both like each other's appearance, they decide to meet for coffee, and the story begins. The stark, cold air of air-conditioning coupled with a waft of cellular breeze – these elements quickly remind me that I am surrounded by all things digital. However, the warmth of nearby human breath, the inhales and exhales all around this densely occupied mall help to keep this air from going to sub-zero. We walk into a bubble of biting coldness, but the warmth that is emitted from your strong arms cuts through it, providing us with shelter amidst this technological blizzard. Cold, warm, warmer, hot. The organic conversations we have help aerate the thick musky smell of internet dating shame that I can see from your posture is something you feel too. My hands are still cold, I slot them both into my insulated pockets to keep them warm. I walk beside you and your body feels real, I look up and notice your facial features. I like your side profile better than your digital profile. You have a sturdy, genuine nose. Just like those ancient Greek statues that stand in museums; like the cornerstone of a Roman cathedral, your nose holds up your face. After a split second, a jolting thought disrupts me, I realise you are standing too close to me and instinctively shuffle an inch away. This feels better and safer, although my heart is still beating wildly.

In the present moment, I hold your hand and reminisce of the time we first met, and I sheepishly apologise for how our first encounter was a digital one.

Connecting with friends

I have always found confidence in being a loner, solitude in small doses was like a refreshing breeze. However, a breeze does not usually last very long. Once I sit too long in the silence, I start to recognise that I crave sound and the company of a friend. Thankfully, there exists friends in my life – those who enjoy my company, just as I enjoy theirs. They make life a joyful journey. Two good friends are better than a lover.

Connecting with our family

The inevitable connection, unasked for, taken for granted, but the most precious of all connections. Mum often calls to ask if I've taken my anti-depressants and at the end of every day, I comfortably and uncomfortably arrive at home. They keep me well fed and I doze off to the sounds of loud talking. This is my lullaby as I slowly drift off to the mental image of a family of sheep, as each sheep leaps over a shoddy fence, I arrive closer and closer to a state of slumber. Family are the people you want to share everything with, the very good and the very bad. They are the nucleus of the cell of life. Family is someone who knows too much, someone who sees your blatant ugliness and still chooses to love you anyway.

Connecting with my maker

Every evening, I never fail to be startled by a darkness, one that is the absolute antithesis of peace. I plead God to help silence these demons that persistently haunt me. I continue to count sheep and try to breathe through flashes of grim and evil melting faces. Thankfully, the darkness slowly subsides and I quietly doze off to the sound of distant mutters that seep through the walls. In the last few moments of my day, my maker gives me the warmest hug I have ever received and my soul is soundly at peace. I finally fall asleep in my creator's powerful gentle embrace. Somewhere within my consciousness, I realise, as a loner, I am not so alone after all.

A Nervous Condition

Cherie Baird

I've grown accustomed to the feeling
that I've left the oven on.
We're old friends now.
It prods at the back of my neck as I drive away –
did I turn the heater off? Did I
lock up last shift? Will my hair
dry by the morning? Has an assignment
spilled unnoticed from my sodden mind?
Is there something I've forgotten to pack?

I nod a brief hello as we pass one another,
this feeling and I.
I miss my train.

Just as it becomes familiar, suddenly it
slips from view; mutating, transforming
into a new threat
with unforeseen depth.
Will we still be here in thirty years?
Am I going to lose my job?
Will my place be ash by tonight?
Can I trust these systems of power?
Are we safe here?

Nerves crackle. A damp mind floods.

It's hard to smile at strangers
when they can't see your face.
If the eyes are windows to something
deeper, everyone I pass
must know that
my soul is scared.

Is it misguided to find myself wishing for
that old friend? To miss merely
worrying about leaving the oven on?
Maybe it's privilege or naivety that
wants to go backwards rather than
stand strong against a struggle.

I learn to bump elbows in the rain,
listen to quiet voices hoarse with muffled volume,
tip the barista extra, wave to the train conductor,
triple check the oven and hope
my eyes crinkle enough
to pass on the message.

My New Paws-itive Pastime

Danial Yazdani

Danial Yazdani explores ... what does he explore?

Yes, you may have just read a very hideous, poorly thought-out pun for a title. Yet, I can assure you that at least one person could not help letting a soft smile take over their lips. Perhaps they even let out a light-hearted chuckle? No, I may have been a bit too ambitious there. However, I think it is fair for me to tell you about a little experience I had, all those months ago in the earliest week of lockdown. What initially started off as a fond memory, followed by quick scribbles has now become an apex of reflection I wish to share with others. And I can assure you that this encounter redeems any form of unbearable wordplay.

I had just finished a three-hour rehearsal on Zoom and was feeling restless. My dog, Bella, a six-year-old, hyperactive Maltese-Pomeranian mix had been barking non-stop throughout my call, so I figured she was feeling the same. A walk was in order. I popped on that brand new tracksuit lost in the back of my wardrobe, and feeling like a mighty Sue Sylvester, leashed up Bella and put on ABBA's *Under Attack* for my first number. I began my walk, turning the corner of my street and onto one of the busiest roads in The Hills Shire: Windsor Road. It's hard to get some peace and quiet when walking along its thirty kilometres length. Cars are always – and I mean *always* – lined up behind one another; the traffic is erratic and a pain in the arse to navigate. No backstreet or shortcut will get you past it. As a matter of fact, such hilarious timesaving detours will bring you right back to it! However, on this particular day, I was blindsided by the deserted place that was Windsor Road, not even a single car in plain sight.

I stood there for a few minutes, and I can safely say that a measly seven cars passed me by. Yep, I counted them. A few black and white ones, the odd red or silver one and one metallic blue. It ironically reminded me of the time we learnt about a *flaneur* – a bewildering observer of society – in English during our study of T.S. Eliot's poetic personas. That was over a year ago – or was it? – and I was a foolish child back then. Now I was an adult, a grown-up, a man and most importantly an initiator of my own choices and decisions. And now, a year on from my first lockdown, I was standing like a stranger at the corner of my own street, bemused by the unconventional silence and lost in my own thoughts. Confusing, right?

Moving further down the road, I bumped into my neighbour who was walking onto Windsor road from the next street down. 'Do you smell that?' he said. 'That smoke, that weird smoky smell in the air.' It was very random to say the least, but I replied respectfully, made some small talk and continued on my walk. Right before we departed though, my neighbour *smiled* at me. Here I was, seeing a familiar face smile at me for the first time in however many years we had lived in the same complex. I moved on.

Further down Windsor Road, Bella and I bumped into an ugly looking thing: a pug. At least at first I thought it was ugly, and I let those personal dog-based biases come into play. Its owner, a stout woman wearing the most fabulous hat I had ever seen encouraged her pug to interact with Bella and set an example by interacting with me. At this point, I had had one too many interactions on a brisk walk that was supposed to raise my twenty steps a day to two thousand. Nonetheless, I made some polite conversation about dogs and lockdown (of course) and said goodbye. Once again, I departed but was taken aback by the beauty of her smile. She had the warmest and most euphoric smile I had ever seen. I had experienced weeks in seclusion from the outside world and from the tangible yet distant warmth of strangers.

That smile stayed with me for the next ten or so minutes, as if I was living a lucid dream. I was in full control, that is, of my words and actions, but was I actually using that control appropriately? Had I smiled at my neighbour, the woman with the pug? I genuinely could not remember.

That walk was truly something else. I came across a diligent gardener, two speed-walkers dressed from head to toe in white, a muscled sprinter, a couple in fluoro orange vests and a lady draped in a purple shawl and jewellery, also with two dogs like mine – these people were strangers, but I encountered them as if they were ghosts or spirits guiding me along the way. Every single one of them *smiled* at me as they walked past, nodded their heads, called out a classic 'G'day!' and chit-chatted. These people were strangers, I tell you!

I got home after fifty minutes or so, walking the length of Windsor Road I was able to conquer in a day's journey. By the time I turned back into my street and into my townhouse complex, I was actively looking for other people. I was desperate to reciprocate the rare charismatic, interactions that I had just experienced in others and had failed to return in the moment.

Flash forward countless weeks later; after weeks of lockdown blues and continued extensions, I have changed my route from along Windsor Road to a place of utter serenity: Bidjigal Reserve. Its closest entrance is less than a kilometre away from home. The reserve was a small, but significant part of my childhood. While at Dad's place, my brother and I would listen to stories of turtles and platypi, of eels and lizards that Dad would fabricate as a way of getting us hooked on bushwalking with him. He was successful (only a few times, though), and we would go to the same entrance, skipping along the tracks like a naïve Hansel and Gretel, actively searching for the not so exotic animals in the bush. At most, a bush turkey and some finches were all we got. I know, what fools we were. And my oh my, what an enthusiastic storyteller (and big-time exaggerator) Dad was and still is!

Anyway, this year, as I randomly took a turn off Windsor Road one afternoon, I rediscovered the old entrance to the reserve. From then on, my walks changed and became bushwalks, sometimes exploratory, sometimes with others and often over two or three hours long. Bella accompanied me from time to time too, making new friends and causing unnecessary dog-related riots. But that's a story for another time. However, as these ventures became more commonplace in my now not so monotonous lockdown routine, the wonders of going bushwalking on Bidjigal's tracks were also accompanied by the regular smiles I had first encountered on Windsor Road. People like me, perhaps with a grain of adventurousness in them, were making the most of a difficult time while savouring the tenderness of spontaneous smiles from others. I took and still take these smiles and put them in my pocket, store them away for a rainy day when I feel out of place in this pandemic world, and I look back on them when I crave the feeling of belonging to a greater group of people serving a common purpose. Oh, and people who are obsessed with their dogs, they're also pretty swell, and their smiles hold a touch more power.

For you see, this short tale of shortcoming, followed by a moment of revelation and change in path, led me towards the light in a time of blurred, continuous darkness. At first, I was reluctant to document my experience because I didn't want to add to the bombardment that has started to become and eventually will be 'pandemic-fiction' or 'COVID-fiction'. But, with my mental health spiralling, and with my days becoming less and less put together, the simple act of a smile reminded me of the little things that can make someone's day, let alone restore their faith during a period of dreaded lockdown isolation. And to me, that is worth sharing with others in the same boat. For others, it may be giving someone a small piece of advice or even grabbing a cup of coffee for a friend, but for me, smiling at others and being on the receiving end of a smile on my now daily bushwalk has become my new favourite pastime. I'm paws-itive.

Goodbye to All That

Dennis Haskell

I walk keenly to the University
for the first time in years.
Through the familiar, narrow streets
but past buildings I've never seen;
my sureness retreats somewhat,
so I stalk casually intent
wild-haired young people ahead
whose manner clearly say 'students'.

Once there, I know the Oxford-
modelled place, or think I do;
the neat quadrangle grass
is officiously roped off,
mocking mere visitors, and
in the far corners
arcs of bark chips
accompany new trees. But
Philosophy is still off
to one side. I remember
its intellectual split
in my undergrad days, a power
strike and the buzzard-like
professor's silhouette
as he paced past and past

the room's stained glass
in the dark, discoursing on Kant.

All history now. Now English
is no longer a department.
To me, all the staff names
are new. In my old office
a young man lounges, reads,
as another does next door,
where a kind tutor, Dave, taught
until the night he OD'd.
I haven't forgotten the shock.
Happier to recall poetry workshops
with now well-known names,
the rich gift of teaching
when literature first seemed
an endless landscape
and its exploration
an endless joy.

Did Chris Brennan, kicked
from his Chair, feel
something like this?
Suddenly it seems
I should not return
ever, never. I have died
away from the place, as
it has died away from me,
surreptitiously. This
is what age really means:
awareness that the places forget you,
that the self you were
is no longer there, and
all the world that you lived

now lives only in you.
Your past is unique
like a language
only you can speak
and who on earth could be listening?

Literary Movements

Grace Ugamay Dulawan

Move / Moveable / Movement

4.

When I go to class, I do not *go* anywhere. I sit where I have been sitting already all day: in my chair, at my desk, in front of my laptop, at home, staring out the window in sympathy with the Jacaranda that does not move, is not *going places*.

3.

I do not know other writers. I did not grow up amongst writers and artists. I grew up in a community, but not a movement. And in many ways, I've left my community and become only an individual.

2.

The problem is a lack of community. I am not *in* a relationship *with* other living writers. I am in conversation with the works of writers constantly, a dialogue that happens when opening a book and reading their words and tracing across disparate works the commonalities, the questions and answers that speak to each other. But I am not part of a *movement*. Movement implies bodily action.

1.

I am a single, moveable object.
    Here and now an object in stasis.

The problem is that I am an *I*.
I've been trying to multiply,
to join up, to turn one letter into two:
I → We.

0.

With whom am I speaking?

Analogue

5.

I borrow books about Philippine literature from the library. I find and buy a children's book called *Ed-Eddoy*, an Ifugao folk song. I seek and find Ilocano and Ifugao epic poems. But who am I in conversation with? I am trying to locate myself in a tradition.

4.

In Hanoi I join a writing group. The first time we meet is in a café by West Lake, the rooftop of a large, air-conditioned chain-café that serves decadent chocolate muffins with green tea ganache, a frothy earl-grey latte they call a London Fog which is a revelation. It is my first time in a circle of writers. They are all a few years younger than me. *Cool* in a way that I don't feel at all.

The second time we meet in a narrow, multi-level building renovated in the distinct, hipster vibe that South-East Asia is so good at curating. We read snippets from our work aloud. I am intimidated, stimulated, needy. After I read a piece I've written about a relationship, a girl says, 'Thank God my relationship isn't like that!' I feel misunderstood. I say nothing.

3.

In Jordan, I try to join two different writing groups. The first is not what I think it is – full of PhD students doing dissertations on international development policy. One of them works for the United Nations Relief and Works Agency for Palestine Refugees in the Near East (she says it as one-word: *UNRWA*) as a Neutrality Coordinator. I think of that quote about neutrality in the face of injustice. She explains it's not as interesting as it sounds.

In the second writing group there are two Palestinian women and me. They are both mothers, I am not. They talk about Palestinian children's books, about Palestinian writers they like and don't like. They talk about the rich expat neighbourhood one of them lives in, they both have strong American accents and have lived in Washington DC.

One of them says to the other, 'I don't like the mums in my neighbourhood. They don't call their maids by their names, they simply say *el-filipiniye* – isn't that terrible?'

They call me by my name, not el-filipiniye, but I am not anybody's maid.

I don't see either of them again.

2.

In Sydney, before the virus throws everything into disarray, after I decide to do a Master of Creative Writing, my friends and I decide to start a book club. There are just three of us. It's not a *real* book club. It starts off as a kind of book summary and recommendation forum that morphs into discussions of short texts, wades into more tangential things like erotica, then the things we read as teenagers. We end up eating junk food and watching old R'n'B video clips on YouTube. Occasionally we discuss books or ideas, but it's more accidental than anything else.

1.

I get a part-time job working at a social enterprise that works on multilingualism, creativity and books. Everybody says it's a great confluence of my interests. I think of the phrase *on the nose*.

Digital

0.

i watch a facebook live stream of filipinx writers. i can't remember when i rsvp'd but the video pops up automatically when i am working from home, toggling between tabs. on the screen there are young women like me across scattered continents.

part of a collective. articulate. passionate. connected.
the verb *yearn*.

1.

soon after George Floyd is murdered, my friend L invites me to join a facebook group called 'decolonise - fil x aus'.
the adjective *aloof*.

2.

where am I located? with whom do i seek to commune?
commune as a verb.

3.

for one class my tutor asks us to describe something that is in the room or something we can see that the others cannot, 'off-screen'. i describe the tree outside my window. i worry later, retrospectively, that i misunderstood the task. that i should have described something inside my room, even though the girl before me described the ocean.

4.

once i turn off the time estimate on my kindle i feel better, read slower, pay more diligent attention. still though, i am conscious of the time.

5.

i worry about the ethics of downloading books.
  i do not pay for them.
    i cannot afford the books i download but do not pay for – there are
      too many of them, they are not available at the library.
        what is the difference between borrowing a book from a library,
          which is free, and downloading it from the internet,
            which is also free
              (but stolen?)
                where do these books come from?
              and how are 483 stored on
                one device?
                  i go on sprees and
                    download books
                      like a woman possessed.
                    as if possession
                  is wisdom.

6.

the screens, the silent claps after presentations, the speaker view, the grid, the breakout rooms, the way people look like stills – so intimate in their rooms – each a modernist dutch painting, a way of watching how the light fades in everybody's life. people empty chairs to go and switch on lamps, flick on lights. dogs come in and out for pets. sometimes the tops of children's heads pop up. a few times a bald-headed baby is handed over by limbs off-screen. black screens appear. others disappear. everybody's face is still, staring. questions are posed into silence. it's a kind of game of who breaks first. all of the social cues are both missing and happening too presently to be legible. the clean rectangles are strange blocks of people, a stranger's version of *The Brady Bunch*. everybody framed with enough space around them, nobody touching, everybody on mute. nobody can see my hands off screen as i scribble, grasp at this strange simultaneous group portraiture. once, when our tutor disappears, her internet cuts out, we all think it is our internet because nobody's face moves, we all look frozen but we are only very, very still.

IRL

There are two photos of the Jacaranda tree I describe to my class. I swipe between the two. The tree in winter, swipe left. The tree in spring, swipe right. As a metaphor, it is too obvious. But then, after semester is done, it looks the same as it did in the first picture, all bare and unflowered.

* * *

Sometimes I choose the easy way out / I am tired / put off by the thought of / having to present myself to others / video off, mic muted / I lie on my bed / supine / listening to the class / I close my eyes / I let my reactions fly / I groan, I laugh, I say / – OH MY GOD out loud / it is exhilarating / when I am called on to speak / the little rectangle with my name in it has a blue outline around it / I prefer this sometimes / words without images to subtract, distract / it's hard to know before you're in it / if something will be generative or not.

Picture all the things people could be doing: taking dumps / making out / driving home from work / grocery shopping / brushing their hair / taking a shower / reading a book / doing yoga / walking their dogs / taking care of their babies / cooking for themselves / their families / Some of these are easy / we see them happen live / Others we have to / take pains / to imagine.

Imagine the urges to groan and yell / that people keep from indulging / the pulling of hair / when the internet cuts out / The hmmms and rights! / And mutterings of agreement / that we never hear / lest we cause an echo / a gurgling underwater / muting of background noise / Hear the debriefs after class / when housemates and lovers and parents / and siblings and friends ask / *how was it?* / See the eye rolls and the lit-up / expressions and the imitations / of classmates and tutors alike / Know that this is all / going on / all the time / in real life / in person too.

Networks

If I asked you to draw a conversation, where would you start?

* * *

if you have ever had the urge to

        have two conversations at the same time

you have two options

      the first: be a girl, a woman amongst other girls and women

see how the volume increases, how we cackle and roar over one another

        the second: zoom. see how you can be mute

and speak to the people around you

        your classmates watching, wondering

distracted by your mouth, opening and closing,

         mouthing words, yet silent

see how you can have two things at once

* * *

A One-Woman Play

Scene: seen
Props: herself up on her arm
Lighting: up the stage

Basic Script:

Oh, ho hum,
Middle child
Westie, Selective School Nerd,
Settler, Migrant, Woman of Colour
Languages: English (Native)
Spanish (Fluent) Arabic (Elementary)
Filipino / Tagalog / Ilocano (None x 3)
Still, always, outsider

Motivation:
i accept these labels
As badges of honour. As if
To better situate myself, to set myself
Apart, to be at ease in the perception
That i move on the outside of things

History:
A good question to try to answer
Is, why do i keep moving away
From places and people
That have a hold on me?

Reworked Script:
i wonder how much
Of my isolation
Is self-imposed
How much of it
i perform
For myself

* * *

My favourite view on Zoom is speaker view. The person who is speaking is enlarged, takes up the whole screen. Everybody else sits in a small row on top. The situation I'm most comfortable in is when the Speaker is presenting, their powerpoint is the large screen, their head in a small box that I can move around - everybody else I can make disappear by clicking on a small little minus symbol, as if they were numbers I could subtract.

* * *

An ode to bookstagram:

Book Materiality   Literary friction   Book soup

      Extreme.Metaphors   Books.in.films

          literary runner   Books.engineer

The more *straightforward*   accounts are people's names plus the
    verb 'read'

As in   Eda is Reading   Rita Reads

We are all   claiming our literacy

Staking out some space   for ourselves   saying,
    come – follow me

* * *

I have a private account on Instagram, yet all the people I follow are public. I can't bring myself to attempt what they do – a following, access to the masses. Part of it is a belief that I'd have to sacrifice something of myself, part of it is about keeping one foot out and one foot in.

* * *

A few months into lockdown, I delete my social media apps. Later I log in again, via a browser, and notice a voice message from a former student, asking me if I'm okay, if I'm still alive. I smile at the sound of her voice, the rounded vowels of her Brazilian accent, the way it makes the sentence a squiggly line that meanders and curves. / It is amazing all the living I do unwatched. I no longer have the need to make space in my phone's memory by deleting videos, uninstalling apps. / The boycott doesn't last. I end up checking it on my browser, first occasionally and then so often I give in and re-download it. Still, I don't post anything, just watch everybody else live their lives. They can see me watching if they check who's seen their stories. The symbol they click on is an eye. Next to the eye is a number that says how many people have been watching. We have all either been the eye or checked on it, pulled to be on either side.

* * *

All the mediums I've ever written in:

- A journal (if I am a man) a diary (if I am a woman) I start when I am a child, so it is both (or neither)
- Notes passed around in high school (in year nine, a secret alphabet a boy named James made for he and I to write in our own secret language)
- MSN messenger (capitalisation wild, numbers and letters mixed together, lyrics chopped and spliced and stuck next to our longing, heartfelt names)
- Emails (the first, from a friend to me, written in Courier New, black background, neon green letters, like the Matrix)
- Blogs – Blogger.com, later, wordpress.com, but first MSN messenger blog
- Medium, for a brief second
- Instagram captions
- Facebook posts
- Long WhatsApp texts to friends that sometimes turn into ten-minute voice notes

* * *

i have been trying to say / so many things / for such a long time / putting myself out / into the void / instead of into the world / now, now / i organise for my classmates / from life writing / to meet at a bar in newtown / our voices echo in the empty / monday night space / some of us are shorter / than we thought / from the screen / we can hear all of the / voices and laughter / that we muted in class / here, in person / we let it ring out.

* * *

A Series of Questions reframed as statements:

1. I often wonder if I can't see what's before me because I've phrased it the wrong way.
2. The suspicion is there, that the only thing stopping me from being a part of something larger, is my perception.
3. If we have language, we are part of something that belongs to all of us.
4. We inherit the apparatus of power that hides in words too.
5. If we contain multitudes, we are rarely ever really alone. We are a *we*.

* * *

Somebody in my life has pointed out that I have started to refer to my writing as 'pieces'. As in *I've been working on this piece*. I like to picture my words as pieces, decidedly fractured things you can hold in your hand.

Something you can behold and be beholden to.

Now

Ruth Phillips

Fleshy magnolias layer concrete paths
somewhere close to spring but early
feeling weather is not a measure of what is to come now
despite earlier daily light there are few bright prospects.
Horizons are ridden – fear and doubt
not for dogs – happy and present
we plod behind their enthusiasm
we, us humans, have mucked things up
for the future and for now
more furious flames and floods will come
as we 'learn to live' with the next mutation
that rips the hands of our elders from our grip
and is cause for polarisation, communities split by conspiracies.
Are we America too?
Unfazed by documented effects, deaths across the globe
construction sites sear into the quiet of working at home
those men say 'do you know anyone who has died?'
It's a conspiracy of rulers – control
of liberty to be individual, to consume
social solidarity lost ideal and whimsical memory
of other times
uplifting moments
where are you today, tomorrow?
Lockdown blues produce
foggy, fleeting spaces to think

where hope struggles to fit
then talk and turn around
the tawny frogmouths are there every morning
and rest all day
beauty, nature sends to soothe
the cerebral
deep breaths
and routine maybe equals hope.

Swimming 2.0

Christopher D. Roche

So, here we are again. The Grand Hotel changed its name, but the swimming pool was still the same. Different water, new grass, the same light reflecting. Same-same, but different. Katie purposefully sat in the exact spot she had been in fourteen years ago. New university buildings peeking over the hill, and new bricks mixing with the old ones. A body which felt the same under her towel but looked different, towel off. Complete turnover of molecules probably, maybe a few unchanged building blocks somewhere in her DNA. A couple of substances put in, a couple of new partners inserted here and there. *I've measured out my life with coffee cups . . . and the rest. – or was it spoons?* The professor from that era had to leave. A dinosaur who knew too much, who didn't fit in anymore.

Yet here she was, same university on the mound, same swimming pool, same tanned six-packs walking past. Not so many eyes flicking her way, she supposed. Less body hair on men these days. The prize of the feminist movement – the male wax. No more Sean Connery chest carpets on parade around these parts. No more Sean Connerys in general.

The jacaranda had died. Replaced. But not the same. Or at least not the same to those who could remember. The new generation probably loved the spindly young thing planted in its place. Still a favourite for making out (underneath) after class hours? There's a cordon now. Keep-off-the-grass. But they probably still do (the students). Not Katie and (probably) not the professors either, she supposed.

She read about that adult actress who went for a shoot. The director inspected her and knocked down twenty percent right there because she was too old. An extra five percent was taken off for a scar on her chest. Katie wondered what her own market value would be now. Did anyone add value for experience? Maybe. Obviously not porn directors. But you have to try before you buy, and no one seems that keen to try a divorced forty-three-year-old, even if Instagram-able big backsides are all the rage.

I must apologise to Sal. If I ever see him again. Katie imagined bumping into him somewhere around Sydney. Maybe he'd be walking past, or maybe about to get on a bus. She would grab him and immediately say: 'Listen, I'm so sorry, I was too young, I didn't know what I was doing.' Then the bus doors would close, but that loose string flapping in the wind of her life for twenty-one years would finally be tied.

The waxed chest finished his set of lengths and pulled himself out of the pool. Almost like a slow-motion advertisement – for wax, or a fitness program, maybe a tanning product. Time-lapsed water dropping onto cobblestones. No look from him to her; but, behind her shades, Katie could take her time. He was probably born in the year 2000, when she'd been popping corks in London. He looked similar to that carefree college boy from England. Circular time.

The worst thing about being in your early forties? The isolation. That barrier between your eyes and the eyes of the person you're speaking to. The battle to cut through the crisscrossed neurons firing off about work, to-do lists, issues in inverted commas, baggage sacks loaded on over the years. Like speaking to people through ultra-thin prison glass. Like putting a hand to a hand, and feeling a connection, but knowing there's glass in-between the two of you. Might catch some warmth radiating through, a voice on the line, but it's not the same as touch. Could smash it, but you might get taken away. Would you smash it, jump through, hug once and be permanently banned? Or would you choose a lifetime of palm-to-glass?

She tried to test the waters from time to time. She told Duncan Tan one of her tamest stories. He listened wide-eyed, then started leaning backwards and forwards in his chair. Was he rubbing his thighs? Katie couldn't remember, but that was how excited he was. 'Wow, how you've lived!' – and he had said that to her at least five times since then. There's no way of moving on to your real uncut history when the test case elicits maximum response. If she were a man, she could probably tell more stories. Still, at least Tan enjoyed himself. Dimitri had just started looking around the place and quickly changed the subject.

The weight of her experience buoyed her up, but also brought her down. The unbearable lightness of being . . . whatever it was that she was. That she is now, and now, then now, and again now. Personality had always been a fluid in motion for Katie. You can't put your finger on a fluid.

Splash. Her thoughts were interrupted by an oversized mother ushering her three children, duck-like, into the pool. The familiar pang of guilt: Katie knew she would only ever manage the one. Light of her life, best thing that ever happened to her. Never again. Probably. Gain a child, lose a husband.

She stood up and walked to the changing room. Towel-wrapped. Faded shades of purple. Possible look from the waxed advert guy as she walked past (no smile). No way of knowing if it was a look or *just* a look. It didn't matter anyway, if he was doing what she'd been doing back then, there wouldn't be time for her.

Slippery phone banged on the locker floor. No network. That'd be right. Not no network, just no signal. Plenty of networks. Too many. Cells have networks inside of them and outside of them, and a network to connect the inside to the outside. Net-worth. Newt-works. No work. No safety net, that's for sure. Networks of air, and invisible things carried in the air, moving between her lungs and everybody else's. The duck woman, six-pack man and Katie were all connected by water and air. The duck woman, six-pack man, Katie, Duncan Tan, Sal (wherever he was), the fired professor and even Dimitri with all of his social media accounts. *Especially* Dimitri with all of his social media accounts. All connected. At a distance. Not Sean Connery (dead). Come to think of it, the professor – probably dead now too.

The changing room hadn't changed. Same smell, discoloured wood, rubber with spikes that hurt your soles. The shower area now had cubicles, though, not a communal area. Same soapy water still flowing from the next cubicle, in the grouting lines, carrying debris between your toes.

As she walked up the hill, dry grass crunching under her shadow, she saw a family in a playground. Children were climbing in a huge web while a parent and grandparent, coffee-bearing, looked on happily. Inspired, Katie crossed the road to Bibi's coffeehouse. A socially-distanced pentagon of people buzzed outside, waiting in the sun.

'Katie Palmer?' said a breathless voice from behind.

Katie didn't recognise the person, but then she did, heart-in-mouth, it was Sal. Sal, but not Sal.

'Sal. Hey. Sorry, I, well it's been...'

'About twenty years!'

'Yeah, crazy, right? Wow,' stuttered Katie. Sal looked more relaxed, but then he'd had the element of surprise. 'Listen, Sal, you know, this might sound weird, but I've actually thought about you a lot. You know . . . look I'm just going to say it, I've been wanting to say it...'

Sal smiled, 'Katie, you don't have to say anything, I know, I get it.'

They paused. The silence wasn't awkward. Or at least, it wasn't that awkward.

Ding. 'Regular flat white for Katie. Have a good one.'

Without speaking they started drifting, Sal and Katie, moving down the road towards the junction.

'You know it's funny how things happen, how things bring people together.'

'Yeah, it is. Like we're all . . .'

'Connected?'

Katie smiled, yeah, sometimes it really does seem like we're all connected.

Hard Lockdown

Dennis Haskell

As if breaking into sense
a wind whisked down a street
and found nothing there
but its fingerprints of air

and its quickstep of invisibility
danced into street after street
where our shops and faces sat shut,
shut by glass, shut behind masks,

an emptiness stark as sunlight,
streets like pieces of bone,
handles hands dare not touch
and faces so sharp to turn,

our mouths too scared to breathe
what chance might care to toss
into the air's droplet dance,
the tense, meaningless nothing

our eyes can't see, nor hands touch,
our ears can't hear, nor noses scent,
the nothing which will make
nothing of us.

Blue Days: Trapped
Wentao Dai

Blue Days: Chaos
Wentao Dai

Blue Days: Split
Wentao Dai

Network on Bicycles I   Qinxuan (Laura) Yu

Network on Bicycles II   Qinxuan (Laura) Yu

Network on Bicycles III   *Qixuan (Laura) Yu*

Arterial Trees
Dyone Bettega

Fatal Fraternity
Yasodara Puhule–Gamayalage

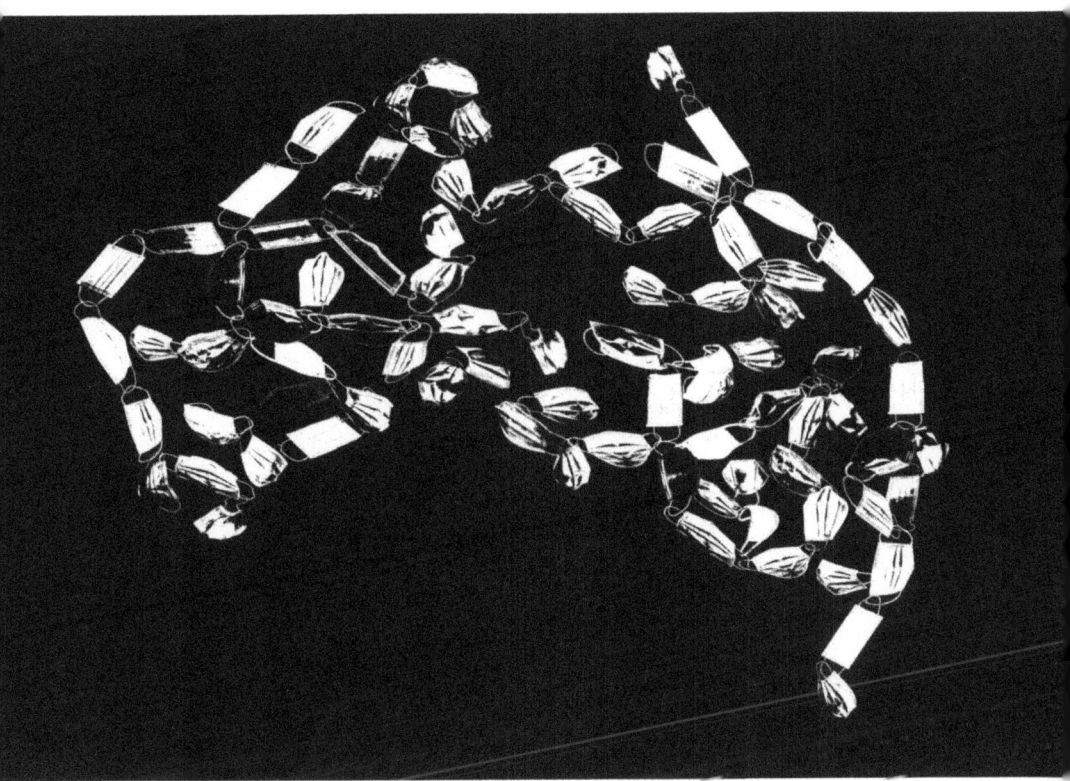

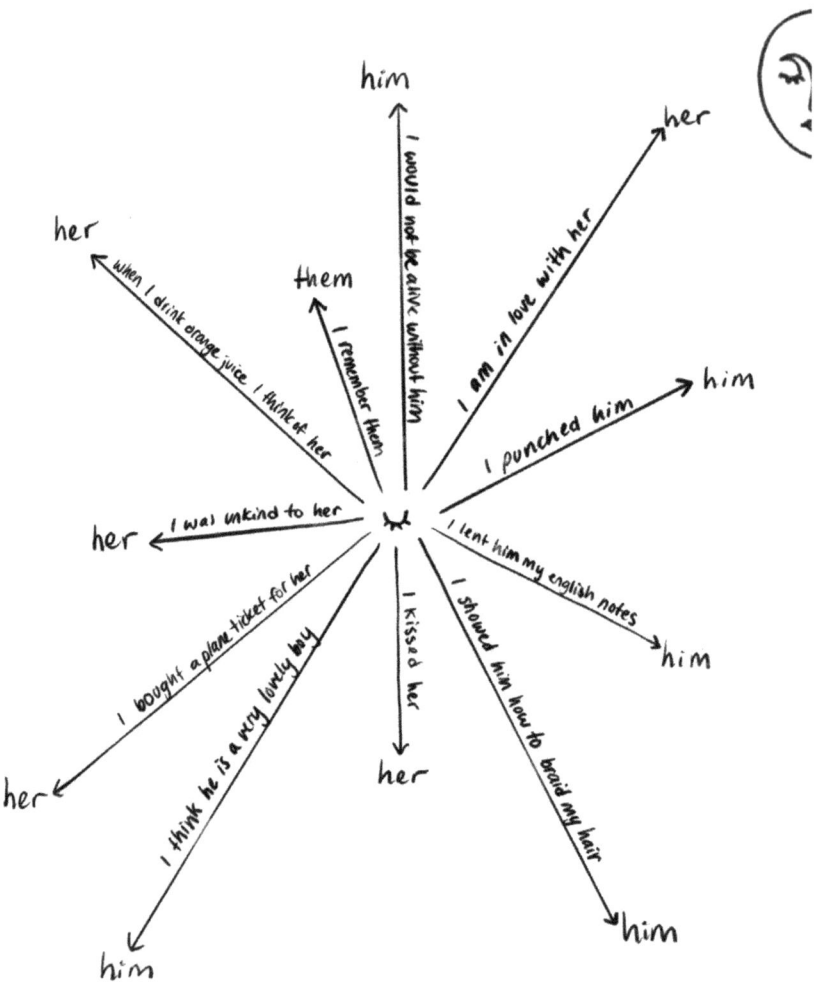

him

I would not be alive without him

her

I am in love with her

her

when I drink orange juice I think of her

them

I remember them

him

I punched him

I was unkind to her

her

I lent him my english notes

him

I bought a plane ticket for her

I kissed her

I showed him how to braid my hair

her

I think he is a very lovely boy

her

him

him

Networks I   Abigail Bobkowski

there is more to your life

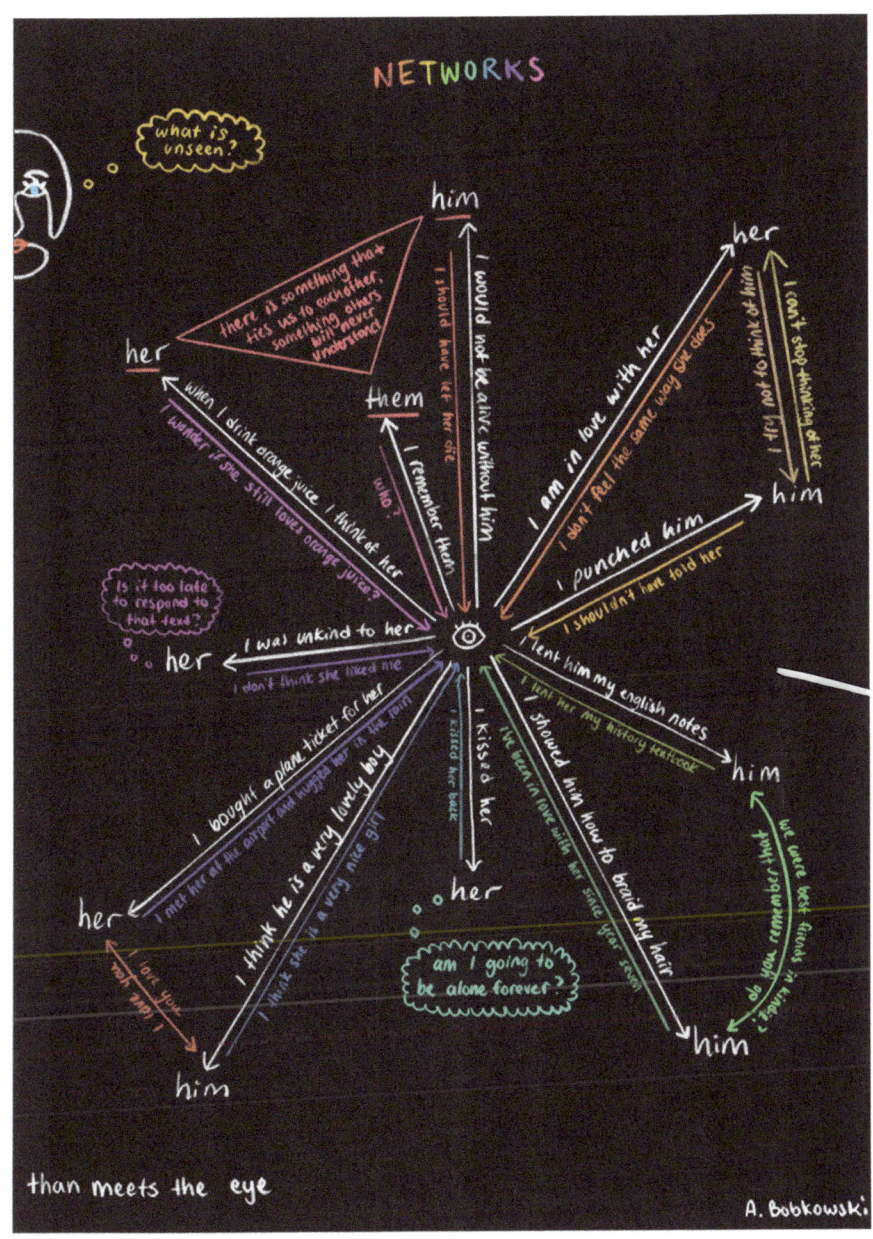

Networks II *Abigail Bobkowski*

Missing Piece
Memi Adams

Uploaded

Allen Chan

We pressed our faces
like passports between a scanner.
Asking for recognition **
a permission to be heard in
this land of adult-
hood.

The shedding
of pages, Tumblr-ing
into MySpace.
Pulling key-bindings
from our voices,
trading our stories for redemption,
our quest for connection,
popping bubble gum. Blue faces
and messy ends.

Bouncing balls into outer space,
we were helium without the decay.
We lived in beds of stepping stones,
pulling and throwing orbits through gravity.
We learnt that life was so much than lines
placed to conform to someone's idea
of language.

This currency of
ourselves, mined and sold
but ever intact.

Linked In

Angela Xu

Can I connect with you?

Plastic grins with shining veneers lie stamped below unfeeling eyes.
Left eyebrow hooked, expectantly,
right eyebrow tense with sincerity.

Beady eyes bore into mine.
The wolves gear up for the hunt,
and the vultures admire their meal.

Walls awaken and pound at my back
as the lights flare blood red
and dissonance feeds the air.

Salted pearls pool at my brow,
metal tints my tongue.
Fight or Flight.

Survival is a deadly game.
Weakness must be hidden.
Fire met with fire.

Yes.
Of course.

How Successful Social Media Marketing Campaigns Engage Active Audiences

Melissa Snook

Would it surprise you to know that every day we spend roughly five to seven hours on our phones, from the moment we wake up until we go to bed.[1] What's even more staggering, is that of that time, eighty-nine percent of eighteen-to-twenty-nine-year-olds browse social media at least once a day.[2] Did you also know that in 2020, social media purchases increased to 5.3 million in that year.[3] When we spend a significant portion of the day on our phones, we occasionally come across businesses and individuals advertising their services or products. We know instinctively, that some are more successful than others, but we don't stop to ask ourselves why; why you clicked on that link for the latest skincare product, but not for the set of kitchenware you just scrolled past.

Businesses have become increasingly more aware of the power and usefulness of social media in marketing campaigns, and their ability to grab your attention. No longer can a business solely rely on traditional forms of advertising. This article will look at four different businesses that have created social media campaigns, and will be introducing social media theories and tools so that we can better understand their failures and successes. Beginning with the Victorian Taxi Association's #yourtaxis campaign, this article will identify what went wrong with this campaign. Through an analysis of Southern Rail's #AskEddie, Marc Jacob's Tweet Shop and the *Deadpool* DVD release campaigns, we can gain insights into how a successful social media campaign is created.

---

1   Dixon 2021.
2   Sensis 2018.
3   Hinton 2021.

Naïve Optimism: #yourtaxis Campaign

With the rise and popularity of Uber, taxi companies have had to resort to new measures to gain customers. In 2015, the Melbourne based #yourtaxis campaign was created on Twitter to start a conversation between the Victorian Taxi Association and their customers.[4] Their quest for customer feedback backfired when an overwhelming number of comments were negative.[5] Customer complaints ranged from safety ('Driver fell asleep on freeway and almost wiped out car in next lane because he'd pulled an all-nighter') to hygiene ('It smelled like a wookiee's armpit').[6] The campaign strategy in this case followed the idea of user or public participation. This means that during marketing campaigns, the purpose of social media is 'more about conversations, connections and shared control'.[7] In this case, the campaign objectively was successful in this goal: it did facilitate public interaction and create a community with similar experiences. Its failure lay in the naïvety that the public would be entirely positive about their experiences. From this case, it seems almost impossible to create a successful campaign with positive public feedback towards a controversial business.

Audience Participation: #AskEddie Campaign

Another divisive transportation company demonstrated that in order to create positive user participation through social media marketing, it is important to constantly focus on the customer. Southern Rail is a train service that operates in the United Kingdom.[8] Labelled 'Britain's worst', the business, albeit unknowingly, rebranded their company image in 2017 using a fifteen-year-old intern.[9] Eddie was a student who was completing work experience at Southern Rail.[10] He was

---

4   Ross 2015.
5   Ross 2015
6   Ross 2015.
7   Lipschultz 2017.
8   Sanghani 2017.
9   Sanghani 2017.
10   Sanghani 2017.

given full control over the company's Twitter account, and soon went viral with #AskEddie.[11] Southern Rail customers began asking Eddie questions, which he would answer.[12] Questions ranged from quirky: 'Would you rather fight one horse sized duck or one hundred duck sized horses?' to questions about his school studies.[13] Unlike the #yourtaxis campaign, there was a clear understanding of their audience. Prior to #AskEddie, the company had been dealing with 'months of criticism from customers for cancelled services and strike action'.[14] The strategy here was to transform the negative comments into a positive interaction between Southern Rail and their customers. The prospect of a fifteen-year-old representing the company allowed a more innocent and organic flow of conversation that deviated away from the negatives, rather than highlighting the problems as the #yourtaxis campaign did.

This campaign was also successful because it acknowledged the importance of an active audience. Web 2.0 is an idea suggesting that successful marketing on social media can only occur when the user is both a creator and consumer of content.[15] By providing a platform where users have the power to generate content and participate in a digital forum, the campaign created a sustainable and powerful tool to market and positively rebrand their image. Through clever communication, users were able to exercise some control when interacting with the company's image. This campaign also exemplifies the use of 'produsage' and participatory culture. Henry Jenkins describes participatory culture as when consumers become involved in the production and sharing of new content.[16] Fanfiction is a perfect example of participatory content, where fans of a show or movie create their own fictional story to share.[17] In a similar concept, Axel Bruns defined produsage as a substitute to traditional producer-consumer

---

11   Sanghani 2017.
12   Sanghani 2017.
13   Sini 2017.
14   Sini 2017.
15   Berthon et al. 2012.
16   Jenkins 2006.
17   Jenkins 2006.

relationships.[18] Instead the consumer becomes producer, distributer and consumer.[19]

Mutual Benefits: Marc Jacobs Tweet Shop

During New York Fashion Week in 2014, designer label Marc Jacobs created a unique social media marketing campaign. A pop-up store, called the Tweet Shop, was built for fans of the brand, who then spread positive reviews of the products.[20] The idea for the Tweet Shop came from a particular insight about the brand and their consumers:

> Marc Jacobs is really active on social media and Daisy is one of the fragrance brands that triggers the highest engagement among fans . . . We have seen people creating drawings and stage mood shots featuring the iconic bottle, so engagement of the fans is already there.[21]

The way the shop worked was that both public consumers and celebrities were invited to the event, where products were exchanged for 'social currency'.[22] The people in attendance were treated as cultural intermediaries who would creatively market their product using #MJDaisyChain in exchange for items.[23] This campaign was based on the idea of social and cultural capital. Pierre Bourdieu explains that 'capital is accumulated labor which, when appropriated on a private, i.e., exclusive, basis of agents or groups of agents, enables them to appropriate social energy in the form of reified or living labor.'[24] This campaign effectively demonstrates how cultural intermediaries combined with the ideas of social and cultural capital can create a successful campaign. In cases like the Tweet Shop, customers use their

---

18 Bruns 2008.
19 Bruns 2008.
20 Murphy 2014.
21 Murphy 2014.
22 Murphy 2014.
23 Murphy 2014.
24 Bourdieu 1986.

status on social media to generate momentum and visibility on behalf of a company. Marc Jacobs received free marketing and labour, while the cultural intermediaries received free products.

Deadpool DVD Release Campaign

Another important factor in the success of social marketing campaigns is the focus on brand. When using social media to market a product, it is important to maintain a specific brand image that aligns with the product. Brand creation is extremely important as Georgios Tsimonis and Dimitriadis Sergios state:

> Brands are increasingly interested in establishing a presence in social media, interacting with their fans, helping shape their experiences and even leveraging their voices for a greater marketing impact.[25]

One such campaign that was extremely successful in creating a social media brand is the DVD release for the 2016 film *Deadpool*. The campaign didn't just focus on the DVD release itself, but instead marketed itself using the clever, witty, inappropriate humour *Deadpool* is known for.

The reason this campaign worked so well could be attributed to the 'Rule of 7'. This theory suggests that encouraging consumer behaviour to take action (in this case purchase the DVD) can be achieved by your consumer seeing your product seven times.[26] The *Deadpool* DVD campaign used a variety of different strategies to market their product, using different forms of social media including Twitter, Facebook, YouTube and Snapchat.[27] Combined with the witty humour, the social media campaign enhanced the visibility of the product and contributed to the production of the *Deadpool* brand.

---

25 Tsimonis and Dimitriadis 2014.
26 Kruse 2021.
27 'Deadpool Gets All The Likes' n.d.

Ballboys Charity
@ballboyscharity

For #WorldCancerDay **make sure u** #TouchYourselfTonight #deadpool #movie #comingsoon @VancityReynolds

♡ 2   6:05 PM - Feb 4, 2016

Tweet from Ballboys Charity which raises awareness of Testicular Cancer, promoting both their business and the release of the first *Deadpool* film in 2016.

Conclusion

When it comes to marketing on social media, there are a number of factors that are crucial to the creation of a successful campaign. Gaining audience participation is key to any campaign. The aim of any social media content is to encourage consumers to interact and participate in discussions through comments, likes and any other forms of engagement. It is also important to encourage users to produce their own content. The Marc Jacobs campaign was highly successful in this, using the status and cultural power of intermediaries with social and cultural capital to promote the brand. Campaigns also need to be tailored and structured in a certain way that promotes positive feedback. By using #AskEddie, Southern Rail was able to steer disgruntled customers away from controversy into a more neutral and quirky discussion, something which the #yourtaxis campaign failed to due to naïvety. Lastly, the importance of brand building cannot be understated. Sticking to your brand and promoting it in a clever manner can go a long way in consumer trust. The *Deadpool* DVD campaign showed how unconventional means of marketing using social media can be highly beneficial. Speaking to your brand community, in a manner that relates to your product, can be a very effective tool for businesses to use in social media marketing. There are definitely lessons to learn from social media theory and these campaigns. A successful social media campaign ultimately makes the difference between average and significant sales. They not only bring in a larger profit, but they create a loyal consumer relationship.

References

Berthon, Pierre R., Leyland F. Pitt, Kirk Plangger, and Daniel Shapiro (2012). Marketing Meets Web 2.0, Social Media, and Creative Consumers: Implications for International Marketing Strategy. *Business Horizons* 55(3): 261–271. DOI:10.1016/j.bushor.2012.01.007

Bourdieu, Pierre (1986). The Forms of Capital. In *Handbook of Theory and Research for the Sociology of Education*, 241–258. New York: Greenwood Press.

Bruns, Axel (2008). *Blogs, Wikipedia, Second Life, and Beyond: From Production to Produsage*. New York: Peter Lang.

Deadpool Gets All The Likes – The Shorty Awards (n.d.) Shortyawards.com. https://shortyawards.com/9th/deadpool-gets-all-the-likes

DiChristopher, Tom (2016, 16 February). Deadpool's Secret Weapon: A Viral Social Media Campaign. *CNBC*. https://www.cnbc.com/2016/02/07/deadpools-secret-weapon-a-viral-social-media-campaign.html

Dixon, Georgia (2021, 7 April). Aussies Spend Almost 17 Years in a Lifetime Staring at Their Phones. *Reviews.org*. https://www.reviews.org/au/mobile/aussie-screentime-in-a-lifetime/

Hinton, Thomas. (2021, 12 August). Count of Consumers in Australia Who Use Social Media for Online Shopping in the Year 2020 with Forecast to 2024. *Statista*. https://www.statista.com/statistics/1256814/australia-consumers-who-use-social-media-for-online-shopping/

Jenkins, Henry (2006). *Fans, Bloggers, and Gamers.* New York: New York University Press.

Kruse, Kathy (2021, 29 September). Rule of 7: How Social Media Crushes Old School Marketing. *Kruse Control Inc.* https://www.krusecontrolinc.com/rule-of-7-how-social-media-crushes-old-school-marketing-2021/

Lipschultz, Jeremy Harris (2017). *Social Media Communication: Concepts, Practices, Data, Law and Ethics.* London: Routledge.

Murphy, Samantha (2014, 6 February). Marc Jacobs Pop-Up Shop Takes Tweets, Instagrams For Payment. *Mashable.* https://mashable.com/2014/02/06/marc-jacobs-tweet-store/#QNeEizMXJgqG

Ross, Monique (2015, 10 November). #Yourtaxi Campaign Backfires as Passengers Share Horror Stories. *ABC News.* https://www.abc.net.au/news/2015-11-10/vic-taxis-campaign-backfires/6927626

Sanghani, Radhika (2017, 15 July). #AskEddie: Meet the Work Experience Boy Who Saved Southern Rail. *The Telegraph.* https://www.telegraph.co.uk/men/thinking-man/meet-eddie-smith-work-experience-boy-saved-southern-rail/

Sensis (2018). 2018 Yellow Social Media Report. *Sensis.* https://www.sensis.com.au/about/our-reports/sensis-social-media-report

Sini, Rozina (2017, 11 July). Work Experience Teen Takes Over Southern Rail's Twitter. *BBC News.* https://www.bbc.com/news/uk-40577155.

Tsimonis, Georgios, and Sergios Dimitriadis (2014). Brand Strategies in Social Media. *Marketing Intelligence & Planning* 32(3): 328–344. DOI:10.1108/mip-04-2013-0056

The Snowball Effect

Emma Murphy

My heart glows with
star-lit sadness,
my thoughts are engulfed
in flickering orange petals
of anxiety.

I run, but they are never far behind,
they catch up to me
like a hunter preying on a fox,
following a trail of pawprints
in the snow . . .

But your night sky
of twinkling lights
steals away that sadness and places it
amongst the others in a constellation
of 'I'm here for you'.

And all those heavy thoughts suddenly
turn cold and are too glaring
to look at.

You manage to freeze my mind's snowball
so it can no longer accumulate

the sticky uncertainty
made from frozen flakes of rain
that were scattered
across different parts of my brain.

Your mittened hands whisper
'We're in this together'
and for a while
the snowball stops rolling.

Once-Friend

Cherie Baird

Dear Once-Friend,
I mean it when I say, 'I hope you're well.'
We used to be so close my family developed suspicions,
but I loved you in a way that meant more
than any lover of mine before or since.
Every anecdote out of my mouth
found its way back to you, if indeed
you weren't where it had begun.
You were my best friend
in all the title's platonic glory,
and I was so afraid of losing you
that I let you go myself.
Isn't that what they say to do?
There was no fight, no fury,
no anger or argument or anything, really.
Just a question, a little helpless acquiescence –
what else could you have done? – and silence.

Once-friend –
you were more than my friend once.
You were my ears and the voice inside them,
the shoulder that nudged me to face fear
with gentle laughter,
the hands that hugged and gifted and wrote
and flailed just a little

when the eyes got excited.
You were my companion, my confidant;
my dreamer and my pragmatist;
my calm presence in the moments
when I felt most stranded.
You grew with me for so many years,
I forgot I was growing up too.

Once-friend, I'm sorry I never explained myself.
I'm sorry I left you to wonder
what it was that made me seek something
different.
Once-friend, you don't need me –
your brilliance is astounding alone –
but sometimes I wonder how it could be
if there was still a space
left for me. Kept for me.
Just in case of emergencies.

Once-friend,
I don't know the details anymore:
the daily updates of nightly dreams,
the most bizarre thing you read last week,
the stranger in the shop who stared for too long.
That doesn't stop me from smiling,
glad you finally got to Pompeii,
your first kiss, that big break . . .

I double tap and linger
before I scroll.

I really do mean it when I say, 'I hope you're well.'

If She Knew

Isla Scott

A blog is a funny thing, you know,
like a diary plastered up for all to see.
Secrets and feelings spread to everyone
like gossip in a playground full of strangers you'll never meet.
I suppose there's an element of separation
that makes it easier than admitting to your then best friend
that you don't care anymore.
You get the cowardly cathartic release of revelation
without having to look them in the eyes.
Pretend you're both all right and happy,
tell yourself you're still real friends,
escape any looks of betrayal or tears, and still
get out of actually trying to make it work.
Maybe I shouldn't have tried to play along.
But let me start a little earlier on.

It wasn't like the blog was a secret,
not officially, anyway.
She always pestered me to read it,
pouting when I said *eventually*.
My personal theory is that she would have been
more careful with her words if she thought I read them.
Wouldn't have made it so obvious,
so clear she had moved on.
Maybe that's why I kept saying I didn't,

because I wanted to know what she really felt.
But I still wonder, if she knew I did read it,
would she want to change what she'd said?

I stopped reading a little while after she moved away.
I couldn't bear hearing about her wonderful, fabulous life
while I was in the middle of hating mine.
I don't know how she found time to write posts
in-between all the exciting things she had on.
She certainly never seemed to have enough time
to talk one-on-one for more than twenty minutes every five months.
Of course, for a while I lived for those minutes,
excited to talk and to share once more,
until I realised they were just all about her.
So I wonder, if she knew how alone I felt when we talked,
would she want to change what she'd said?

I once tried to tell her –
I don't know how well I did.
Through tears, I practically told her
I needed more confirmation of our friendship
than a self-absorbed message every few months
(in hindsight, I should have been as clear as that).
She had thought she'd been doing well.
She said she would do better.
She did not.
And I wonder, if she knew she raised my hopes for nothing,
would she want to change what she'd said?

The other day I found some old cards she'd written me,
before she moved away and during the first couple months.
She was all assuring, promising she was there for me,
and always would be.
I remember I felt comforted by the words,

for a while. Until the conversation dried up,
and her assurances fell flat,
and I realised it was all just lies
we both once thought were truth.
I don't know when, or if, she ever realised,
but it hurt to know that she no longer cared,
and it hurt to remember when she did,
and I wonder, if she knew that her words made me cry,
would she want to change what she'd said?

For a long time I thought it was temporary,
that things changed but would change again.
I kept telling myself just wait a bit longer,
she'll come back and it'll be the same once more.
So she came back and I waited and I tried and I fought.
So she came back but it didn't change at all.
Eventually I knew it had to end,
because I was tearing myself to shreds inside,
and she didn't even fucking try.
So I shrugged, and smiled, and told myself
to never hope she might try again.
But I wonder, if she knew I'd given up on her,
would she want to change what she'd said?

A poem is a funny thing, you know,
like a diary plastered up for all to see.
Secrets and feelings spread to everyone
like gossip in a playground full of strangers you'll never meet.
I suppose there's an element of separation
that makes it easier than admitting to your then best friend
that you don't care anymore.
You get the cowardly cathartic release of revelation
without having to look them in the eyes.
Pretend you're both all right and happy,

tell yourself you're still real friends,
escape any looks of betrayal or tears, and still
get out of actually trying to make it work.
I wonder if she knew this poem was for her,
and I wonder if I'll ever know she's seen it,
and I wonder, if I knew that she'd read the words I wrote,
would I want to change what I'd said?

Honey Bear

Seth Robinson

I was born around the corner from the Honey Bear Bakery. I can't tell you too much else about those early days, but the bakery I remember. There was a bear statue that guarded the door. I remember it being fifty-feet tall, looming over the rooftops, when it was probably only five or six. But memories are shapeshifters, ever present but never concrete. At times I remember him like a honey squeeze bottle, cartoonish and cute, with a painted face and a nozzle on his head. In other moments, he's a grizzly, furry to the touch, with teeth and claws that break the skin of wandering hands if Mum isn't quick enough to catch them. Honey Bear was the gatekeeper, whatever form he was in, the last line of defence between me and the fluffy-sweet Madeleine cookies, or, on a really special day, carrot cake. Those smells, those flavours, one whiff, one bite, and it all comes rushing back.

* * *

There's another story from around the same time that Mum tells. It's one of those ones that could be a memory, maybe, or maybe I've just heard the story retold so many times that I have a vision of it in my head. I'm standing at the kitchen counter in our little unremembered house, on a plastic stool. I've got a mixing bowl in front of me, and I'm trying my hardest to do a good job, with plenty of breaks to sample the batter. Mum and I are making carrot cake. It could be the recipe they use at the Honey Bear Bakery, or it could be something of Mum's own devising. Either way, my little heart is full of joy, because it knows that soon my little belly will be full of cake.

Then tragedy strikes.

Mum – who has spent this time grating the carrot cake's titular ingredient – comes over and dumps the vile shredded root into my bowl. The batter that little me has whisked to perfection, given all his attention and fortunately none of his blood or sweat, is ruined. This toddler is now very happy to add his tears to the mix, because – and I'm aware this is a horrible paradox – while I *love* carrot cake, I *hate* carrots.

I don't think my mother understood that until this moment. I don't know if she does now, but there are only so many ways to explain that carrots are an essential ingredient to a screaming toddler. I can't remember how that story ends. I don't know if we ended up having cake that day, but I can tell you now, almost thirty years later, I still hate carrots. Ask me in an adult conversation and I'll tell you I don't like the texture, which is true, but I think there's something more innate in the mix as well; a moment of perceived toddler trauma I've never been able to reconcile.

* * *

I have a soft spot for a certain Ms Sara Lee, and the way she does carrot cake. It comes in a foil tray, with a peel away cardboard top. There's a ritual to opening the thing, you have to run your finger around the edges, folding back the little foil lip. When you lift the lid, you're presented with a slab of no-frills carrot cake. There might be a few walnuts, but I usually pick those off. They're an ingredient I only sometimes like. It's another carrot cake paradox, another something I could do without, that is so often seen as essential to something I love.

If it's been in the fridge, Sara's cake is cold to the touch. It's dense, and moist, and if you ask me it's the perfect road trip snack. I doubt it was ever intended this way, but sitting in the passenger seat of a nineties Fairlane on the way to the coast, it makes sense. Amber light pours in through the window, and the sky ahead is bruised black. The wind of an oncoming thunderstorm whips the poplar trees and the long grass by the side of the road. It's got an apocalyptic, end of the world vibe – and a promise that our coast trip is going to be rained out. But riding with cake and plastic fork in hand, that doesn't seem like such a big deal.

'Are you going to eat that whole thing?' a friend's voice asks from the backseat.

'Maybe. Probably. You want some? Better say now before I start.'

'Nah. Carrot cake is gross. Waste of a cake, I'll take chocolate any day.'

I don't respond to that, because this is the kind of debate we seventeen-year-olds have most days, and I know I won't win. We're still trying to settle whether Superman or Godzilla would win in a fight – and that debate has been going for the last three years. Instead, I go through the ritual, manipulating the foil, peeling back the card, going to work with my fork. Between bites, I gaze out the window across the field at the end of the world. My eyes land on a hay bale, a golden hulk zooming into the past, and for the briefest of moments, I think it could be Honey Bear lumbering along in his most ferocious form, sniffing out my cake.

* * *

On a rainy day in Melbourne, walking through the city, I stop in a café on a whim. It's not the first time. It won't be the last. I'm lured to the glass case by the till, where a lone chunk of cake sits patiently. I can't speak to its quality, or the comparison to cake from the Honey Bear or even homemade, but its sheer existence – its identity as 'Carrot Cake' with its hand-drawn cardboard sign, dollops of cream cheese icing, and the barely visible orange traces of its offensive namesake – that's enough.

'Can I help you?' asks the moustachioed barista.

'Could I have one of your carrot cakes, please?'

'Sure. Any coffee?'

I dodge the judgement that responds to my lack of a coffee order, and a moment later there's a brown paper package in my hands. It's sans string, but it's still a Julie Andrews moment as I carry it – undoubtedly one of my favourite things – out into the rain.

It's a juggle, managing my umbrella and my cake as I reach the three steps down from the café door, and my foot finds a slick spot on the granite. My feet go up, my butt comes down, and suddenly I'm sitting there on the steps, wide-eyed and wet. The cranky barista is there in a moment, along with a couple of the café's other patrons.

'Are you alright?'

Surprisingly, I'm fine. And perhaps more importantly, I've managed a circus-worthy balancing act, keeping both hands up, and my cake perfectly level. It's even managed to stay under my umbrella, so it hasn't been rained on.

'Uh yeah, I'm all good. Thanks.'

I hurry off then – two sets of cheeks reddening – avoiding any further discussion. I don't really have anywhere I need to be, and I'm unsure where I'm going, but eventually I find a doorway where I can shelter from the rain. I curl up, and shred the brown paper, finding a little wooden spoon inside. It's much more environmentally-friendly than the plastic spoon I used in the Fairlane all those years ago.

A tram bell rings from the next street over, and I'm aware of distant voices and feet, their inner city rhythm blending with the rain. I take my first bite, and let it melt in my mouth. Things slow down for a second as I taste and critique, feeling my separation from the city around me. It'll be fleeting, but for as long as it takes me to chew I appreciate the distance of time, and how it can bend and flex. One bite, and the years disappear.

My eyes settle on a 7-Eleven across the street, and I briefly wonder if they sell honey in squeezy bear bottles. I haven't seen one in years.

* * *

For my birthday, my partner brings me cupcakes. It's one of the little things that tells me how well she knows me, because while I love cake, I think cupcakes are the bee's knees. It's about the texture, more of that moist-muffin top to body ratio, and of course, on a cupcake your icing vs cake percentage is significantly higher. It's a box of twelve, and I'm sure they're meant to be rationed, but seeing as it's my birthday I give them three days at the most. When I open the box and look inside, I approve. There's an assortment of flavours: vanilla, cookies and cream, red velvet, chocolate – the essentials – but of the twelve, four are carrot cake; each marked by a little orange and green hard-icing carrot.

This particular breed of carrot I have no problems with. In fact, they're encouraged. I even approve of their texture, the little pop between your teeth, followed by the sugar rush.

I plan my attack, so that the carrot cupcakes will be interspersed throughout, as well as being the first and the last I eat from the box. The other flavours are up for grabs – I'm happy to share – but the carrot cakes need a coordinated approach.

They don't last long. I was too generous in my estimate. It's only a day later when I find myself sitting in front of my computer, sipping tea and eyeballing the last cupcake. I pluck the sugar carrot off the top, crunch it between my teeth and consider my laptop screen. For the first time in thirty years, something has occurred to me. I have Google, and most businesses – even long-ago bakeries – have websites. There's potential here, for what's been partly remembered and the rest of the way imagined to become solid.

I pluck the bottom off the cupcake and sandwich it on top, making a little burger – it's the way a guide on a food tour in New York told me was the 'correct' way to eat a cupcake – and one handed, I punch in my search words.

Honey Bear Bakery.

It's there a moment later, complete with website and Instagram page. I click the link, see their feed, and then stop, mid-bite and swipe.

There's something holding me back. I'm sure Honey Bear is there, probably just a scroll a way. The mystery will be solved, and I'll know once and for all. I'll know what he looked like, fearsome or friendly. My memories will be solid.

But by the same token, he'll no longer be a shape-shifter, hanging at the periphery of my vision, there when I take a bite of cake. That memory, which has carried me through so many years, through the hard times and the chaos will be gone. I wonder if I know, if the cake will lose charm. The threads that hold my sense of self together are so fine, the sniff of a cake in the oven, the taste of cinnamon and cream cheese icing, memories of rainy days and home, before I even knew what that meant; those are precious things.

They're all tied to that sense of wonder and curiosity, always asking myself, was the bear really fifty-feet tall? Was he friendly, or was he fierce? All it takes is a bite of cake and I'm back there, the earliest place I can remember, standing at the feet of a shape-shifting bear, with everything still ahead and the only choice that matters; Madeleine cookie, or if it's a special day, carrot cake.

There's magic in that, and what's the point in eating cake, if it doesn't come with a little magic?

Gutom Pa

Harold Legaspi

Lumamon ng adobo – pork and chicken slowly cooked in vinegar,
oil, crushed garlic, bay leaf, black peppercorns and soy sauce.

Kumain ng crispy *pata* – portions of pork legs, knuckles,
served with chilli and calamansi, dipped in vinegar and soy sauce.

Gusto ng lasa ng sariwang lumpia – freshly rolled with meat filling.
Inubos ng mechado – larded beef cooked, sliced, served with tomato.

Don't these dishes wait? *Where's Lola?* She eyes the morcon, a beef
    roulade – thin
sheets of cooked eggs and marinated beef layered one on top of the
    other, tied

around carrots, celery, cheese, pork fat and sausage, then cooked in
seasoned tomato sauce. *Where's Lola? Where is she?*

Tinikman ng paksiw na isda – simmered in vinegar broth, seasoned with
patis and vegetables. Also, *pinakbet* – with okra, eggplant and bitter
    gourd.

Lamunin ng sisig – sizzled chopped bits of pig's head and liver,
milkfish, seasoned with calamansi and chilli peppers, topped with an
    egg.

Gutom pa. Lola dishes *pan-de-sal. Tita, buko* roll.
Mga lalake kumain pa ng banana cue. *Mga babae, biko* and *puto.*

We want to thank Christ for the blessings of this fiesta.
We want to thank Christ for the offerings that we chew.

We shall eat with our hands and hearts.
We shall eat till the last melt has dried in our stomachs.

Kumain na.
Gutom pa.

NOTES

Kumain na in Tagalog translates as 'Has eaten'.
Gusto ng lasa in Tagalog translates as 'Likes the taste'.
Gutom pa in Tagalog translates as 'Still hungry'.

What Eyes?

Hannah Roux

> And what shoulder, & what art,
> Could twist the sinews of thy heart?
> And when thy heart began to beat,
> What dread hand? & what dread feet?
> William Blake, 'the Tyger'

Inside this red orchid
are beaded, glistening particles
trembling at speeds eyes cannot see,
in glittering, gleaming, golden specks
which circle in concentric rings,
and know the complex dancing moves
exchange their partners in one blink
and keep the time. Their dancing groups

(one atom)

are as slender as the fine hairs
raised on your forearm, as the lashes
fluttering on the rim of your eyelid,
whose movements my eyes
could see when I was close –
so close my lashes touched
the small goosebumps I raised
along the smooth cord of your throat.

These things are: they are inside
the cells and pulsing living things
that are your body, your mind, your eyes
they move in water-currents,
senselessly unseen
and seen and making sense –

making speeches, love poems and break-up songs,
marching bands and teacups,
oil paint and coal mines,
pencils and factory farms: moving matter
as though it were nothing
of your own volition to enter
a dance that never ends
and end it, change it, the moves of the will,
absorbed – like something natural – into nature.

These move like water in the brain
are also a dance, an unseen dance
we dance, with eyes on us.

(Or can we really say we dance?
since the moves are the sudden light –
felt in the heart and in the mind:
the woman pruning in the garden,
the roses trembling
under the dew's caress, dreading
the winter. Sheets of rain in strong black lines
from sky to sea and fluttering sail
between the sky-water and the ocean-water

and fear – felt in the stomach or in the heart –
of the lion, the kraken or the raven)

Within each drop of rain, the atoms
cluster like spider-eggs
and dance a gleaming, glittering dance
and this, we say, is the world:

in this are supernovas, every star,
the galaxies which swim for miles
across the debris-scattered dark
in rings caught by power of weight,
swinging in pendulums: planets and asteroids.
All made like this, all made so small,

and all plummeting
at speeds we can't control
nor stop through wishing or wanting.

(If stars could wish, would they cry out
on the last day: 'I want to be light?')

I saw this procession
flooding through the city gates
in which the smallest atomic speck
of hydrocarbon, ash or dust,
was older than a thousand worlds

(had been within a thousand worlds)

and came to light, once that I saw,
one golden afternoon on a path.
This speck went first through the city gates.

I thought: whose eyes behold these things?
The dust, the toenails of this child,
the crumbling bark on paper-gums;
consider the grass, each blade of it,
the direction it turns in the wind;
who holds in some enchanted gaze
the turn of worlds and the mad descent
of this autumn leaf in the driving rain?
What eyes the movements of our breaths
have grasped, and slipped eternity
into each cell, have known the fall
of every star, have held and cupped
their hands around the distance and time
it takes their light to travel?

My seeing stills, your breath still stirs
upon the fine hairs on my cheek
and I must ask what dreams you dream
then ask, still more: what eyes, what art
can grasp the measurement of hearts?

To Go

Zoe Coles

There is a car spot that I can drive straight into. I have to cross two lines of traffic to get there, but when there is a break, I simply go forward and find peace. I look like a fool, not indicating left or right, but I am simply going into nothing. Now you're the fool for thinking so poorly of me, the small blonde girl in her beat-up car not knowing how to drive. I know how to drive. I just don't like going places.

I slot into the space like a coin into an arcade machine, effortlessly. There are only four shops on this strip. There's the corner store, specialising in outdated American candies, the fish 'n' chips takeaway, the café and a second-hand shop called *Again and Again*. I'm here for the café. It looks out of place after its recent rebranding, but locals know it's just the same stipple ceiling with chalk paint splashed over. It's filled with mixed imagery, as though the store were a convoluted metaphor itself. There are chalky doodles of planets and stars, but also flowers and cartoonish worms. Inspirational quotes contradict one another. Sure, it looks a lot nicer than it did before, but it has always been the sun that's kept the café in business. The sun does not need a rebranding. She is here, again and again and again and again, adorning the garden patio that the café's tables and chairs soak in, leaves and chatter thriving. Like a stage, she holds the space to let the networks of people spin their glorious webs, translucent and intricate. When it rains, the webs are torn down, and the café simply doesn't open.

It is vaguely cloudy when I drive down, but the sun peeks out from the cloud often enough for them to open their French doors. The line for takeaway is speckled with the usual subjects: twenty-something women my age in activewear, an old couple and their Bichon Frise, a dad's weekend with the kids. The script has changed, but the characters stay the same. All the better. They are the perfect audience members for my plan. One of the women chats to the barista, holding up the line. From what I can gather, they used to date. They exchange their lines in the script of conversation unconvincingly. She is selling him the utopian lie of her life too hard, and he returns the favour.

'Oh yeah, I quit the business long ago now. Actually, me and Marnie . . . you remember Marnie, right? . . . set up our own creative consultancy a couple months ago, so.'

'I left mum's place. Got my own apartment, you know. It's actually got ocean views, which is pretty sick.'

'Nah, I'm totally off dating apps. The guys at the club seem to find themselves all over me, so no need to manufacture that myself.'

I hear her activewear friend let out a snort, but I'm too far back in the line to work out if it's in response to the lie her friend just told or if she's loving the fact that her bestie is letting this douchebag of an ex know what he missed out on. I listen to this conversation of networks falling apart only to reassert themselves once more, destined to ebb and flow just like the very queue we stand in. They shuffle to the small crowd waiting for their coffees, and a few minutes later, I am at the front.

'Two apple-carrot juices, three decaf flat whites, and one mango smoothie to go please,' I pronounce, pre-emptively wavering my credit card over the machine.

'That'll be thirty-six dollars, thanks.'

A supercut of all the different ways I could have spent this money plays in my mind's eye. Charities, birthday presents, plane tickets to faraway places, coins to toss in ancient fountains for when I get there. But I tap my card and join the myriad of customers waiting, petting the Bichon Frise on the way.

Everyone here is in twos. Couples, running buddies, old friends, co-workers, mothers and daughters. They interact in their networks like atoms, programmed with such a familiarity that I want to congratulate them for remembering their lines so well. They hint at old events, future plans. My lines, well rehearsed in the days spent constructing this scheme, are two-dimensional, existing only for this space. In the past, I have come here in a two, but it is better when I don't. I feel I am split into two already, the disparity between what I think and what I say. Once my plan plays out, I will be synthesised.

Like a mosaic, a full image will form that is so clear, one would never think to pair it up with anything else.

My drinks are called out, and they are placed in a cardboard carrier that almost makes them more difficult to hold. I carry them to the car, which is only a few steps away, overexaggerating the uneasy movements of keeping the drinks upright while fishing for my car keys. I get a few smiles. Good. They are watching.

I place the drinks, all six of them, on the roof of my car as I find the keys at the bottom of my tote. The car unlocks and I cocoon myself inside it. The drinks are still balanced on top, but not for long. I reverse back onto the street with vigour, and fleetingly catch a few eyes from the strangers in front before the kaleidoscopic tapestry of coloured liquids pour down my windscreen.

It is brilliant. It is beautiful.

Before I get out to reap the rewards of my plan, I momentarily hide behind this sheet of spilled drinks and praise myself for the magnificence that is caking onto my car. There are the candlelight hues of the smoothie that drip down to the bonnet, with flecks of fern green blending in. The best of all is the creamy goodness of the flat whites, a sandcastle being washed away. I recall that the average colour of the universe is one called *cosmic latte* as I am encased by this little universe I have created. With space and sand, I mix my metaphors, and out of the car, I rise.

They are all looking at me. It is so wonderful. They are looking at me with sympathetic smiles and they reach out their hands to help. They touch me. They are laughing with me as I choke out practiced words of embarrassment and insecurity. One man tells me how his wife once did the same thing, and the wife rolls her eyes at the story but places a hand on my shoulder in solidarity. The barista brings out a cloth and explains how he saw the whole thing happen. I bask in hearing my story told, and I know that they will go home and tell their children and their parents and their friends again and again and again about it. About me.

The prior week that I had spent in bed did not matter anymore. All the words and touch that I am being decorated with now makes up for the people I pushed away. The days I had spent with this plan, brewing and fermenting inside me as I clung to my bed and refused to leave the house, matter no more. These people – these beautiful people! – love me. They love this story. And I wrote it for them! I do not need to come here in twos, I am wholly one. I am the mosaic of stained-glass windows that they can see through, looking beyond everything else to arise at the truth that I am the girl who once spilled her drinks all over her car. That is all I am. I am just a clumsy accident, nothing sinister, nothing sensational. This is my rebranding, and I am the brilliant architect.

This story is like the sun.

These little in-jokes, amusing tales, myths, legends – they keep the café alive. I keep these people alive.

Eventually, I unslot myself from the car spot and back out onto the road, the scent of fruit and dairy wandering into the interior. I take the first left, and then the third right, down to the beach. The coffee van is still there, with a dozen or so cars parked around it, and an equal amount of people in line. At the front of the line, I repeat my little spell for companionship that I am so desperate for. The networks expand, and I slither my way in.

'Two apple-carrot juices, three decaf flat whites, and one mango smoothie to go please.'

For Bonnie, with a Granddaughter's Love

Emma Murphy

I knew you from airmail
packages
and ripped birthday
wrapping paper,
from the long journeys
Barbie dolls and jewellery
endured.

I knew you from faint, delayed phone calls
where time with you was priced
at thirty-nine cents a minute.

I knew you from half-way trips
to white sand beaches,
palm trees
and coconuts.

I knew you for owning
flawlessly delicate shades
of lipstick,
that I was too young for
but you let me try on sporadically.

For Bonnie, with a Granddaughter's Love

I knew you as Oz,
I pictured you
living in an emerald green castle
with yellow brick roads,
with hearts, and brains, and bravery.

I begged my parents
for a pair of ruby red slippers
so I could walk
to where you were.

But most of all
I knew you from stories
of a childhood
I was never present for,
but know better than my own.

These narratives will outlive
your ninety-three
and we'll tell them with grace
and with accuracy.

Where I Belong

Janika Fernando

My world is a rushing river,
Enormous, feeling
Claustrophobic as the glaring light
Makes me privy
To blindness.

                             Pain plucks the strings of my heart,
                    Surmounting, surmounting, surmounting!
                                     I scream.
Night cloaks in black, hiding the sharp sky
                     Moments of silence as I shut my eyes
                                 But soon,
                           Everything shakes,

Smooth, mellifluous
Music flows gently through
The glass windows.
This feeling,
My own tongue cannot capture.

I remember the golden glory,
Homesickness floods me.
I long for a place that never was
What I dreamed,
Never.

                             I still cry when I wake.

The longing feeling of home,

Unshakeable, in the air

> *All because I followed but a Dream.*
> *The voice of every immigrant that I know,*
> *Their story is told through my eyes: the daughter of an immigrant.*

* * *

Kiyoma is dreaming about her home. She envisions the waves, as they break around the rocks in the shallows. Their foam crests become a chaotic lace around the deep blue ocean. See how she watches them twirl, mesmerised by their movement, their rhythm steals her heart, and arranges her regular contemplations. Maybe many can relate to this feeling and maybe some should try. It is what characterises us. Home. We can decide to overlook it and embark on a quest for our dreams. We will consistently discover a way to feel incomplete without it.

At least, that is how Kiyoma feels when she wakes in her Sydney suburban home to the ripple sound effect of her phone alarm. Wait. No. She hits snooze at 6 am and with great trepidation, she faces another Monday morning. Time is ticking. She needs to cook breakfast, pack lunch for her daughter, pour an espresso coffee for herself, and be dressed by 8.20 am. They are late. She drops Kikky to school. My, how she walks just like her father Neythan as she disappears through the school gates. The same routine flows seamlessly each day. If one could compare Kiyoma it would be to Mother Nature, who nurtures her children's branches before herself.

Kiyoma is at work at 9 am. Her mind swims in different directions, reminding her that she has to complete the monthly stocktake and supplier invoices. Having multiple screens sends waves of pain into her weary eyes. Oh, how her shoulder aches from clicking her right-hand mouse. There are times when she rises every now and then, to grab a snack from the lunchroom. Often, she wonders whether the current that she drifts along in each day would be different back home. Despite these lingering pools of thoughts, her mind has learned over the past years to accept and cherish ascertaining numbers and algorithms. If this sustains her, like a cup of water, why does she feel half-empty? After all, her job gives her nourishment enough to provide for her daughter and herself.

Her boss strolls into her room once more.

'Kiyoma, have you finished this report for me?'

'Not yet, I'm onto it.'

'Okay then,' her boss replies, returning to his office.

My, gracious. If Kiyoma had not assumed control over her own current, she would not be playing her role in the accounts department. Goodness, how her ex-husband Neythan did not even want to study hard enough, let alone bother to get his college level Accounting certificate to attain a good job. How stupid, really. He always wanted to move; a change of current is all. A change of heart? No. He only has his own mind.

Neythan promised Kiyoma the world, you see. She thought Australia would be incredible with him. She thought that he had graduated from Business College and was working in an office job. He would chuckle at her when she used to call him from Sri Lanka, inquiring as to whether he had returned home from work.

'Oh, office. Yes, darling!' he would tell her his blatant untruth.

After showing up in Australia: consternation. Disturbance. Shrouded outrage that became released outrage when he confessed the reality of his lie, that he was just a taxi driver. When she asked for money for something, she got nothing. Neythan could not have cared less – reckless. She wanted to see, to hear, to think, to feel but what did Neythan want? He wanted the opposite. The tangible over the intangible at any cost – the big mansion, the fame, to win the lottery, the millionaire dream. This is precisely why he spent countless dollars hoping there was the tiniest chance that the lottery show would announce his name on live television, and in turn prove her wrong for thinking he was an idiot. He cherished his horoscope readings that told him all these acts would make him renowned as Mr Popular. Mr Popular must be in the dumps now that she had left him. After all, he did not concentrate on what should be accomplished for Kiyoma and Kikky. Goodness, how she hopes Kikky does not wind up like him and instead becomes more honest like her.

'Kiyoma, are you going out for lunch?' asks one of her work colleagues.

'Yes.'

She leaves her screen where it is and rushes out to meet the balmy air of Strathfield South. Her eyes hide behind her sunglasses and her hair flows freely in the breeze. Gone is the gloomy hustle and bustle of people in winter, where everyone is dressed in warm bundles of wool and puffy jackets. Now, people caressed by cotton clothes show off the figures they were hiding in those dark and dripping months. Kiyoma passes by crowds cheering at St Anne's Catholic Church on her way to Oporto. Goodness, how sweet! The church is having a wedding on this fine Monday morning. Kiyoma never had that. A proposal, that's all that it was. Kikky has the photograph of them after she accepted the proposal. Kikky wants to climb into Kiyoma's skin and comprehend why they live the way they do, without Neythan.

Kiyoma remembers catching her first glimpse of Neythan on the Sri Lankan bus. His eyes refining focus on her, standing in her saree like a pretty mannequin. The perspiration sticking to her lips. Yet, she was enough in his eyes. Pretty enough to follow her. To promise her the Dream that, surely, she would not regret. Pretty enough to wind up here in her office, back at it again in front of her multiple screens, devouring the so-called legendary chilli sauce of her double Bondi burger. It is the closest that Kiyoma can get to chilli in those fast-food outlets. But it is not real chilli, not at all. It is the kind of chilli that makes her heart slump, that carries with it the bitter taste of freedom she remembers from her first arrival in Sydney.

Freedom has a price, you see. The price is leaving the teardrop island laden with the familiar fumes of turmeric, chilli powder and cloves. The price that Kiyoma soon discovered when the ebony-carved elephant that her ammi[1] gave her, shining with specs of gold, broke after arriving in Australia. All because Neythan had slammed the delicate boxes excessively hard on the floor. She was truly broken, robbed too early of the tape and glue necessary to piece together the elephant. Her heart, ineffectively stapled shut, was thumping hard, her skin extended over her throbbing muscles, like a well-used canvas. Her

---

1   'Mother' in Sinhala.

mind was a lost soul adrift, trapped in that marriage, and urgent for a loving memory that might be decent, warm and inviting enough to make her happy.

One loving memory is the wafts of spices that floated in the air along with the frying of papadums,[2] tickling her nose as soon as she woke up. The banging and clanging of pots and pans as her ammi stirred a chicken curry. Her knife slicing onions to make a more than decent meal – a wonderful dish because she loved Kiyoma. Loved her sisters – Amaya, Dilini, Roshida, Giyani, Malsha and of course, her thathi,[3] Sergeant Marco. Sergeant Marco was always there to wake her up at four in the morning to study. Oh, but the cheekiness of Kiyoma when she turned her bedroom light on under the guise of studying, but in reality, she curled herself up under the covers and continued her dream of travelling to Australia, roaming the globe's horizons – to escape, to be free.

* * *

My mother once gave me this message in a bottle:
'Listen carefully to my tongue,' she whispered.
                         This bottle: tossed to   and   fro
By the enormity of the waves,
Scratched and cracked,
By the rough reefs,
Does it not remain a bottle?
Life seeps through
Your graceful, glass barriers,
But you know better than to let life break you.
This is your boat,
Command the currents like a Sergeant would,
Listen to your heart   for it is more than just a beat,
The hope that you seek will find you,

---

2   Sri Lankan flatbread appetiser.
3   'Father' in Sinhala.

And it will give back what the Dream has taken away.
Do not be sorry and shy for the faults in your stars:
For they make us human.
Dwell no more, no more,
Because all will lead you to the greatest chapter of your life.

* * *

Kiyoma is sitting in her office, typing up the final touches of her work. When the clock hand reaches 5 pm sharp, she gathers her bag and heads out, rummaging for her car keys. *Click-click,* and she starts the engine of her car. She drives forward, the wheels creeping at an agonising pace. Goodness! How the car's engine persistently whimpers and moans, it is practically identical to an inhabitant of any nursing home. She thinks about the whimpering and moaning of her stomach when she was on the plane, her first plane ride to good old Sydney. Adrenaline made her heartbeat quicker, redirecting blood to her muscles and away from her gut. She hung in mid-air, the rotors murmuring in the midst of the reddest of skies. Hearing that defying pause – when the pilot reported, *'Ladies and gentlemen, we have been cleared to land at Sydney terminal. Please ensure one final time your belt is safely fastened.'*

The wheels shrieked on the ground. She covered her ears from the speedy, ear-splitting sound and –

Honk-honk.

'WOMAN, MOVE!'

Oh! Kiyoma's mind shifts back to the present as she continues the rhythmic movement of her engine, the other cars flowing with her through the peak-hour traffic. She turns up the volume, and the familiar rhythm of *Ammawarune*[4] soothes her soul. Watching out her window, Kiyoma drives past the hustle and bustle of a million different faces.

---

4   Song by Nanda Malani – an elegy for all mothers.

The gataberaya[5] instruments make the black, yellow, brown and white faces disappear for just a few moments. She is happy to be living in a multicultural nation – surely she should be used to it by now? How long ago was it when she arrived on that first flight to Sydney? All so long ago. Kiyoma was not used to travelling, while Neythan, next to her then, had encountered everything previously.

Kiyoma parks her car at the shopping centre. She moves along on the escalator with the thick current of faces. Every now and again jarred by the smell of espresso coffee, she turns right and weaves her way out of the crowd. In contrast to a child, there is no mother, father, sister or sibling to pull her away. Rather, she inches sideways until she is in the current again. She veers into the Country Growers shop, where she will purchase a couple of vegetables, some to bring home to Kikky.

Her daughter is waiting at home. Goodness, but what will they eat tonight? Unfailingly, it is the sheer assurance and shrewdness of Kiyoma that she manages to cook a decent meal. Stir-fried vegetables, white rice with a side of steak to place on the table. A meal for two. Gracious! If it were not for her daughter, Kiyoma would not know where she was presently. Kikky's birth in the world gave her a profound melody of hope. Hope that she would not be alone with silly Neythan. Through her, she could have a more purposeful life here in the nation of dreams, by devoting her soul to her child, just as her mother does from Heaven, singing the lyrics, '*Amma pamanai laga inne*'.[6]

Yet genuinely, Kiyoma could not have stopped herself from holding Neythan's hand and taking the plane ticket to Sydney, to what would be paradise. Glancing out the taxi window to the city that surrounded her, the world had never felt so wide and free to her. Lights sparkled like stars dropping to the Earth and tall structures made her eyes gawk in insurmountable wonder. Taxis, buses, cars and motorcycles hurried along tangled lines of avenues, making winding strings of light. They all interlaced together in the magnificent mess of a dream.

As they drove under the wonderful, arched Sydney Harbour Bridge, this amazing, sublime, practically terrifying dream made her,

---

5   Hill Country Drum.
6   'Your mother always stays near you' in Sinhala.

as an immigrant, feel fortunate. Goodness, how she wondered how many arms it took to build such an extension, to stand still despite everything. Solid and undaunted.

Kiyoma shifts her brain to the present and pulls up into the driveway of her home. *Click-click.* The key chain jingles and clanks in a cadence. Gracious! Her daughter, Kikky, is sitting at the dining table reading her books. Kiyoma grins. Books. *Wonder where she got those genes.* Like mother, like daughter. Indeed, it is generally the nose, the eyes and the mouth from Neythan. Gracious, and do not forget the walk as Kikky rushes to give her ammi an embrace of warmth, love and appreciation. She knows in a split second that her girl has showered, as the lavender lingers in her hair.

Then Kikky continues as she is, sitting and reading. Kiyoma is cooking a decent meal yet again. If on the off chance she paused this very scene and replayed it, it would be the same as every day. If she reminds herself of the beginning as she stares out the kitchen window, into the lost oblivion – she would be back home. Back on that teardrop-shaped island singing out of tune. She used to climb the old tree and reach for the cashew fruit that fell from her hands. Land on the ground while the cashew fruit hit her head and hear her sister giggle at her daring, her valour, her bravery and her fun-loving nature. She is the youngest sister out of them all – the baby.

'Ammi?'

Goodness! Kikky is calling her. What does she need? Is she hungry? Did she get an awful mark?

'What time was I born?'

Overall, that is a clever and inquisitive question. The appropriate answer is 22 December 2002. Sydney Hospital at the stroke of ten o'clock. After the agonising pain, she was there. Incipient eyes opening, mouth pulling for milk. She needed to drink this second in. This second where Kiyoma watched her newborn peer through the earthy-coloured eyes that were more splendid than she could have imagined. In that second, Kiyoma realised that she was her defender, for whatever length of time that she would live, and her affection would last forever. Kikky had started to fret and cry. If her sister Amaya were there, she would reveal to Kiyoma how irritating that would be. It was charming to the point that she cried, her grin filling her with a daylight she thought would not exist after she left her home. All the painful moments that came before softened endlessly.

But the misery of change. If only she could hit replay on her life back to the Nil Manel[7] flowers. She remembers the flowers' otherworldly bliss of indigo interwoven with brilliant sparkles to form a sweet aroma. She pulled a lily out of the lake only to wind up in the water, snickering at the sprinkle, the solace. Her youth, so boisterous, and the creations of an underhanded kid stealing desserts from the kitchen bench and the 'shoo-shoo' wave of her ammi's hand to leave. Yet, Neythan set her daughter's childhood apart as not so thrilling as Kiyoma hoped. Unsurprisingly, Neythan did not want to take them out anywhere. He did not want his daughter to become a social creature with other kids and to see the world the way Kiyoma dreamed about before landing in Sydney. Goodness, how they moved from room to room, villa to townhouse to house. Her husband was always changing the tide yet did not stop to consider her desires. Their needs. What was best for their child. Never. Yet she had nobody, when she first came to Sydney, to confide in about her misery. How alone she was. There was that late night, you see. Kiyoma was with her baby – breathing inside her belly – and Neythan decided to leave her to do a taxi job.

'Oh Lord, I'll be back soon!' he yelled against her requests to remain.

Soon, she cried – for she had never been so distant from everyone else. Never felt like this. She recollected her ammi and thathi never letting her go anywhere alone or to stay at home in solitude. She was constantly close to her sisters, who safeguarded her while she slept, studied and worked. Always there. But that very night, it dawned on her how much she missed home. It opened her eyes to the warm fires, clammy embraces and reassuring faces. Never thinking for a second that it would end this way.

But it did.

It did in light of the fact that she shuddered that night – wondering how a man could do something like this. Leave a pregnant woman such as herself all alone on a Tuesday night.

---

7   National flower of Sri Lanka.

'Ammi? You didn't answer my question.'

'Sorry, Duwa.[8] 10 pm.'

But no matter how she acknowledged the obvious issues, it didn't make a difference. It never mattered. She and her daughter were alone and always would be. Truthfully, she can never return permanently to Sri Lanka because to return means to surrender this paradise. This opportune bridge, which she has planned to build for her daughter here in Sydney. Ahh, Sydney. Kiyoma thinks about the style of the curved Harbour Bridge. It is impossible to miss the peculiar-shaped Opera House, the koalas and the kangaroos. All so ostentatious, and these people long for large stadiums and theatres. They fabricate ice rinks and spread out parks with soccer pitches. Unlike Sri Lanka, obviously. No. Sri Lanka does not have numerous clever structures to signify its country and character. It has people.

People. They are the very waves of Sri Lanka, full of power and brilliance. If Kiyoma was feeling sick, if she needed someone, she need only speak a word and just as the white stream of a waterfall cascades over the rocky stones, the next-door neighbour would come rushing. Rushing with warm smiles, a cup of gratitude and food. That is just how it is in Sri Lanka. From a young age, people serve their neighbours even though they are complete strangers. No matter how wet they became with poverty, it could not dampen their spirits to flow towards another's deafening roar of misery.

Kiyoma finishes cooking their meal and her daughter sits with her at the dining table. She admires her beauty, and her instinct to be studious and ambitious as she slowly eats her mashed potatoes and gravy. Yet Kikky reminds her of Neythan and she wonders how she must feel not having a father around. It could do to have someone help with carrying the groceries, driving them places, paying the rent and fees because in fact – she has to do this alone. She has her daughter of course, but her daughter will not always be around. She is busy studying. Soon, university. Soon, career. Soon, marriage, and well, Kiyoma will never be free from worry, will she? Each moment ties her back, like a knot made of her and her daughter. They became two after they were three. Just two. What rather low numbers, some might say,

8   'Daughter' in Sinhala.

but two can be powerful in some ways that some might not understand. Her daughter adores her. Does she miss Neythan? Who knows? But what is more important is getting through every single day without setting herself on fire.

A Viber call from one of her sisters in Sri Lanka.

'Hello Akka,[9] can you hear me?'

'HELLO NANGI!'[10]

It happens countless times. The voices echo repeatedly as the connection grows poor and then it comes back, as time is wrestling between day and night – past and present. An indescribable strained quality to her muscles yearns for a melody of comfort. If only she could just drift into the universe of dreams.

She remembers the fields in Sri Lanka where there were quick flashes of bright green, as her friends drove her up the winding staircase of the mountains. Sticking her head out of the roof of the jeep, the cold mist gently soothed her skin. Goodness, how emerging out of the mountains, the sudden gust of hot wind slapped her face. How she just could not wait to leave the humidity of summer behind her, and head for what she thought might be bearable. Now, the skies might be blue, but her world is grey. The winter penetrating her every time it comes around. Just thinking of the cold can make her think of home, of the humidity, of the mountains. It fills her lungs with fresh air and reminds her of those she left for a better life. Now the forest of home is in the walls of her mind. How tired she was of the forest, how tired without them she is now.

Yet her brain is swimming in different directions, trying to arrange her daily contemplations. A stranger no more but not even a visitor to her home, like many of her friends who visit Sri Lanka every year. Her mind is constantly whirring with how to pay school fees; how to pay rent; how to pay food, water and electricity bills; and how to buy a house on her shoulders alone. How can she go to Sri Lanka each year? That itself is another cost. Not just to buy the thousand-dollar tickets but also to buy presents from the land of the Dream for her family and relatives waiting back home.

---

9   'Older sister' in Sinhala.
10 'Younger sister' in Sinhala.

What a dream.

The subconscious part of her brain detects the need to protect her daughter, to ensure survival for both of them. What she really needs to endure tomorrow is sleep, at least six hours would be nice. Sometimes, she wishes the dollar after dollar were rupees, with transaction after transaction. She is a lone, solitary figure in supporting them and her daughter insists that she can work; she is old enough, but no. Kiyoma says, 'Studying is the richest thing you can do', translating the lyrics of *Ma Bale Kale*.[11] She gives the best advice to her child, shaping her into what she was when she was her daughter's age.

Kiyoma understands that children cannot see suffering without suffering. Goodness, the number of times she tells her daughter of the fortunate food and life she has here in Australia. Kiyoma knows the life, marked by great distress and poverty, that she had with her sisters. She knows that her ammi was simply exhausted every day from her frail hands kneading dough, cleaning and struggling to place meals on the table for all five of her sisters. She remembers how they had to carry buckets of water on their heads, careful to not let droplets spill onto the ground, and journey on for miles. She knows her mother and father would have loved their granddaughter if they had been still alive when she chose to fly to the Dream.

Gracious, yet her youth resembles a snapshot out of time. She can see her jet-black hair blowing in the spring breeze, her energetic face moved in the direction of the sun. Despite everything, she moves like the delight of life inside her cannot be subdued, in that handmade flower dress her ammi made for her; she could be anybody. There is nothing her family would not do to keep her safe from hurt, but they cannot ensure her safety for eternity. She must be there for herself when she falls and stands up again to reach for the stars, when she lets her daughter go after them, out of her love.

'Ammi.'

'Hmm.'

Kiyoma is laying on her bed, after wrapping up all the cleaning and cooking, when Kikky opens the door and bids her goodnight. Kiyoma checks her mobile for any calls but understands it is past the point

---

11   Song by C.T. Fernando.

where she can answer any of them. Time is still ceaselessly ticking. She shuts her eyes and nods off. In her dreams, she envisions her sister driving her back to where everything started. Sri Lanka. She is going for a stroll and there is a door. The door that was once a splendid navy blue is now fragile, as it has blurred in the daylight; the years passed mean it has incurred significant damage. Venturing from home is so difficult, with such a significant number of recollections, and now every one of them collects in her chest. She traces her hand down to the doorknob. Thin at the edges, thicker in the centre, remembering the cottage. Then she seizes it, ramming the door shut. She almost hears the apparition of her youth whine, as she turns to the slight breeze of summer. The beach is stretching out its cool water, lapping at her feet, bubbling like brine, these constant family and friends chattering, as the water comes in its consoling way, as though Kiyoma's bliss is to relive the profound bronze sand of her home. It is 6.30 am when her alarm rings once more. The place where she belongs disappears, and as her eyelids are wide open, Kiyoma knows that she cannot go back.

* * *

Who made you afraid, my love?
Always afraid of the future,
  Dwelling in the looming reminder of the past,
For neither exist in but the creative mind.
      Indeed, memory must reign on.
Fear is madness, but valuable, if you know how it works.
Let the trepidation wake you up, let it show you the way,
      To your true self.
To the bold soul whose love
      Dared enough to chase a solitary dream.
Let your own love become a lamp in obscurity,
Comfortable gleam, you overlooked what is inside of you.
Figure out how to rest there, in time trusting to move nearer, for the genuine
    spark needed to leave its cave, to search for an alternative light.
For there was a period we were one,

It will come back once more and we will burn as one flame:
A light enough to arrive at each dim corner,
A freedom that desires to remain,
The fragrance of the fields,
the melody of the winged creatures,
your arms that vibrate like a butterfly
bursting from a cocoon,
an asylum from even your internal tempests.
Be strong as a genuine person,
one with roots rather than feet that run,
                    Take the jump for you are the fortunate one.

Georgia Restless

Joshua Klarica

There is the way Alex smiles, the melee of freckles in the squash of her face and her eyes half-lidded, like the sun is trying to get through. She makes soft some part of you watching her, forgetful for the moment of course deadlines and student loan applications and where your friends are, or the swaddling heat that chokes the air of the unending and low cerulean above you. Alex takes a sip of pale wine and motions for me to do the same.

We have abandoned the hot flat in Marrickville for the shade of the city, although Alex looks as if we have come further than the 430 could take us. She sits with a single arm akimbo and propped on the railing beside her, watching people move sluggishly along the walkway. From the gardens behind us stroll couples pensive or parents exhausted, while tour groups challenge traffic for use of the road and the pavements either side teem with chatting adults and ambulating toddlers. A young man with a clipboard and a bright blue vest splits groups of travellers like a river around an obtrusive stone, but he looks hopefully at the doors of the gallery that chew out art-goers with the routine of clockwork and the beat of summer's diurnal rhythm. Alex is amused and puzzled and intrigued, as though she were playing tourist, and not they.

Around us, clumps of shiny people sit and eat but mostly drink, the passage of voices turning languid in the heat.

'I bet London feels like an age ago,' says Alex. There is an airy quality to the way she speaks, like she is never rushed for time.

I pinch the hem of my shirt and yank it away from me several times. The relief that comes, cool air on damp skin, is short-lived. I take a long drink of the sticky wine and tell her it does. Even though the days between then and now are so few, they are long.

Alex speaks again but she is a mime, drowned out in the moment by the traffic of the skyline as yet another plane trundles in and shakes the sky above us and then resets into oblivion's vacuum, ready again. She smiles and offers a little shrug, as if to say, 'Well, what can you do?'

'When's the deadline?' she asks, when the sky has cleared. Only tiny swallows inhabit the space now. They are like balled fists that fall through the air, only to sprout wings and skip from our view.

'Tonight. Don't look so worried – I just have to hit submit.'

Alex makes a show of puckering her bottom lip.

'But I'm glad you're back,' she says. 'I don't want you to go again.'

'Sure you do. You'll get your apartment to yourself.'

'What's so wrong with being home?'

Alex grabs at her chest in mock paroxysm, but she expects me to apply all the same. It is almost alarming, the ease with which we have become symbiotic since my return, like two wives retired down south, making dinner plans and watching one another slowly erode with the coastline. Its comfort is cloying, but there is much to enjoy about living with Alex. The eagerness to be young and intimate with her, like we are teenagers sleeping over, surprises me often. We vacillate between watching B-grade horror films and cloying rom-coms, argue about whether we should have gender-fluid toilets (Alex is opposed: 'Men can't aim for shit.'), relax Alex's vegetarianism as we hunt for fried dinners at four in the morning. Then there are the smaller moments, like the way Alex giggles like a child when she hums and you drum her back and her voice shakes.

'Besides,' I say, emptying the wine between our glasses, 'what else would I do?'

The options have opened up for me this last month, however few they may be. I am in the crossfires between further study that will somehow sate the anxiety of the one just passed, or re-joining my parents at the nursery, or, rather improbably, hitting the designer start-up jackpot, all screaming with the dullness of other people's dreams. I am not like Alex, who seems to have avoided the inexorability of a career that follows obligingly the bachelor's graduation and a well-endowed student debt.

'What if I don't get in?'

Alex is surprised by the suddenness of my question. Then she leans forward, uses one finger to drag her glasses down to the tip of her nose. Her eyes are jade green and knowing.

'Hush,' she says simply.

'*Hush?*'

Alex nods vigorously and repeats herself. 'Hush. You will get in. Don't tell me that old crone is in your head again.'

Abigail Price, she means, the gaunt course coordinator from London, her spine jagged and hunched so she may better scrutinise the ground before she walks over it. Her thin voice comes back effortlessly, in the dark workroom replete with students doubled over sewing machines and garments of bleeding-thumb couture, asking, with the concern of a mortgage broker, 'Are you sure this is the course for you, dear?'

I pull out my phone and open my email. I scroll through the promotions and words of the day, until the unread white turns to forget-me grey. I star an email from my parents and the reminder from the admissions board, check the junk folder and trash folder and then I scan the inbox one last time for their names. I type them in. Toni, then Mary; Kim A and Kim T, down the list. Finally, I type in Elton.

'Like the singer,' he had said. 'It would have been much cooler if they'd named me Benny instead.'

There had been nervous laughter in the group of strangers as Elton pushed a hand through his black hair. The debutantes, local and international, had toured the design faculty and now sat running introductory drills and name-sharing activities. Elton swallowed his T's and K's when he spoke, bearing the lazy, charming glottal stop like so many of the English.

'Not Jane Austen's Elton, then?'

He had looked across the circle at the small, huddled body that had spoken, her chin resting on knees pulled to her chest. 'Actually, that's right,' he said, surprised. 'My mum loves Austen, but she convinced my dad it was after the singer. He thought it was real rock 'n' roll. Still, probably better than being called Knightley.'

'Or Emma, I suppose.'

Elton had laughed.

* * *

There are no new messages, nothing that has slipped by. The most recent correspondences from the cohort are greyed out and dated a month ago, read and responded to and re-read.

'They're busy, Georgia,' harps Alex. 'They're in *New York*. I'd ignore you too.'

A note on Alex's effortlessness: one summer, three years ago, Alex sat down and wrote a short play. A friend of ours knew a director who put it on at a local theatre, and in time the play gained enough traction that Alex found herself in New York, watching her play being performed 'off Broadway'. She has a few short stories of repute online somewhere, a chapbook and once guest-edited a budding literary journal. She doesn't write so much anymore, working as a court stenographer on Downing Street. Alex possesses one of those enchanted lives, whose mere existence seems evidence to its inevitable success.

'Elton is meant to call me tonight,' I say. 'Before I submit. To go through the application.'

Alex pouts.

'*I'll* look over your portfolio, George. You don't need his eminency to give you advice. Don't give me that look. What's the name of the school again?'

Some nights, Alex slips into my bed and pulls herself into my side. 'Tell me about London,' she says, so I tell her about the students and the course and about Abigail Price, the long days and late nights in the workroom, of the terrible food and relentless food chains, Scousers and Mancs and cockney rhyming slang. Then she asks if I miss it and I shrug, although I do. But memory is a thread looped around the places we have been, and to return, all one need do is pull. At Alex's request I tug gently at the thread, but it continues to unravel long after she has succumbed to sleep, and alone I recount the student movie nights and discount places to eat that were open late and on the bus line; recount the Friday nights armed with cheap bottles of wine from the off-licence and packets of crisps, playing drinking games among the cohort in anxious, equal part to get on with and on top of one another; recount the close cold of that morning beside the Thames, watching Elton laugh at Marcella performing before the doors of the Tate, a self-announced entrée to the art inside, while we waited for the others to arrive. I wonder why it is that I can only shrug when Alex asks if I miss it, why I cannot bring myself to either explain or dismiss my fondness for London's lurid anarchy, its never-drying-clag and the permanent question of *is this damp or just cold?*, London staunch and dirty and under your fingernails, on its haunches and boxing you in, furious and tremendous and exhilarating.

To discern salt from sugar is to taste both and learn the difference, just as to know love is to have seen others ridiculed by a shape they could not fill: so does the experience of one thing fulfill the completeness of another. Knowledge makes things smaller when we look back over our shoulder, changes the shapes we knew, so we can't understand what exactly it was that made it so great back then. It is like a language you once knew, but one you can only summon now in platitudes and genericism. *Parlez-vous français?* Because I don't. Lost are the small, acute knowledges we once had, along with their certainty. And so is it difficult to ricochet through the boundless streets one has always known, calling grocers and baristas and bartenders by name, and not compare the relentlessness of East London with the closed circuit of home, where everything is routine, and nothing is quite real enough.

'George?'

Alex is watching me. She drains her glass and stands, moving behind me, so for a moment she looks out onto what I see. She rests her elbows on my shoulders, drapes her arms in a garland that joins in the small valley on my chest. I glance up at Alex. She is smoothed by a branch of apricot light.

'Let's get out of this heat,' she says.

* * *

It is easy to lose her among the crowd. The foyer is dense with faceless bodies; throngs of child apparitions hurtling past us with their composite screams of play terror and thrill, their parents from the ticket booth calling weakly over their shoulders while haggling prices with stone-faced ticket attendants. There are tourists armed with cameras at their chests and throats, the locals more obvious and pronounced by their nonchalance, milling about the periphery sipping iced coffee and juices offering only a mild interest in entering the exhibition. The chaos of voices clambers through the gallery as Alex returns.

'We're skipping the free stuff,' she says, brandishing two tickets. 'My treat.'

It is the last weekend of the Streeton retrospective that consists almost entirely of painted landscape pieces, mountain ranges and the ports of seaside towns, wide parched fields with hewn trees as old as the world. A point is made of the presence of the brushwork, if only to blur one's vision, rendering the works with the inexactness of a dream. The impressionists, Alex explains, borrowed the term *en plein air* from the French, which translates to 'outside', which is what they tried to capture. Do you notice the fleeting light?

There is a sole room dedicated to Europe, where the sparse and long expanses of his home landscape are replaced by overcrowded market scenes, vivacious colour and sharp lines. In this room Alex mentions to me that Streeton, obsessed with his life abroad, only returned home to milk his celebrity and finance his return.

On Streeton, Alex pinches beneath my rib and mutters, 'Total Anglophile.'

We move in a dance, swapping squares and returning to one another, a small language of smiles and nods and gestures towards the artworks passing between us, careful not to disturb the experience for others. Short-lived murmurs fall back into silence, into the deferential fold, each work met by private judgements and purring contemplations and then passed over.

I watch Alex step through the room as though roaming a garden and grazing on the melange of colour, a single hand raised and trailing the wall beside her. She skips past three landscape images and sweeps into the next room. Instead of following her I stand by the largest of the three paintings, behind two middle-aged women whose murmurings are unintelligible to me. They stand with battling fingers running hurriedly across the breadth of the image, back and forth, like Streeton's brush once did.

There is a sharp quality to their voices when they share with one another. I realise they are each taking a turn to add some contribution to their conversation, each scurrying finger identifying another component of the work the other may not yet have noticed.

Peering closer, the artwork consists almost entirely of sky, speckled marginally with lazy grey clouds. The view is from one narrow, privately owned dock that looks across a brief cyan flash of harbour to another small, but slightly larger, dock. The second dock obscures the base of a bluff that would go on to form a headland. The action of the piece takes place below the heavy sky, an inch above the frame. Presumably, to the left and out of picture would be the curve of the land that connects the two foreshores, or a bridge or an isthmus. To the right there is a sandy promontory, rising from the ocean or falling from the sky. It is impressive, and unexceptional.

Still the women face the piece and discuss it between them. A second wave of viewers has passed through this room of the gallery and looked over the shoulders of the two women and muttered their acknowledgement and moved on. The woman on the left giggles. Moments later, the woman on the right turns to face her collaborator and speaks urgently. An amendment? A reprimand? The woman on the left returns fire; her voice breaks the octave and goes beyond a whisper. They turn from one another like sullen children.

What is it about these brushstrokes, the perpetually fading light on the walls of this gallery, that captures some essence these women cannot bring themselves to pass without an exegesis that turns bitter?

It is true, then, as Abigail Price says, that art is more than aesthetics, more than strokes and colour schemes, fabrics and techniques, that art plucks some internal commentary we did not know that we possessed and discharges it as expression, involuntary and hopeless. What is it in this piece that speaks of the same idyllic, prosaic landscape echoed in its neighbours but about which they each have something nuanced and different to discuss?

The artist, his moods and proclivities, time and designs, stood on one dock only to see something inarticulate yet indelible on the one opposing, something he sought; and if he were here now, would he look on this work and find it again? There is some secret in this vignette of the coast, but I cannot help but think I have seen this innocuous harbourside one hundred times in colour and reality, and it has been sweeter than this. I am unmoved.

Alex bundles into my side and holds my arm with both hands. 'Did you really not notice me, this whole time? You must like this one.'

The women turn and shake their heads at Alex, marching away and continuing to bicker between themselves.

'Dilettantes,' whines Alex after them. 'Did you hear those two?'

'I tried to.'

'They were taking an age to point out things they could see, like a *Where's Wally?* They started arguing about whether there is a shopping centre, or just a carpark, on that hill now. This is from Cremorne, you know, just down the road. Art really is lost on some people, George.'

Alex takes a step back from the painting, pulling me with her, and sweeps her hand across the three large frames. She begins to stab her finger furiously toward them, one at a time.

'That's a cloud of smoke, you see?' Alex adjusts a monocle and speaks with sardonic, gentry diction. 'Very important, that. And here, if you look closely in the middle-ground, you'll see evidence of a choo-choo train, no less. It was the, shall we say, *calling card* of the artist, don't you know?'

It is hard not to laugh or know when it gives way to crying.

* * *

Darkness gathers at the windows of the apartment, looking in. Bronze light from the hall slips in, rounds the furry edges of the room. The residue of day hangs dense, like a scent, like a hum. Alex sleeps nearby.

My fingers drum along the shapes of things present: the dry, gauzy texture of old novels beside the newness of smooth matte editions, a frameless poster from *Wicked*, dresses and shirts and skirts and jackets purchased in the throes of London's deep winter, useless now and hung like skins over wooden clavicles. From behind them I drag the mannequin torso out into space. My hands palpate the garment worn by the plastic chest and shoulders, hesitate over its double helix thread, should it begin breathing. I peel it from its rest and lay it over my chest, push and prod and examine myself in the mirror, only half seen in the second-hand light, and I remember Abigail Price looking on others' work and seeing something I couldn't, then her eyes on my piece and not seeing what I could, as though she were in possession of some congenital homing device for excellence that I was not, a bevy of details optioned only to her, like the colours available to the tetrachromat. In this poor light the garment looks unfamiliar, the thread work rushed, callous and rough like miniature, mangled tree roots.

Behind me, on the floor, the leather suitcase, a relic, lays open. Its contents appear to have escaped and crawled across the floor. There are notepads and sketches and magazine cut-outs, deadstock yarns and lengths of denim, a sliced and refashioned A-line dress from my high school collection, needles and pins and thread. Artefacts. And beside it all, still opened, is my phone and the email from Elton.

It reads:

G.,

Apologies for the late response. New York is a beast! Having a brilliant time, but the workload is unbelievable. By comparison, we all slept lots last year ha ha. Think you might still come visit NYC at some point? Yes, let's organise a time to chat over the phone. Perhaps when things are a little less manic?

Gotta run. Everyone sends their love.

E.

When I pinch the hem between my fingertips, when I make the initial tear, and the second, much longer, rip, I am mostly surprised by its compliance in coming apart. I pause, listen for Alex's coming, her explosive entrance to stop at once what I am doing, but she doesn't stir. I tear again, a single, composed tear that splits a wide smile down the length of the garment. The minutia of the fabric, the tiny grids, undoing.

We had gathered in my flat the day the results were announced, drinking gin from mugs and plastic red cups, the letters of offer released at midday. Someone suggested we stand in a circle, and none knowing any better, we did, and one by one we read aloud our futures to the shared horror of one another. One's condolence letter raised the odds for the next, because fifteen candidates do not go into nine spots, so we calculated and sighed and calculated and cheered until, prematurely, the spots had dried up, the candidates allocated, and there, waiting to read aloud her result, I stood, a sudden yearning opening in me, a mild confusion; belief that someone must have lied matched with hope for an exception, and all the while the dawning, advancing, heartbreaking relief.

When the plane passes overhead the walls of the room quiver. Silence resurfaces soon after, water finding its level. It is a visitor, this silence, a curious boarder; it overstays its welcome, and the hum pours in, getting louder and closer and going away, clinging to the wall like a fly in the dark and watching, listening. It comes back, and in the darkness it is inches from your face. It proliferates, it blossoms.

* * *

They stand along the walls of the room. They are all there, shadowy forms that do not speak, the Kims, Andrew, Mary. Elton is there too, holding hands with Marcella, watching as it begins. I fall back and close my eyes.

It starts with the toes. They dangle and curl and go rigid and outstretched, and when they come back, they are not my toes. It keeps growing, this sensation, like an anaesthetic pushing up through my blood. My legs disappear entirely, my chest vanishes. Up, out, it pushes through my extremities. And when it all comes back, I have traded my body for theirs, my name for theirs, and when I read their results, it is their rush that I feel.

I am Vincent, the weight of his feet stepping forward. Feel the breadth of his shoulders, the swing of his sex heavy between his legs. It gets firm as he reads. Kim T next. Fitting into her frame is easy. Wrap her paws around the mug and announce the verdict with a squeal. I am Marcella, swollen and wanted, now proud. Around the room I go; they go out like a sigh.

But I am cavernous and leaking and they are not enough, so I take Alex next, from the point at which her hips swell, down the length of her body, recumbent and yawning, effortless and lithe. Pull her skin over mine, cool and wet from the shower, an emollient to sate the heat. I sit at the computer, writing with electricity that spits from fingertips. Elton now, Elton last, and we must balloon to fit him. Wear that knowing smile, like the time Georgia asked him if he'd ever been in love. Watch her approaching, this peculiar and small woman, like an overgrown child, her eyes wide with uncertainty and hope. Watch her take your hands and calm them. Smell her, smell you, smell the scents cauterise on one another as your lips orbit. Why do you step back, Elton, watching the light douse in her eyes? Hear the words: 'I'm sorry, and, I can't, and, I am sorry, G, truly.'

We go back further, watching from somewhere above.

From another room in another time: muffled voices chiack and shout but the din does not come closer. She shows Elton the garment she has been working on, slipping it from under her bed. The orange light is bright but it is not harsh, so he can see the work in its entirety. Georgia watches his strong brows unfurl. Her heart crunches in her ears.

'This is fantastic,' he sighs.

Her skin bristles and inflates, for the softness of the adjective strips it of its platitude, its glamour and excess and its hackneyed use. It is an admission, humbled and breathless, quietly fantastic.

Reality's Conquests

Dennis Haskell

Narrow and slightly ovalled
as a castle's, the apertures
your gaze arrows through
reveal the ruffled, massed clouds of Turkey,
like a flattened English lawyer's wig.
Until a short while ago
it was hours and hours of Iranian sand,
mud-coloured but apparently dry,
a country that sheer height
rendered surrealist art.
Here the film's brain-numbing,
Boccherini introduced *auf deutsch*,
find your legs, stretch your head,
stare down the precarious wings . . .
nothing speeds up time
once relentlessness is its choice.
Down there, in a land I think of,
I confess, as veils and *fatwahs*,
radicals and moderates fight it out;
up here, in an eternity of air,
everything is quite right, and nothing quite real.
Who below ever thinks
there are engines slumbering above them
day night day night, even the sunlight
stretched like a strange elastic.

On Lufthansa's maps red criss-
crossing lines clutter the world.
To a pragmatist reality
is as you find it
but here all is theory
that somehow doesn't work
and technology's mystical perfection.
And yes, here comes dinner
yet again, as immediate as truth.

The World in a Seashell

Julia Peng

I used to hear the whole world in a seashell.
I don't remember much when I was a child
except a particular scene
at Surfers Paradise,
a sea that stretched down between the rocks and the cliffs
in the distance
that looked like rusted posts of sailboats.

There was a night that I snuck out
to watch the waves furl and unfurl like a stop motion film.
Of course, my father was right behind me,
and chided me for going out alone.

He heaved me upside down into the sky
until the southern cross became a descending kite.
Turns out, the adults heard me as soon as I left the room.

He'd take me down the shoreline
grabbing shells as we went,
each one a telephone receiver
that I'd place next to my ear
to listen for stories left behind.

It was only recently that my father started to leave voice messages.
'Happy birthday', 'Merry Christmas', 'Happy New Year'.
Each little grey bubble beating
to the syllables of his voice –
little remnants of him
since he returned to a place
eight thousand kilometres away.

I respond, 'Thanks dad', 'You too', 'Happy New Year'.
The stories have dried up
but secretly I hope
that we'll be able to go back on the northward drive
to find stories in the seashells.

Half-awake

Harold Legaspi

I cannot sleep, lying on the kama, past the bedtime hour
        a thorn kept underneath my concrete pillow
    where my crown ought to be
the moths drawn to my lamp, gas burning, to light the corner
        near my bedpan.
      The tangled ink spilt by my quill
          bears news of a family feud,
        avalanches of silence from Mother
    over the disappearance of her husband.
     News he has left her to be with the bruha of the Capital.
They come at us
        like so many insects picketing, banging, wailing
     against the too literal door
as the tails of their dogs
        wag discriminately, snitching gossip
         from leaves and twigs spoken of after mass.
     Foes and friends cue the poison of words,
       butchering truth, a torrent of stories, loose in their gaps.
A blur, a pricking song, ripens to stuff their mouths with hearsay.
         Aren't they sore from muddied waters?
   Our skin is brown, ambiguous and blind,
     locks in the chaos
of a grand bed of nails.

Notes

'Kama' in Tagalog translates as bed.
'Bruha' in Tagalog translates as witch.

A Juggle of Fruit in a Yellow Bowl

Helena Bryony Parker

Having turned and missed
a thousand little things, I'm sure
I ask myself, what if I had not seen you?

Suppose I never checked the news
six years ago, or never owned a dog.

Perhaps if I gazed into my lap as a child
rather than out the window of Mum's white Honda.

All the things I may have missed
that could have built this sandcastle differently.

The fact is, I wonder if we are not made of much.
A riddle of happenstance, arranged playfully,
a juggle of fruit in a yellow bowl.

On a day cooled to porcelain
from a bright breeze and
a jacaranda sky – was that it,
when you turned my way?

I might have remembered
the weather back then,

lined up my cherries and apples,
had you looked towards me that day
and this time I looked away.

Sorrow on Barney Street

Kiya Elphick

I stand in front of the bay window casting a shadow over the sunny day that has put everyone on the beach in a happy mood. The rays dance on the peaks of the water washing on the sand; it must be infused with serotonin. It brings about a good feeling over everyone who can get out of their house. There must be something in the water; that's the only explanation. Like how I was convinced there was something in the summer fruits last Thursday when I jealously watched from this same spot. A man was sitting on a blanket near the shore; he watched the sun go down while I observed him with the massive Tupperware container on his lap. It was filled with peeled mangoes, strawberries, oranges; he was mindlessly shoveling them into his mouth, the fruit juice covering his hands making the sand stick for dear life, but he didn't care. He kept digging into the container until the fruit was all gone. He looked so content in that moment . . . like nothing bad had ever touched his life. No evil grey clouds could have ever kept the sun from him, and I became convinced these fruits were laced with secrets that I didn't know about.

I once loved the coast. I loved running on the shore, my swimmer bottoms filled with wet sand from the surf. I even loved getting smacked down by the waves, I have this particular memory of being knocked down by the water, and tumbling towards the sand. A part of me thought I might die, then I felt something catch me. My hand was grasped around an ankle that belonged to my pop, who would pull me to the surface and back into the sun. I was gasping for air, but I realised I was safe again. The saltwater began falling from my tiny eyelids as I looked up to see my pop's face covered in partially rubbed-in sunscreen and white or blue zinc lining his lips. Behind him, I would see my nana in her fancy swimming costume, paddling her feet in the shallows, the sound of my siblings splashing around in the waves pulling my attention back to where I wanted to be. I would be let go again to chase them into the deep end. It was slightly scary, but somehow in the wild sea, I knew I would be safe because I had my guardians waiting on the sand for me. When it got too deep, my mum or dad would be there to hold me above the water; I felt almost weightless in their arms, my aunty encouraging me to dive under the waves myself. I would watch her descend beneath the rolling surf and emerge on the other side from my mum's arms. The summers were a family affair, an event that I never thought would end, one that I thought I would always have.

In my dark house, I watch the water become angry, dangerous, a sea far from the one I once knew. I shiver as I think about facing the large waves, knowing that I may never come out alive this time, that I won't be able to fight away the sea monsters that lay beneath the surface. I reach for the blinds and pull them shut, blocking out the sunshine portrait of a summer's day. I now face the dim-lit room behind me – we need to get a better light bulb for this room. I pull out my phone to make a note of it. I also make a note to tell Mum to bring her vacuum down next time, the smell of dust thick in the air, and as I walk into the hallway, I see our family's memories caked onto the walls. I stop in front of the photo of me, my siblings and our grandparents. When this photo was taken, I never would have thought that one day it would be the only way to see my grandparent's faces, slightly distorted by the photo paper and locked behind glass to keep the memory from rotting away. Before I walked into this house, I thought I wouldn't feel a difference, that it would still feel the same as when he was alive. I thought this because everything was left untouched – his clothes were still hanging in his wardrobe, the kettle still full of water from when he last boiled it. But as soon as I pulled into the driveway, it felt like a foreign place I'd never been to before, certainly not a place that my loved ones once lived. It feels wrong to be here without him, to not hear his heavy footsteps come down the hallway or his voice beaming throughout the house trying to get my mum's attention. It was strange to not hear his breathing machine hum; I didn't realise I had gotten used to it in the short time he had it. Now everything was just quiet, still, finished. I make my way past my mum in the kitchen, organising paperwork with my dad, sorting out the business side of the end of life.

Mum's eyes are puffy from crying and tired from doing this once again. What was it now, number five? We should get this funeral for free, right?

I stay out of their way and find myself on the front balcony. I take my seat on the closest chair, the cushion inviting me to take a break; I wiggle a bit to find a moment of rest. I watch people walk past, I recognise a few faces and a man my pop would always wave to, I brace for his voice to call to the man 'Hey Mate, how are ya?', but as I close my eyes waiting, it doesn't come. When I open them, a few tears rest on the brim of my eye line, but I brush them away with my finger. The man was now gone and the street was quiet, left to my shocked mind, my tired heart and my disbelieving brain. In the corner of my eye, for a moment, I thought I saw him sitting on his chair closest to the window, his legs outstretched and crossed at the ankles. I swing towards the vision; the memory is mistaken for reality, dissipating as I'm met with an empty chair with his cap sitting in his spot. Is this normal? Memories taking human form and tricking your grieving heart into thinking everything's okay. That my pop is still sitting there in his denim shorts and jumper, sandals on his feet and yesterday's paper in his hand. I can still hear him complaining about football and the smell of his hair gel; it feels like if I reach out hard enough and wish until my heart starts bleeding, he will be here. But alas, I'm met with thin air.

'I'm going for a walk,' I yell to my parents in the kitchen, throwing the door open and walking into the street, my face thick with tears and anger boiling in my blood. I make my way down the quiet road – I don't even know where I'm going, but I'm determined to outrun this feeling. After this many losses, you'd think I'd understand how these moments would feel, but instead every time these things happen, it gets worse, and I get weaker. Not only am I sad now, I'm just left with anger and wanting to throw hands with God himself. People who come to the funerals, the wakes, who visit with food or send cards always say that God is watching over us and that the loved ones we lost are at peace with God or in whatever afterlife they believe in. But in this moment of storming away from the house, I feel the most alone I've ever felt; I feel like I have a target on my back that God, the universe, or whoever keeps shooting at.

I pass the local bowling club and turn right towards the train station, passing the flag they've flown for my pop. I pull my attention away from it and power walk towards the platform. When I make it there, I take a seat in the empty station, only now realising my feet are bare. I curl them up under my crossed legs and just focus on breathing, on not bursting into flames.

I try to get my racing mind back to reality, but it's distraught, replaying the last time I saw my pop. Believe it or not, it was five weeks ago at my grandad's funeral. That moment of grief was my last memory of my pop. Now, if I get into the last time I saw my grandad, I wouldn't be able to say it because, for the life of me, I can't remember, and that makes me want to smack my head against the pavement right where it says, 'STAY BEHIND THE YELLOW LINE'. As I spiral inwards, I clock a station worker sweeping the platform staring at me. He looks like he's wondering if he should call their small-town police to come and rescue me, he even has his phone in his hands, but he puts it away when he sees that I'm staring at him and walks back to the storage room. I must have scared him. I must look like a wreck.

I stand up and leave the station before the worker comes back out. I walk the streets thinking the same things repeatedly until the sun starts falling from the sky behind the horizon. When I come back to my body, I'm facing the ocean with my feet sunken into the sand. I push my feet through it, the grains slipping through my toes and the heat from the fiery sand smothering my skin. I watch the sand move beneath me, turning from dry particles to wet soupy sand. I let the waves wash over my feet like I'd watched my nana do years ago before dementia got to her, and I remember a few years later running along the shore with my baby cousin, my mum, and my aunty before the cancer took her away from us. Our shadows distorted in the water as we splashed it at each other; for a moment, I believed she'd make it out of that hell on earth alive. Once again, I was still wrong, much like when my grandmother was admitted to the hospital and the fatal straw was already pulled. The anger within my blood boils over and is now flooding my body.

'You're a naive idiot,' I whisper to myself as I wade into the water, the saltwater splashing against my clothes until they're completely soaked. On the horizon, I see a big wave brewing; I brace myself as

I hurtle forward, running through the water to come head-on with it as happy childhood memories come whooshing past me. I run faster, hot tears falling from my eyes and mixing with the cool sea. As I dive headfirst into the big wave, I hear a phantom voice shout 'Dot!' and then my vision submerges in the tide. I'm pulled further under, being tossed around and thrown back towards the shore. I push up towards the surface, but I'm met with another wave smacking against my head, pushing me back down, my hair plastering to my face, my lungs starting to burn. I reach out into the salty darkness, but there's more of nothing, water washing between my fingers; I'm alone, an adult stuck in the tide with nobody to save her.

When I stop fighting against the tide, I find myself being slammed onto the wet, hard sand. My back smacking against the ground, pushing the seawater out of my lungs. I lay on the shore breathing in the air I longed for, soaked, water rushing over my body, very much alive. I watch the clouds move along the blue sky, parting to let the remaining sun come through like a beam from the heavens. I lay there wondering if the ones we love become our guardian angels when they die. Like the man with the Tupperware container. I engorge myself on the hope that my lost loved ones aren't so lost to me after all. We will always be connected by a thin piece of what was.

Ma or the Final Word of Harper

Grant Hawkes

There were some muted colours that floated in front of Harper. Soundless. All feather-edged and of a remote reality, one where form was nascent while the conscious mind observed it developing. Tinnitus sat like a needle sideways in the cradle of the man's occipital bone, seemed to bring all sound from all time to a singularity. Allowed the silence depth and breadth, allowed the space profundity. The synapse is the space between cells across which information passes.

Creation is the sum of theory, but the manifest laws go on forming, writing, spelling in new ways, so creation must always be submissive to theory, plastic to the idea that it may exist or that now it must.

Muted colours floated. They could be named by what they didn't contain, by what absence they held. All things hold absence. All things are in relation to that which is around them. To say this is not, is to say this is. Soundless. Tinnitus. Creation. Harper reached over with habitual blind proprioception and lifted up his spectacles off the bedside with his thumb under the bridge. He opened the wire arms, exhaled through his nose, then rested his clasped hands on his knees so the lenses were dormant and directed toward him.

(Sartre) I suddenly realised that anyone could be anything.

An extension added already to the theory so Harper felt atomised. Blurred back to a nascent orb, to the floating muted colours, to creation. He denied that they made a certain sense about him. Intentional distraction made him aware of his own acrid odour, his scent of bed-sweat rose like thought up into the air that had previously been odourless.

Odourless. The horror of being odourless. I am.

To say this is not, is to say this is. I am not. Not I am. At a short distance the feather-edged colours held together patient, enduring. There was no other, yet Harper still formed thoughts in dialogue:

Do you ever get the sense that you can see yourself in everyone else? As if they're just a manifestation of another you? A reconfigured you from the same elements just placed slightly obliquely to your own life.

He rolled the arms of his spectacles through his thumbs and forefingers so they rose and settled slowly. He hung his head towards them as if beckoned, then placed them on his face and lifted his head with his eyes closed. Harper sat there in a dark space. Tinnitus. He tapped out iambs on the surface of the bedside with the knuckle of his bent pinkie finger. The tinnitus threatened to cease while thought poured into the vacuum, then trailed off completely.

Prose is the refusal of poetry, the refusal to commit to pattern, to rhythm, to beat. A betrayal of preverbal naturalness.

He removed his spectacles with his left hand and pinched sleep out of his eyes with his right. He held the cupped hand over his nose and mouth. He inhaled through his nose and exhaled out in lengthened cadence. The treble to his heart's bass that he knew in this state would be around forty-eight beats per minute. Bradycardia. The sensation was delicate in his chest, but discernible.

I am. Breath, beat, bradycardia.

The fuller breath he took through his mouth brought the taste of sweat, again, off his palm. When he arched his neck, his cervical vertebrae made a disconcerting fluid creak he could hear internally. He then turned his head obliquely and raised his chin. He wouldn't know his own resemblance here to the silhouetted figure in Cignaroli's *Death of Socrates*, though his body held Socrates' same aspect by virtue of some subordinate memory. Harper's left hand still held his spectacles, lying dormant in the operative yet nether harbourage of the mind that holds in obscurity menial awareness until external forces call for it. His right hand drops to his shoulder and presses fingers into the meaty trapezius muscle, or was it the buried splenius cervicis that he sought to alleviate? Astereognosis. He understood the misapplication of the disorder yet allowed the abstract exchange as his fingers pressed about his back as if into a sculptural substance, he considered his own body as an object that he could not discern.

I am not.

The muted colours, tinnitus, creation, iamb, I am, beat, beat, breath, bradycardia, the death of Socrates, astereognosis, I am not. His heart beat at greater depth, allowed profundity. The muted colours would make sense, the spectacles turned in his left hand by one arm like a weathervane. Harper's bare feet had been on the timber floor, yet only now as awareness shed dormancy did he realise they were cold. The cold feet of Cignaroli's Socrates.

I suddenly realised that anyone could be anything. (Had I remembered that right?)

Harper braced himself then stood. The wall should be there and it was and it was white and it was cool under his spidered hand. His faintness spun as if a weighted marble the size of a man's brain rolled the internal curvature of his cranium until the marble dissipated like forgetting, like memory, then he slid his hand down the wall and away. The hand dropped by his side to be called upon later, then was raised immediately to pinch the other arm of his spectacles to balance the motion of placing them on his face. The feather-edged colours all lay certain and conspicuous about him as objects with unobscured meaning, no longer muted. Harper left the bedroom where he'd slept, went with his beating heart.

A sudden blow at the door, then rapping and rapping. Harper pressed hard on his temples, pushed his fingers up through his hair so they felt feathered. The space within the cranium bone made the man.

間 *(Ma).*

The word uttered like a regressive cry for help. Light poured into the room through two windows. It all poured in. And none left, never brimmed or spilt from the room. The walls and the roof formed the room, yet the light was the room's essence. The space in-between, this was *Ma*. The silence between notes, the gap between the artist's intention and what of themselves they reveal, the time between action and consequence.

Ma. Ma.

I chased down to Daphne's garden
Wet in the white rush
Bay leaves billowed on the bush
Then tore themselves free
Free, unfettered in the wind

On ma the bay leaves sailed
Escaped sweet bay

Ma is made up of the kanji 門 (*mon*) meaning gate or door and 日 (*hi*) meaning sun or daytime. 日 can also mean to fuck in Mandarin. Harper dug his hand back into his shoulder. The pain tempered by force as in equal measure force inflicts pain. He wouldn't know he traced the fingernail lacerations across his naked back writ there like cuneiform.

The great wings beating still
Beating,
Still,
Beating,
Still
At the door the rapping beats
Ma-beating-ma, Beating-ma
Still. Ma. Still.

There are voices that he doesn't register, as if they were never intended for him. In the sounds somewhere are new accents ascribed by diacritics that he knows not their nuance. Harper moves towards the window so now his chest is wholly in the sunlight. His chest is tanned, an organ changed, the sunlight stored within him, but never does it spill. His sinewy upper limbs have a definition that enables the imagination to believe they once held other form, other semblances. The exposed arm of Socrates. Astereognosis. The skin pulled tight over another being where there were once wings. He feels the sunlight draw the ache off him, runs his palm up his long neck, pulls the back of his skull into a bow that resembles humility or shame or grace.

They're just a manifestation of another you.
Who was she?
She was you.

Leap the rupture
Her rupture / Your rapture.
Our Helen

Satkāryavāda. Inherent in all cause is the effect prior to its origin. I am always. I am not between beats, *ma*, I am, iambic, beat, bradycardia, I am not, astereognosis, Helen, always our Helen. Always this thought, the epiphenomenon of this poem kept quiet:

Leap the rupture
Her rupture / Your rapture.
Our Helen

To keep quiet is not an admission of guilt or shame or humility. Along the length of the swan's neck, there was time enough to cut off its head. *Before the indifferent beak could let her drop.* The gate it beat, it beat. Harper threw his hand from his head as if thought were born there and could be expelled in simple kinetic fashion. Him, the space within the cranium bone. Helen always, Helen the effect and consequence, Helen the cause. He turned his back to the light so the nail indentations turned in dark crescents, shaded bruises darkened like mares on the moon. White tails of comets in scratches. Harper, his name between the dead beats on the door. *Ma.* He stepped toward the door, the sweated skin of each foot caught in the slightest stickiness on the floorboards, two fingers on his radial artery.

But your heart beat beat beat beat against the asphalt
The body a drum

The cry and the quiver, the shiver, the giver
The fever of,
was it love that beat?
Her rupture / Your rapture

Before him pierced the singularity of light through the peephole. More light. Harper, Harper, his name in *ma* between the beats. Inherent always in the door was the beating upon it, the bellowed vibration of his name against it. Through Harper surged the night, the history of the night, this morning always held the cause of the night. *Ma*, the Cappadocian moon goddess, she was struck there in the dark sky, full and unashamed like a pervert. Goddess to the Anatolian lunar god, Mēn. *Ma*, Harper, Mēn, just sounds, beat, beat, beat, an auditory agnosia that could signify anything. The sound and the fury of the door that beat and beat. Sīn was the Babylonian god of the moon. Sīn, just sound and fury. There was Harper with her, beneath them all. Arched over her like a fermata, the death in-between heartbeats. *But feel the strange heart beating where it lies?*

Leda I loved your beauty.

Beauty, that *incidental product of some process, that has no effects of its own.* Helen. Upon the door, Harper beat back in Alexandrine metre with medial caesura. *Ma.* Fermata in the beat like the nail marks writ across his back. He put his eye to the peephole in every expectation to see a brace of bluecoats, but it was not policemen that beat. The fisheye enlarged the figure's dark, hulking, pulsing state. Harper's pulse raced in realisation, synchronised now to the figure's heaving shoulders. Brother, father, bridegroom, it didn't matter. Time paused like a curse, *fermata*, the snapped horsehair that held the sword of Damocles. *Ma.* The brother saw the shade pass across the lit peephole like the shadow of the earth eclipsing the moon and blew a hole right through the door. All the light poured in. He wouldn't wait to assess what had become, what was personality to him. Inherent always in the dead body of Harper was his crime; that much the shooter already knew.

To be aware of *ma*, there must be an end or a vessel either actual or abstract. When the vessel is broken there is no *ma*.

The cranium was broken and all the light poured in.

Extracts

Leda and the Swan – W.B. Yeats

- *The great wings beating still*
- *Before the indifferent beak could let her drop.*
- *But feel the strange heart beating where it lies?*

Epiphenomenon – Simon Blackburn, *The Oxford Dictionary of Philosophy*

- *… incidental product of some process, that has no effects of its own.*

A City in Sleep

Jemima Rice

At the tumbling edge of the sea,
built over but bare
in a thin, net-like truth,
its pulse flaps into me as I breathe
stretching out
becoming part of the blood in my organs
as I exhale, tethered.

I cringe at this way we describe –
our visions of landscapes always
clung round our bodies
and off-beat minds;
a papier-mâché of the soul.

For every building I see
it is catching myself in the glass
that prompts words;

wandering stunted monoliths
twice rebuilt
and twice deserted,
I note when the veins between them
are slowly reclaimed
but in doing so, sometimes,
forget the earth.

People are blood
amidst concrete and slivers of cloud,
yet nowadays I watch
these buildings stand alone.

This city in the midst
of a triple heart bypass;
veins emptied of the fluid
from which they once drew life –

still bracing for us
but melding with the deepening soil;
blurring in,
becoming old.

We're no longer bodies to buildings,
but an indiscriminate hum –
a fleeting flash of cars,
then gone.

Meanwhile the skyline
emerges like a silent canopy –
wondrous thing whose heart we can't control,
creature whose secrets
we no longer know,

hot air balloon that has
cut all tethers to its grass-bound gods;
now soldered to sky
and whispering
to sky alone.

Has it swallowed all the
umbrellas and cups,
computers, jackets
left carelessly as offerings
in offices
and squares?

All I know is,
it's looking across the water
with a spirit that splays out
as air reaches into my throat:

this thing we like to think
is a corpse without us
is in fact a brushstroke
of memory
bleeding on eternal page,

rooted down by the sun
and ever-falling leaves,
bulging with all the human crumbs
it just ate.

I see in it – almost –
the silken glint of life;

the web of existence
weaving
while we wait.

Collaborating During COVID-19

A Reflection on Our Interconnection With Trees

Diana Chester and Ann Jyothis Raj

> For a seed to achieve its greatest expression it must come completely undone. The shell cracks, its insides come out and everything changes. To someone who doesn't understand growth it would look like complete destruction.
>
> Cynthia Ocelli

The Trees of Afghanistan Project is a collaboration between environmentalist and artist Ann Jyothis Raj, and sound studies scholar and artist Diana Chester.

We began this project in 2019 and have spent much of 2020 trying to navigate the complexities of creative collaborations over distance during the pandemic. In this article we will discuss the process of collaborating this year and highlight some challenges we have experienced. COVID-19 has created separation, isolation and loneliness for many, including us, and it has impacted our practice and ability to collaborate. We are both women who are currently living alone because of the pandemic. Ann has worked between Afghanistan, The Netherlands, Hungary and India this year, while Diana has been based in Sydney, Australia where the international border has been closed. The international nature of our collaboration, proximity to Afghanistan, the geography where the research is based, and shifting creative mediums and output plans for the project have led to redrawing timelines, challenging time zone negotiations and general difficulties we could not have anticipated when we began. By looking at the experience of trees and what we know of their life and communication, we will attempt to communicate the challenges we have faced this year through this lens of trees. We have held close the idea Ocelli communicates, that while what many of us went through in 2020 may have looked like complete destruction, it was in fact complete transformation.

Isolation

Due to the pandemic, many of us have had to remain in the same place for long periods of time without the mobility we are used to. Diana, who typically travels for research, has been unable to leave Australia for this project and others. This is similar to trees, except a tree often remains in one place its entire life. Some of us have lost loved ones and many of us have experienced major disruptions to our daily lives, social networks and our daily activities. We asked ourselves what we can learn from looking at how trees navigate their lack of mobility, in some cases their movement from place to place, and how this can shape our understanding of our own circumstances.

Trees do better when they are together, in a forest or the woods. Ecologist Suzanne Simard has shown how trees use a network of soil fungi to communicate through underground root networks and rely on their interconnected nature for support and survival.[1] We also know that when a plant is moved from one pot to another it takes time to acclimatise to the nutrients and new environment. Humans require these same support networks and the same adjustment to new environments though we may not always give ourselves the permission, the time or the space for this. People sometimes place trees ornamentally in relative isolation, for example in pots in their homes or on terraces, these trees become entirely dependent on the person to survive, they may even shrivel and 'die' but life is still within them invisible to us. In this same way the isolation many of us have experienced due to lockdowns or distance from loved ones may contribute to feelings that we are not receiving the type of nourishment, tactility or support we need to feel alive and present. What happens to us when we are distressed?

---

1   Toomey 2016.

Young trees inside a home in the northern part of Herat province, in Afghanistan. These trees are almost cocooned within the home of this family, sheltered and cared for by each of the humans living in this earthen house.

Initially this project was envisioned as an in-person exhibition, a space where visitors could roam within a room filled with visual, sonic and text-based narratives about the trees of Afghanistan. The exhibit would include stories and memories of trees as told by Afghan people, how they relate to trees, and stories about the space trees take up in their lives. We realised around April that we were going to need to move from an in-person exhibition to something virtually accessible. When we started thinking through the possibilities it led to several interesting outcomes. The first is that we began working with a 3D concept artist, Kushaan Chavda, who used a number of photos from one Chinar tree to create a highly detailed 3D visualisation that can be projected like a hologram in a space or shared virtually. This was a bridge for us, allowing us to think about the physical and tactile aspects of trees in a virtual space. Kushaan's model highlights each knot and ridge in the tree's bark, so that it feels as though you can reach out and feel the Chinar. This led us to want to focus more on the tactile than the virtual, leading to the development of physical objects and practices that happened by hand rather than our initially conceived computer-based manipulations and expressions. Perhaps this move to the tactile was aided by the distance we felt in our daily lives from human touch and the realisation we would need to take this project into a non-tactile environment. Ann shifted her focus to embroidery of trees from the project which allowed her to be physically present with the project materials. Her logic was that all materials come from the earth in one way or another. Even synthetic materials are made from chemicals and materials that come from the earth. When we are so isolated and working over distance it can be complicated and confusing to understand the circumstances in which we are all existing, which can cause an unmooring to occur. This focus on the tactile provided a grounding force.

Tree of life and its invisible narrative(s)

Ecologist Suzanne Simard has warned us that threats like clear-cutting and climate change could disrupt the critical underground networks that trees and plants rely so heavily on.[2] But what does this mean for trees in war-torn Afghanistan?

While working in Afghanistan, a country suffering from decades of war and conflict, Ann frequently contemplated the nature of human narrative, especially its impact on our own growth, life and death. When you meet someone in Kabul, you'd never guess that they went through years of political instability and war, or that they may have lost a dear one. The trending news about Afghanistan is about conflict and death, with rare glimpses into the lives lived or the lives lost. Can you comprehend an eighty-year-old tree? It takes twenty to fifty years to grow from seed to full adult and it is gone in an instant when it is chopped down. A living, breathing being is gone. Is this like the human experience?

We borrow everything we need to survive from the earth, as do trees. If a tree is allowed to die in the forest, there is a process it goes through. It passes on the data it has to the other trees and then it dies nourishing the soil as it goes. Can we say the same for human beings? Do our ceremonial actions of cremation and burial support our return to the earth in the same way as trees?

Although we are not alone in expressing or perceiving the metaphor of a tree in our lived experience, who indeed understands trees? Who celebrates their life and learns their secrets, and who mourns their death? We asked these questions of the trees in Kabul, which is how the Trees Project began.

During the lockdown, Ann was happy to be 'stuck' in her hometown, in Kerala, India. Through the months of lockdown, she reconnected with the trees on her family's farm that had witnessed the lives of the family over a century. These trees surrounded the space where her mother and later Ann herself ran barefoot. One of the oldest trees on the property is the Anjili Chakka tree, the Wild Jack Fruit of Kerala. One evening before departing India, Ann went up to the terrace to take a good look at all the trees, to thank them and bid them farewell.

My eyes gazed toward the beloved Anjili tree, my eyes were fixed on it, I wondered what it would tell me if I could speak with it,

---

2   Simard 2010.

Trees standing tall in the middle of Kabul city. Cedar is abundant in Afghanistan and below the fir and cedar lines, oak, walnut, alder, ash, and juniper trees can be found. The trees in Kabul stand testimony to the juxtaposition of 'normal life' and the days when the city reverberated with bomb blasts and gunfights. War and conflict is tremendously destructive, not only in terms of its effects on human populations and the cities in which they live. There are many voiceless witnesses and casualties of this war, including the trees pictured here.

> I hoped that it felt my love. Suddenly, I found myself in tears, it felt as though the tree was bidding me farewell too, somehow I knew I would never see it again.

A few months later, her family informed her that they would be cutting down the tree as it would fetch a few thousand dollars as lumber.

Perhaps it is a blessing that trees don't speak human languages. Our collective use and skills of linear language systems may not have the capacity or depth needed to hold the information, poetry or story of a single tree, let alone an entire forest. Those of us who perceive beyond language and who study trees may be able to say more, but it may only be one leaf from an unwritten book about a tree. The Trees

Tree rings can tell us how old the tree is, and what the weather was like during each year of the tree's life. I can't help but wonder if the trees that have survived across Afghanistan can tell us about their lives without being cut down to be investigated. This geometric pattern on the bark gives me pause to imagine how the sound frequencies may have translated onto the surface of the tree.

Project is one humble attempt to express some broken perceptions and assumptions about a few trees in Afghanistan.

Conclusion

The lockdown across the world has made us still, within the parameters of our chosen walls. What many of us went through in 2020 looked like complete destruction, but it was in fact complete transformation. We look toward trees as an example of how to live in a time that seems so chaotic. Let's conclude with a quote borrowed from Hermann Hesse's one-hundred-year-old love letter to trees:

> In their highest boughs the world rustles, their roots rest in infinity; but they do not lose themselves there, they struggle with all the force of their lives for one thing only: to fulfill themselves

according to their own laws . . . to represent themselves. Nothing is holier, nothing is more exemplary than a beautiful, strong tree.[3]

* * *

This article was originally published by the Sydney Environment Institute, 11 January 2021.

References

Popova, Maria (2012, 21 September). Hermann Hesse on What Trees Teach Us About Belonging and Life. *The Marginalian*. https://www.themarginalian.org/2012/09/21/hermann-hesse-trees/

Simard, Suzanne (2010). Climate Change and Variability. In Austin, Mary (ed.). *The Role of Mycorrhizas in Forest Soil Stability with Climate Change*, 292. Intechopen.

Toomey, Diane (2016, 1 September). Exploring How and Why Trees 'Talk' to Each Other. *Yale Environment 360*; Yale School of the Environment. https://e360.yale.edu/features/exploring_how_and_why_trees_talk_to_each_other

---

3   Popova 2012.

Mangrove Roots

Hannah Roux

Here, the mangroves grow. Here the plovers
softly shelter. Here, the roots are
raised and taut. Here, the sea-salt grows
tough on their skin. Here, we sought
a pleasure – here it lies discarded
raised in roots, the carded fish
breathe in bursts of bubbles. The breaths
you took beneath the mangrove trees
were quick and sharp as salt. Your hair
rose up, distended in the water,
all your bones, displayed and ribbed
by coral, looked like they once did
in the garden where the mangrove roots
divided one in two. The sea
breathes in and out, the streams
turn fresh to salt, although
the sea is never full, the roots
are never sated, always thirst
for air as if for water. Stay here
with me, where the mangroves grow
the shy plovers shelter, where the roots
encase us in their ribs. We sought
a pleasure here, it lies suspended
salt-like and aerial. Fish eat at it,
like grass. Your hair floats distended

by water like the plovers. Here,
it is here the roots are.

Becoming Indigenous

Future Cities as a Network of Waterholes Connected by Songlines

Steven Liaros

According to Isaac Murdoch, an elder from the Serpent River First Nation in Canada, the process of reconciliation with First Nations people begins when we reconcile with the land.[1] This is a call for all of us to become indigenous – to find our connection to Country, to feel at home on, and to love and respect, the land upon which we live.

Yet there are many obstacles. How do we find our connection to this Country from the air-conditioned comfort of urban life? For people who have come from other parts of the world, how do they connect with this continent? What about their descendants, like myself, who feel the tension between their ancestral culture and the Australian culture? Most importantly, has the dominant Anglo-Celtic culture assimilated itself with the land upon which the idea of Australia has been constructed?

Early European colonisers brought with them their European seasons, which do not align with the actual seasonal changes on this continent. Australian Indigenous weather knowledge is far more nuanced, with different calendars in various parts of the continent, each determined by local conditions. In Nyoongar Country, in the southwest of the continent, there are six seasons. In Yirrganydji Country in the northeast, north of Cairns, there are two major seasons, Wet and Dry, divided into five minor seasons. To truly integrate with these environments, it is necessary to observe and understand the land upon which we live locally – not just with respect to the changes in weather but also how other species respond to these changes.

---

1   Murdoch 2016.

Political economy of Indigenous Australians

There is an abundance of evidence regarding the complex political and economic life of First Australians in the journals and diaries of the early European settlers. Bruce Pascoe synthesises much of this evidence in his 2018 work *Dark Emu: Aboriginal Australia and the Birth of Agriculture*:

> as I read these early journals, I came across repeated references to people building dams and wells; planting, irrigating, and harvesting seed; preserving the surplus and storing it in houses, sheds, or secure vessels; and creating elaborate cemeteries and manipulating the landscape ...[2]

First Australians designed this economic activity through a deep understanding of the cycles of life in their local environment, which then informed the many systems of land management and community governance. In *The Biggest Estate on Earth: How Aborigines Made Australia*, Bill Gammage describes how hundreds of different cultures and languages across the continent were bound together by a common worldview:

> The Dreaming and its practices made the continent a single estate ...
>
> There was no wilderness. The Law ... compelled people to care for all their country ... an uncertain climate and nature's restless cycles demanded [a] myriad practices shaped and varied by local conditions. Management was active not passive, alert to season and circumstance, committed to a balance of life.
>
> ... Means were local, ends were universal. Successfully managing such diverse material was an impressive achievement; making from it a single estate was a breathtaking leap of imagination.[3]

---

2   Pascoe 2018, 1.
3   Gammage 2011, 2.

This is an example of plurality and diversity bound together by a common narrative. Local communities were autonomous, while also being respectful of the autonomy of their neighbours. There was no central government enforcing its views over the entire continent, but a network of societies all choosing to be responsible for their part of the country and their local community. Borders followed natural bioregional boundaries, so the law varied from one jurisdiction to another because the ecosystems in different bioregions functioned differently.

For Indigenous Australians, the land teaches people the law. Law is based on understanding and managing the land to ensure an abundance of life. To learn from the land, it is necessary for each community to align works and activities with local natural systems. Systems can vary from place to place but the objective is the same everywhere: to create abundance. Unlike capitalist objectives of endless extraction from nature and endless work for people to power endless economic growth, the objective of Indigenous communities is to create an abundance of food, minimise work and maximise play and ceremony.

A network of waterholes connected by songlines

In the arid parts of this continent, Indigenous communities navigated the landscape along songlines that connected one waterhole to the next. Uluru was a spiritual centre because it was a permanent waterhole and so provided a wide array of foods, as well as shade and shelter. It therefore became a place for teaching, learning and ceremony. The landscape was perceived as a network of waterholes connected by songlines – also called storylines or dreaming tracks. The songs referenced features in the landscape, thus acting as a system of navigation, guiding the singer through the land. Therefore, although there were hundreds of autonomous societies, they were all nevertheless connected into a network through trade and other activities.

Imagining the landscape as a network of waterholes connected by songlines offers an ideal framework upon which to build future human settlements. Rather than creating evermore congested, polluted and unaffordable cities, while simultaneously depriving rural townships of resources and infrastructure, perhaps we could let go of the coastline and distribute human settlements more evenly across the landscape. Each settlement would be a waterhole that supports a discrete community. That community would be responsible for managing the land, ecosystems and infrastructure in their locality to ensure these remain in balance and create an abundance of life.

Waterholes as integrated systems of energy, water, food and shelter

Small-scale renewable energy technology now makes the development of such new settlements possible. An energy micro-grid can power a water micro-grid, cycling water through the site via a chain of reservoirs and wetlands. This water cycle could then irrigate a diverse regenerative agricultural system. All these systems would be tailored to the geographic and climatic conditions of each locality, integrated and optimised to minimise energy demand.

Food-water-energy infrastructure ecosystems would be enmeshed around passively designed co-living and co-working spaces, allowing a discrete community to manage the systems that provide their basic needs. They would manage their shelters while harvesting, storing and distributing food, water and energy within their local catchment. The energy micro-grid could also power a fleet of shared electric vehicles, also offering the charging infrastructure for passing travellers.

Scale and complexity would be achieved through the organic networking between settlements rather than growing the population of one settlement. The virtual connectivity of the internet allows us to form a globally connected estate, with a wide diversity of cultures.

The wisdom of relational philosophy

According to academics Mary Graham – a Kombumerri person from the Gold Coast area – and Irene Watson – who belongs to the Tanganekald, Meintangk Boandik First Nations Peoples, of the Coorong in South Australia – the Indigenous worldview is fundamentally different from the Western worldview and is based on a deep appreciation of relationships.[4] Graham suggests that there are two dimensions to this relational philosophy. The principal relationship is between people and the land, the secondary relationship is between the people themselves. This guarantees that the land is the source of the law, rather than the land being subjected to laws created by people. The pre-eminence of the land over social relationships, has broad implications for our understanding of the world around us.

Some of these implications[5] are noted by Watson in *Raw Law: Aboriginal Peoples, Colonialism and International Law*. Binaries, contradictions and competitions become opportunities to find useful relationships in the zone of conflict. When we are present in the landscape and become aware of the cycles of life, time itself becomes cyclical.[6] The past and future diminish as our awareness of the present expands. The present becomes a point in a repeating cycle of life that clarifies the past and defines expectations for the future.

Logical thinking – with its assumptions and consequent externalities – becomes systems thinking. Hierarchical and centralised systems, become egalitarian and distributed governance systems based on community consensus. Ownership and control of the land becomes responsibility for stewardship.

New stories for navigating life and the land

Perhaps the most powerful aspect of the Indigenous worldview is the acknowledgement that we navigate both the land and life with songs and stories. Our current prevailing story is that 'Jobs and Growth' will bring prosperity to all. This is so embedded in our cultural worldview that it is almost impossible to question it. Yet this narrative is destroying both the people it is intended to support and the ecosystems and climate upon which we all depend.

There is a need for new narratives, new songs to guide us. Perhaps the most important is the story of a transition from a linear to a circular economy – that is, from an endless growth narrative to one

---

4   Graham and Maloney, 2019, 389.
5   Watson 2015, 14.
6   See also Abram 1997, 183.

that acknowledges the natural cycles of growth, decay, death and regeneration. Another is the transition from an extractive to a regenerative mindset. Rather than just taking what we can, how can we give more than we take? This is the circle of life. Rather than always aspiring for more, how do we seek moderation, harmony and balance? How do we think beyond our bubbles or silos, and see the world more holistically as a system? Unaffordable housing, climate change, plastic pollution, inequality, droughts, floods, loneliness, stress, traffic congestion, food insecurity, no free time – these are all symptoms of a systemic problem. We solve all these problems together only by thinking in systems and creating a new system.

The stories we live by guide the work that we do and so shape the human settlements that we create. The transition from hierarchical social structures to egalitarian ones will be reflected in the changing pattern of human settlements from highly centralised cities that dominate the land and its people, to a distributed network of settlements. This change will also be reflected in a change in lifestyle. From being permanently settled in a home and anchored to a job, we would instead be free to travel, explore and find the place and people we connect with, who help us be our best and who value our unique contribution. We would also be free to find our own balance between the mobile, nomadic life and the settled life.

As we create the songs that guide our transition – from linear to circular, from extractive to regenerative, from silos to systems and from centralised to distributed – perhaps we might also reframe the founding Story of Western societies. Certain truths are self-evident: that we are all created equal, and that we are all endowed with certain inalienable rights and responsibilities. Life, Liberty and the pursuit of Happiness could be understood as a responsibility to enhance the land and make it viable for an abundance of *all* life. Living amongst this abundance of life would liberate us from unnecessary work and give us all the time and space for the pursuit of Happiness.

* * *

This article was originally published by the Sydney Environment Institute, 6 June 2019. Significant changes and additions have been made.

References:

Abram, David (1997). *The Spell of the Sensuous: Perception and Language in a More-than-human World* (2nd ed.). New York: Vintage Books.

Australian Bureau of Meteorology (n.d.). *Indigenous Weather Knowledge.* http://www.bom.gov.au/iwk/

Gammage, Bill (2011). *The Biggest Estate on Earth: How Aborigines Made Australia.* Sydney: Allen & Unwin.

Graham, Mary, and Michelle Maloney (2019). Caring for Country and Rights of Nature in Australia: A Conversation between Earth Jurisprudence and Aboriginal Law and Ethics. In La Follette, Cameron and Chris Maser (Eds.). *Sustainability and the Rights of Nature in Practice*, 385–399. Boca Raton, FL: CRC Press.

Murdoch, Isaac (2016). *Reconciliation Begins with the Land.* https://www.youtube.com/watch?v=3pwHxmGU58U

Pascoe, Bruce (2018). *Dark Emu: Aboriginal Australia and the Birth of Agriculture* (2nd ed.). Broome: Magabala Books Aboriginal Corporation.

Watson, Irene (2015). *Raw Law: Aboriginal Peoples, Colonialism and International Law.* Oxford and New York: Routledge.

Being a Part and Apart
Fragility and Belonging in Wild Places

Claire Moser

16°08′59.0″S, 130°16′32.8″E

I drive through a muted pastel bushland, alone on a stony track, rough and hot. It is Judbarra National Park, Northern Territory, 12,882 square kilometres of scrub, where for millions of years beings have come and gone – boab, rock, sea, footprints, birds. Since, it has been trampled (even by the well-meaning), it became open-run cattle country; now grave or home to a few remnant wild Brahman and brumbies. I move slowly, a maximum speed of thirty kilometres per hour, in a stop-start progression along rocky 4WD tracks, assuming the lines of foreign dominance, yet knowing myself small, insignificant. A perfect speed to observe – stopping often, getting down on haunches, barefoot, to scrutinise tiny plants, or endless variety of rocks, or lizard tracks over sand. I see no one, and almost no creature, save a small, white-dappled falcon – it watches as I climb a jumbled rock-strewn hillside, so that I can observe the sweep of the escarpment and valley, a fraction of its own aerial view. I seek its secret pattern, worn by water, wind, fire, time. The breeze up here reminds me of the cool morning air that sometimes comes before a hot day back home, far away down south. Smell is supposed to be the strongest catalyst of memory, but this is more than smell, it is a feeling across the skin, and I'm back there, a child. I try to see with a child's eye, to feel with honesty this place.

16°47'33.7"S, 130°22'05.0"E

The hills are flat-topped, an expanse of pale slate-grey and green, patched with the dusty ochre and pink of the earth. I cannot see the track. Here are boabs, fat grey giants sitting quietly, leafless in the dry season, swimming in yellow grass seas. Some boabs are so ancient and knobbly they seem to be subsiding into the soil, with trunks almost spherical, crowned by a scraggly crop of branches, bone-grey and twisted. The trees look exhausted – or perhaps content? – rain-starved and fire-scarred, surrounded by a matting of vari-coloured leaf-fall in a rolling carpet. I can name very few species, but that does not stop them from being themselves. Large yellow-gold leaves are interspersed with smaller leaves of deep russet through purple and pink-mauve and terracotta, and the beige-grey-cream of gum leaves. Between flow eddies of palest yellow or mauve tinted grasses and spinifex, tall and thick in places, low and twisted elsewhere. The round blue-grey leaves of squat silver mallee release their scent, crowns blending into the blue of the sky. Bare, thin-limbed kapoks cluster in places, with their bright yellow blossoms and egg-shaped seedpods in place of all foliage. Long-dead hop-bush and acacia shrubs are wind-scalloped into leafless bundles, desiccated question marks dotting the land. My mind weaves through this seamless mass, where silence hangs lightly, and I cease to feel my own thoughts – they drift outwards from me, waning into quietude. After travelling through this country for several days, to emerge from the park into fenced cattle country is a shock – barrenness, shrubs eaten down to limbless stalks, eroded grey-dust cattle tracks starring out from water points and huge herds of sad looking beasts in the shadeless expanse.

17°24'51.8"S, 130°48'09.8"E

Here is another kind of place, a human place that confuses me, makes me feel ignorant, brings up an un-squashable shadow. This place is Daguragu. It is a remote community, a tiny satellite of tiny Kalkarinji, some way up the track. I didn't mean to come here, it was a wrong turn. I feel like an intruder. It is just two streets, a scattering of houses, worn-out, some graffiti, a mangy dog, calf and fat old goat in a crumbling one-swing playground, all surrounded by the rusting carcasses of a hundred-odd cars and 4WDs, disembowelled for parts, propped here and there on bricks where wheels are gone. An old Aboriginal man and woman sit on the concrete step of their verandah and watch me pass. A young man in a basketball singlet and cap walks down the dirt road ahead of me; I stop by him for directions, 'Nah mate, you gotta go back up the road a bit there, no shop 'ere'.

Where did the feeling of peace go? Why should I feel it only in a place that I think I understand, that accepts me, because it says nothing? But that is a fabrication – the bush is a living web, but it can feel for me no more than an ant, or the moon. And I do not understand it in any deep sense, though I think I can feel it. Daguragu is just a place for people to live, just a place for them to be. I am not judged. I am only watched.

17°28'22.0"S, 128°22'31.2"E

A beating sun and the final pages of *Desert Solitaire* brings questions. Is this a place of belonging? Do I belong? I wonder what kind of inescapable hypocrisy washes over my face, as I flee the swelter to sit in air-conditioned comfort on four wheels. Yet it is completely necessary to be here – a compulsion to go and see what's out beyond the borders, under the skin, to exist in this world. Then comes the compulsion to write it all down, to capture a little bit of this alterity. But to Aboriginal people, this land is not otherness. I linger in a state of contradiction as the invisible life of the bush continues on, indifferent. I do not know where I stand in this map, both a part and apart. As the hours pass, my questions recede over the spinifex covered hills, drawn down with the insect-bright flash of the setting sun in a molten amber haze. I hope I can remember this. And so I will travel onwards, into the future, to find places and moments all new and unique but which may be triggers for the memory of past places. But I am already here – the search for meaning dissipates, I cannot stay, but for the moment I can just *be*.

About the Contributors

Memi Adams

I enjoy creating illustrations and I am expanding my skills into graphic design. The artwork *Missing Piece* was designed in reference to the growing concern of the effects of technology on our relationships. The adverse effects of technology on connections between children and their parents has been voiced by many of the students that I teach who are as young as eight years old. I believe it is important to see the value of family connection and to learn to listen to each other's stories again. We won't ever regret spending time with our loved ones, and this has become even more treasured in a digital age.

Cherie Baird

I am a graduate of the University of Sydney, holding both a Master of Publishing and a Bachelor of Arts (English and Philosophy). In 2021, I was a winner of the inaugural Ultimo Prize for my poem 'Passer-By'. I had two poems published in the October 2019 issue of *The Wild Goose Literary e-Journal*, entitled 'Let's Pretend I Exist' and 'Celestial'. I also received a high commendation in the Dorothea Mackellar Poetry Awards for my poem 'Filing Cabinets'.

Dyone Bettega

I have recently completed a Bachelor of Medical Science (Anatomy and Histology) and have commenced honours study in Pathology. I am a member of the Elite Athlete Program (rowing) within the

University of Sydney and have represented the university and Australia in the Trans-Tasman Regatta in New Zealand (2016), Royal Canadian Henley (2017), U23 World Rowing Championships in Poznań, Poland (2018), World Rowing Cup III (2018), U23 World Rowing Championships in Sarasota, Florida (2019) as well as four Australian Boat Races (2016–2019) and was crew captain for three (2017–2019). I have been the Women's captain and Chair of the Events and Communications Sub-Committee at the University of Sydney Boat Club (SUBC) in 2016–2021. I am also a recent recipient of the Geoffrey White Scholarship for Medicine as well as the Bill Caldwell Scholarship (all-round) from St Andrew's College within the University of Sydney.

Abigail Bobkowski

I am a first-year English and Management student at the University of Sydney. I love anything to do with language, linguistics or the creative arts. My (very originally titled) piece, 'Networks' explores the limitations of isolationist thinking. I feel that an important element of life is realising that the world exists with you versus revolving around you, and that we have the opportunity to appreciate the complexity of relationships within our lives. The idea of coloured threads weaving a web between individuals came to me as soon as I heard the anthology's title, and the piece 'spun' off from there! I hope you enjoy the piece as much as I enjoyed making it!

Ellen Burke

I am a Geography and English graduate, living and writing on Dharawal, Wangal and Gadigal country. I currently tutor for the School of Geosciences at the University of Sydney, and also work on a flower farm.

Diana Chamma

I am a publishing industry professional with over eight years' experience across a variety of roles. I completed my undergraduate education in visual communication and a minor in literature in 2009 at the American University of Sharjah. In 2011, I finished a master's degree in literature and philosophy at the University of Sussex, Brighton, England. During my career, my main role was as an art director and a rights executive at the Kalimat Group based in the United Arab Emirates. I attended Bologna Children's Book Fair, New York's Children's Book Salon, Frankfurt, London, Beirut and São Paulo book fairs during my time at Kalimat. In 2021, I completed a Masters in Publishing degree at the University of Sydney and now work at the Australian Society of Authors. I am also a Creative Producer with Sweatshop: Western Sydney Literacy Movement.

Allen Chan

Simple – I write what I don't say.

Grace Cheng

I am a new and young writer, most defined by my Christian faith. I hope to continue to write honest and hopeful stories in the future.

Diana Chester

I am a sound studies scholar, multimedia artist, composer and educator. My work draws from sound studies, archival studies, and the ethnographic study of expressive culture in religious festivals and traditions. Currently my scholarly research includes three primary strands; the study of sound and culture focused on religion and the environment; the audio essay as a form of sonic scholarship and pedagogical innovation; and new artistic research methodologies and practices at the intersection of Spacialized media technologies and scientific research. I have recently completed my first book, a sonic exploration of the Islamic Call to Prayer, I am a lecturer in the Department of Media and Communications at the University of Sydney.

Sally Chik

I am published in *Australian Love Poems*, *Cordite Poetry Review*, *FourW* and more. I was lead poetry editor for three publications from the Sydney Arts Student Society: *1978*, *Zami* and *ARNA*. I have a Bachelor of Creative Arts (Hons) and Master of Information Studies. I work in the University of Sydney Library and like to wear cardigans.

Zoe Coles

I am a nineteen-year-old Arts student, identifying with she/her pronouns. I write and learn on the land of the Gadigal people of the Eora nation, where sovereignty was never ceded. My works include published pieces of the creative non-fiction, short story and cultural criticism form. Most of my time is spent reading, sitting on the beach or both at the same time, with favourite authors including Jia Tolentino, Sally Rooney, Rebecca Solnit and Ocean Vuong.

Wentao Dai

I am a third-year Design in Architecture student. As a beginner in photography, I carry my DSLR almost everywhere. I am passionate about street photography, enjoying the experience of capturing pedestrians' interaction with the city. Framing through the camera lens gives me the opportunity to explore the world from different angles. I continued with my photography practice at home during the recent lockdown to catch every little moment in my daily life.

Karen Davids

I am an avid geographer and writer. I enjoy long walks in nature, reading history books and sharing my experiences through poetry. My suite of poems explores the complex networks of emotions entangled in one's conscious mind; the piece attempts to reconcile with the experiences of bereavement, enlightenment and a reconnection to family. This concept was brought to light by my mother's decay following her diagnosis with Lewy body dementia; this experience propelled me to explore the extent to which the disease challenged, but also strengthened, my love for her.

Kiya Elphick

I am a Master of Publishing Student at the University of Sydney and am also a writer. I have previously been published by the University of Canberra in their 2018 anthology while I completed my bachelor's degree. I've wanted to write this story for a while but didn't have the courage to until now, and I'm so excited to have this amazing opportunity to share it with you all.

Tom Evans

I am in my first year of a Master of Publishing at the University of Sydney. Working to promote stories for others and reading as much as I can, I hope that I can share the joy of words with as many people as possible.

Janika Fernando

I am a first-year Law/Arts student, majoring in English literature at the University of Sydney. My short story, 'Where I Belong' focuses on the impact of the Sri Lankan Dream, to search for an opportune future in Australia, and the experience of my protagonist, Kiyoma, a Sri Lankan mother. Having grown up in Australia, my purpose was to use short fiction as a tool to empathise with the experiences of my mother. This is represented through Kiyoma's longing for home through culturally infused memories heavily contrasted with the independence found in Sydney, Australia. I hope my inclusion of fragmented poetry speaks to the interior uncertainty of immigrants following the Dream and their devastation upon their realisation that they cannot return home permanently. As an author, I am interested in writing culturally diverse stories and hope for my stories to become a source of hope, motivation and wisdom for readers.

Djuna Hallsworth

I completed my PhD in the Department of Gender and Cultural Studies at the University of Sydney in 2020 and have taught units in gender and media since 2018. After several years of rigorous study, I am enjoying the chance to slow down and pass the days by baking vegan snacks and chatting with my cats. With my thesis on track for publication as a monograph, I am focusing on writing prose fiction and poetry.

Dennis Haskell

I completed a Bachelor of Arts (Hons) and PhD at the University of Sydney and taught there until 1984, when I moved to Perth. I am the author of nine collections of poetry, the most recent *And Yet …* (WAPP 2020) and *Ahead of Us* (Fremantle Press 2016) plus fourteen volumes of literary scholarship and criticism. In 2015 I was made a Member of the Order of Australia for 'services to literature, particularly poetry, to education and to intercultural understanding'. My website is dennishaskell.com.au

Grant Hawkes

For the past fifteen years, I have travelled or been based in various parts of the world, during which time I have written collections of short stories, poems and novellas. I currently live in Sydney.

Xian Ho

I am in my third year at the University of Sydney, undertaking a combined Bachelor of Science in Immunology and Bachelor of Laws.

I enjoy writing prose and poetry in my spare time and have a weakness for chocolate strawberries, french fries and stairs. All my life, I've drawn comfort from the words of others that eloquently capture feelings I cannot express myself. I hope to strike the same connection and provide the same comfort to others through my writing.

Ann Jyothis Raj

I am an artist and development professional with a master's degree in Geographic Information Science for Development and Environment and a bachelor's in Environmental Studies, from Clark University and Mount Holyoke College respectively. I have worked in the non-profit sector for over fifteen years in various parts of the world. I was an educator at my alma mater, United World College of Mahindra as a Faculty of Science and Head of Project Based Learning. I currently live in India and am focusing on creative collaborations on the environment and nature.

Tahira Kale

I am a science student in my third year, but I have always found a home in art and creativity. Since I was a kid, you would always find me with a piece of paper folding intricate origami, painting complex miniature artworks on my nails or moulding a piece of clay into jewellery. Despite my hesitancy to pursue English after the HSC, solace was found in my academic life through the artistry of words. It's so simple yet unfathomable how a string of delicately placed letters can change a perspective, heart and soul. I hope that my poetry brings someone these transformative visions, and changes their realities.

Joshua Klarica

I am a writer from Sydney's Inner West, completing my Bachelor of Arts (Hons) in 2021. I write poetry and prose, and my work can be found across the internet or more recently in the journals *Riverbed*

Review, *Bluebottle Journal*, *Mantissa Poetry Review* and *Wild Court*. In 2020, I was the recipient of the Cosmo Davenport-Hines Poetry Prize.

Michael Kowalczyk-Barker

I am an alumnus of the University of Sydney, having graduated a decade ago with a Bachelor of Science degree with Honours (First Class) in Biological Sciences. In high school I wrote extensively and creatively, but soon put down the pen as life dragged me in other directions. I stumbled upon this anthology while browsing the Sydney Alumni Magazine this year, and thought I would give it a go. Luckily, I had two good sources of motivation: my sister Emilia, a current student (double majoring in Ancient History and Archaeology) and fantastic editor who helped me with smoothing the structure and catching those slippery punctuation errors, and the Sydney lockdown, which helped me to stay indoors.

Harold Legaspi

I am a poet writing in Darug land.

Steven Liaros

I am a strategic town planner and author of *Rethinking the City*. A polymath and futurist with expertise in civil engineering, town planning, environmental law and political economy, I am co-creating a new model for living in a connected network of regenerative villages.

Claire Moser

I completed Honours in English and Australian Literature at the University of Sydney in 2019. I am interested in how environmental issues and marginalised perspectives can be understood through the lens of literature, especially in the dominant global context of capitalism and instrumental valuing of science over the arts. My Honours research explored contemporary literature's representation of

Indigenous relationship to and perspectives on Country through an ecocritical and decolonial lens, centring on Ali Cobby Eckermann's recent poetry collection *Inside My Mother*.

Emma Murphy

I am a University of Sydney student completing my Master of Publishing, with a completed bachelor's degree in English literature and creative writing from the University of New South Wales. While I love working through the intricacies of other people's words, I also like to create my own.

Libby Newton

I am a queer twenty-something, in my penultimate year of study at Sydney Law School. In 2020, I received the Editor's Choice award in the fiction category of the *Honi Soit* Writing Competition for my auto-fiction piece, 'billie: circa 2010–2020'. I like writing silly little poems and reading LPTs (literary page-turners). I live and write on unceded Gadigal land.

Helena Bryony Parker

I am an emerging poet based in Sydney. My work can be found in the women's journal, *Not Very Quiet* and *Baby Teeth Journal*. I write on unceded Gadigal land.

Julia Peng

Born and bred in the leafy suburbs of Sydney, I majored in psychology and physiology in my undergraduate degree and am currently studying dentistry – all at the University of Sydney! I write poetry as a hobby and also teach English to high school students and hope to inspire them to appreciate the beauty of literature. Inspired by poets like Gwen Harwood, Kenneth Slessor and Robert Gray, I aim to capture the little moments in every day life in my poetry, an intensely personal medium which I see as a reflection of the soul.

Ruth Phillips

I started writing poetry as a child - then later had a couple of poems published – always linked to political beliefs and concerns. I have been working as an academic at the University of Sydney for nearly twenty years! Poetry is a creative emotional outlet – we are in a time of great emotionality. I am a political scientist and an Associate Professor teaching and researching in Social Work and Policy Studies.

Yasodara Puhule-Gamayalage

Frankly, by now, you would think I would know what I truly am, but I do not. I am an artist one day, something completely different the next, eternally struggling to label myself as just one thing. When I feel strongly about a subject, I will almost always express and explore it visually using whatever medium I find around me; that much, at least, I know defines what I do.

James Max Puterflam

I am a current PhD candidate researching a digital sleep intervention for a chronic musculoskeletal pain population. Passionate about both learning and teaching I take great joy in tutoring undergraduate and postgraduate students with the Anatomy and Histology Department at the University of Sydney. Since finishing high school in 2013 I have travelled to many countries in Europe and Asia. Of these I have developed a profound connection with Nepal visiting the country six times since for leisure and spiritual reasons. I was the president of the University of Sydney Buddhist Society during 2018–19. My exploration and understanding of outer science fuels my desire to understand the inner science of existing for which I believe is best understood through personal experience.

Jemima Rice

I am a first-year student and have always loved expressing myself through writing. Currently majoring in English and Philosophy, I hope to write professionally in the future. I have spent most of my life in Sydney and am deeply drawn to its natural and artificial landscapes. My pieces often explore the ways people interact with these surroundings amidst mental, social and environmental upheaval. Other interests include visual arts, languages and music.

Seth Robinson

I am the author of *Welcome to Bellevue*, published by Grattan Street Press (GSP) in 2019. In 2021, I was selected as one of the inaugural winners of the Ultimo Prize (fiction). My other creative works have featured in *Aurealis Magazine*, *TCK Town*, the *GSP Flash Fiction Anthology*, *The University of Sydney Anthology*, *Farrago* and *Woroni*. I received a Master of Creative Writing, Publishing and Editing from the University of Melbourne in 2018 and a Bachelor of Arts from the Australian National University (ANU) in 2014. I am currently working on my next novel, and on completing my Doctor of Arts (Creative Writing) through the University of Sydney.

Christopher D. Roche

I am a cardiothoracic surgeon doing a PhD at the University of Sydney. My research is focused on generating heart patches to repair heart muscle. These patches are fabricated with a 3D bioprinter which deposits cells in 'bio-inks' made from gels. The patches are then transplanted to the surface of the heart. I have mentored many students, and am involved in UTS' humanitarian mentoring programme and founded underdogmentoring.com. Before converting to medicine, I completed a Master of English Literature at the University of Sydney (2007–08) and my first short writing piece, 'Swimming', was published in the University of Sydney's 2008 student anthology entitled *Cellar Door*. In 2021, I revisit the same character, back in the same place fourteen years later for 'Swimming 2.0' under the theme of 'networks'. Fourteen years of science have not dulled my passion for the arts – hopefully I am still able to access my imagination!

Hannah Roux

I wrote – or, rather, dictated to my long-suffering mother – my first story at the age of four: it was the epic adventure of a pair of mice. They ate a lot of cheese. I have been writing ever since. In 2020, I completed an Honours year in English, mostly from my couch. I am now – terrifyingly – writing a PhD. I am – also terrifyingly – working on a long story which, for superstitious reasons, I refuse to call a novel. Poetry, in this context, is a sane and peaceful release. My poems have been published, mostly by this anthology, and soon by *ARNA*. I am a bisexual Christian Sydney-sider owned by a border collie named Lucky. She regards all this writing nonsense as a distraction, and wonders why I don't spend more time snoozing, or running in circles round the garden. She may well have the right idea.

Isla Scott

What can I tell you that you haven't heard before? Sometimes the best stories are familiar. After an undergraduate degree in Literature and Psychology, I have recently graduated from my Master of Publishing. My work was also published in *Earth Cries*, the 2020 University of Sydney Anthology. I've never been able to decide on a favourite book, there are simply too many, but I love fairy lights and the sound of rain and plot twists.

Melissa Snook

I am a former University of Sydney student, having spent nine years of my life there, collecting degrees. What was meant to be four years studying education, turned into an arts degree majoring in History and American Studies; and an Honours degree in American Studies (with a thesis I am still editing even after submitting it three years ago); and a Masters of Publishing. I fell in love with American Studies in my undergraduate degree and quickly committed to another year in the field, writing a (roughly) twenty-five thousand word thesis on American stand-up comedy. My works in this anthology represent this fascination with America, and reflect my love of comedy. I have also been published in the Anthology's 2020 edition *Earth Cries*.

Grace Ugamay Dulawan

I'm a writer of Ifugao and Ilocano descent living and working on unceded Gadigal Land. My lyric essay *An Ifugao Speaks* was longlisted for the inaugural LIMINAL & Pantera Press Non-Fiction Prize 2021.

Kelly Ung

I am a University of Sydney graduate, having completed my Bachelor of Arts majoring in Art History and Psychology in 2020. I've always loved reading and writing, so I am now a Master of Publishing student and a part-time bookseller. Over the past two years, I've enjoyed annoying my loved ones with my astrology knowledge. When I'm not at work or studying, I can be found reading, playing sudoku or hanging out with my dog.

Claudia Ware

I am a performer, arts educator and Master of Publishing student at the University of Sydney. I work professionally in Australian theatre and have performed with several major companies, including Queensland Theatre Company, Sport for Jove and Darlinghurst Theatre. Over the last decade, I have worked part-time as an English literature tutor for high-school students across Sydney.

Tori Wills

I'm a postgrad student at the University of Sydney. I write short stories and other things, on occasion. When I was an undergrad, I studied politics and planned to end up in an important job, but then I became disillusioned and moved overseas to work in the arts instead. I'm back here now, focused on all things books. I spend my days studying, reading, scrolling, bushwalking, making hummus, sewing things and procrastinating from being a more productive writer.

Angela Xu

I am a second-year Law/Arts student majoring in History. Having been involved in editing several journals for Sydney University Law Society and Sydney Arts Students' Society, I took up writing more seriously at the start of 2021 to deal with homesickness, having moved away from home for the first time. My culture and family are major sources of inspiration for me, as I love capturing in words a culture that is full of practices and traditions that are non-verbal.

Danial Yazdani

I am in my first year, studying English, Theatre and Performance Studies and Education. I write in my spare time or, more importantly, when I am struck by an overwhelming feeling or sensation that I can only express to others through the written word. I hope to be a teacher one day and plant seeds of wisdom and curiosity in the hearts of teenagers as they find their place in the world. However, if opportunity strikes, I would like to be a multimodal writer across the literary, poetic and theatrical fields. My favourite quote is, 'Hope will never be silent'.

Qinxuan (Laura) Yu

I'm a second-year international student completing my Bachelor of Arts and Bachelor of Advanced Studies (Media and Communications), majors in Media and Film studies. I have always had a passion for producing videos, taking photographs and other media production making.

About the Editors

Sophie Amos

I fell in love with storytelling through long nights reading under lamplight, audiobooks on cassette tape and Saturday morning cartoons. I fell in love with editing through high school essays, journals filled with poetry and rewriting plot holes in the TV shows I loved. I am glad to say that this will be my second year as a part of the anthology editorial team and now nearing the end of my studies at the University of Sydney, I hope to continue the good times into future publishing endeavours.

Cherie Baird

I grew up as a classic bookworm, pleading with my mum to let me read one more chapter before I went to sleep. I've wanted to work with books since I was thirteen, when I realised it was indeed a real job. Tertiary study has taught me how to be less of a stickler for perfect, prescriptive grammar and more of a believer in finding the right way to express things. I love learning in all its trying and stumbling forms. When I'm not reading, I enjoy songwriting, playing board games and watching trivia game shows.

Ashleigh Cuthill

When I joined the anthology team, it was to gain insight into the editorial processes involved in making a book, but I have learned so much more from this experience. As an editor on this project, I have been able to expand my abilities in this area, but also explore other facets of the book-making process. I have come to understand that my interests lie in book production and am grateful that I have been able to be part of the process once again. As a lover of books and reading, I can confirm that there is nothing more satisfying than seeing your hard work manifest itself in the form of a book on the shelf.

Emma Murphy

While I was in high school, I struggled with the 'where do you see yourself in five years?' question. I had no idea what I wanted to do for tertiary education, let alone a career. Books have always been a huge part of my life. You could always find me, as the cliché states, with my nose stuck in a book. After researching different careers that involved literature, working in a publishing house became my dream job. This led to a degree in English literature and creative writing, a current Master of Publishing and now the anthology team.

Isla Scott

I've enjoyed reading, writing and having strong opinions since a young age, so pursuing a career as an editor seemed like a perfect fit. I have a passion for getting things right, and devour any good book in a single sitting. Amid freelance editing and interning work, I spend my time baking elaborate sweets, criticising adverts and cat-sitting for friends.

Melissa Snook

I started seriously collecting books, yes, it is an actual hobby, in 2014 on a trip to the US and visiting Barnes & Noble. I fell in love and spent way too much time (and money) in there. Since then, my collection has grown from a single bookshelf to an entire room that I affectionally call my 'library'. It's no surprise that my love of books and reading has turned into a career in the publishing industry. Being able to create something as special as a book, from start to finish, has been one of the best experiences. When I'm not reading, I'm usually playing video games with friends or watching my favourite shows.

Darcy Song

As someone who speaks English as a second language, it wasn't until I was well into my bachelor's degree that I started reading my first book in English. If you'd asked me then to help edit someone else's work in English, it would have been unthinkable, but I am glad to be here now and share this fantastic anthology with all of our readers. My background is in journalism and social media management. If not reading, you can find me museum hopping or embarrassingly playing tennis on local courts.

Lucinda Thompson

Books have been a constant source of inspiration, escapism and companionship for me since I was a child. Coming from a creative arts background, I love all things design, production and marketing. There's something so special about holding a physical book in your hands and stepping into someone else's mind in a brief pause from the world around us. Being a part of this anthology team has been such a rewarding experience and I can't wait for you, our readers, to join in experiencing the wonderful talent of the University of Sydney community.

Kelly Ung

I've been a bookworm since I could read. I love jumping into someone else's world and living in their words. As a publishing student now, working on this anthology on networks and connection has been a great first publishing experience. I feel really privileged to be able to read and edit so much incredible work and feel connected to the wider the University of Sydney community during the rollercoaster of lockdown in 2021.

Cassandre Varella-Chang

I first realised how consequential stories could be when I read my grandma's copy of *Anne of Green Gables* at the age of nine. Anne taught me to pay attention to the world, to hold on to wonder, to choose again and again to be both brave and vulnerable in the face of new adventures. I have thought about her ever since. I was interested in writing first, then editing, and am now wholly dedicated to the overarching storytelling process with its bigger and smaller steps. I am most content when working with words and am deeply grateful for this anthology experience.

Jenny Welsh

I love stories and it has been a pleasure to be part of this anthology and showcase the very best writing from the University of Sydney community. Editing is my passion, and after changing careers, I feel am lucky to be able to work doing something I enjoy. I think the theme of this anthology will strike a chord with many; after living through a pandemic, we have all come to appreciate connections with others, however fleeting. Through this project, I have gained a greater understanding of the writing process, and of course how to create books. I hope to have the opportunity to work with many other authors in the future.

Tori Wills

I joined the anthology team in order to get some hands-on experience in book production and the editorial process. I've loved having the opportunity to feel connected to the wider University of Sydney community via the project, especially during this difficult period of remote learning. I love getting lost in stories and expanding my knowledge of niche topics, so I spend a lot of my time reading, listening to podcasts on bushwalks and falling down Wikipedia rabbit holes.

www.ingramcontent.com/pod-product-compliance
Lightning Source LLC
Chambersburg PA
CBHW041750010726
47507CB00009B/347